THE
FURIES

THE
FURIES

A NOVEL

N A T A L I E H A Y N E S

ST. MARTIN'S PRESS ⚏ NEW YORK

For Dan

ὅδ᾽, ὡς ἔοικε, τῇ γυναικὶ συμμαχεῖ.

Sophocles *Antigone* 1 740

www.stmartins.com

Library of Congress Cataloging-in-Publication Data

Haynes, Natalie, 1974–
  [Amber Fury.]
  The furies : a novel / Natalie Haynes. — First U.S. edition.
    p. cm.
  ISBN 978-1-250-04800-4 (hardcover)
  ISBN 978-1-4668-4830-6 (e-book)
  1. Teachers—Fiction. 2. Teenagers—Fiction. 3. Canon (Literature)—Fiction. 4. Grief—Fiction. 5. Edinburgh (Scotland)—Fiction. 6. Psychological fiction. I. Title.
  PR6108.A9686A63 2014
  823'.92—dc23

                                                              2014016596

St. Martin's Press books may be purchased for educational, business, or promotional use. For information on bulk purchases, please contact Macmillan Corporate and Premium Sales Department at 1-800-221-7945, extension 5442, or write specialmarkets@macmillan.com.

First published in Great Britain under the title *The Amber Fury* by Corvus, an imprint of Atlantic Books Ltd

First U.S. Edition: September 2014

10 9 8 7 6 5 4 3 2 1

ACKNOWLEDGEMENTS

Like anything of merit I ever do, this book wouldn't have been written or published without help from all kinds of extraordinary people. Firstly, the research: I'd like to thank all the teachers and counsellors who gave up their time to talk to me, especially Carl Hendrick and Becca Howard for trips to their respective schools, and everyone at the Brent Centre for Young People. I also owe a deafening shout of thanks to the staff and students of Boroughmuir High School, especially Ailsa Stratton and David Dempster.

On the subject of deafness, thanks to Anita Doughty for the advice on hearing loss and hearing aids.

My Edinburgh friends answered endless questions, and hardly ever mentioned that they did have jobs to do. A million thanks to Corin Christopher, Mark Crossan and Susan Morrison for their help. The surviving mistakes are all mine.

I'm not sure I would have begun this book without encouragement from Rebecca Carter, continued it without kindness from Andrew Motion, or finished it without advice from Sarah Churchwell: thank you all.

Much of this book was plotted in Regent's Park: the most beautiful place in London. And yet, keen park visitors will note that I have flattened the ground beneath The Hub, removed it and replaced it with a new building of my own invention. My apologies for the vandalism.

ACKNOWLEDGEMENTS

I'd like to thank everyone at Conville & Walsh for their ongoing brilliance, especially Alex Christofi, Alexandra McNicoll, Carrie Plitt, Henna Silvennoinen, Jake Smith-Bosanquet and Kinga Burger. Patrick Walsh is the best of all possible agents, and I don't care who knows it.

When Patrick was finding a home for this book, I was blown away by the Atlantic crew. Many months later, I still am. Many thanks to everyone there: you are simply and objectively tremendous. My special thanks go to Sara O'Keeffe, the most thoughtful of editors. She never suggests anything without considering every possible consequence first: this book would be half as good without her suggestions and thoughts (at best). Thanks too to Hilary Teeman at St Martin's, who also contributed excellent editorial advice. I'm lucky to have them both.

Thanks to Michelle Flower for the constant moral support and frequent pictures of rescue rabbits, which would raise anyone's spirits. Christian Hill is always saintly and perfect in every regard, particularly running my website for all these years in exchange for the occasional gin.

My mother has read this book more times than I have, including when it was still a draft that only a mother could love. (And she loved it. She's good that way.) My dad read the finished product and said all the right things, which was a relief as I'd lost track of how it would read for the first time by then. My brother, so far as I know, never reads any books I write beyond the acknowledgements, which means as long as I don't screw these up, he'll think it's terrific. There's a lot to be said for that.

And then, of course, there's Dan Mersh. There is nothing I ever do that you don't make easier and no fragment of my life that you don't make better. Thank you.

PROLOGUE

L,

So this guy came today, and he says you sent him. Did you? I'll talk to him if you want, but he seems kind of annoying. He mostly talks in clichés. He's all, tell me what happened, in your own words, take your time, whenever you're ready.

He is pretty hot, though. So if you did send him, thanks for that. Let me know if it was you.

Love, D

ACT ONE

1

The first thing they'll ask me is how I met her. They already know how we met, of course. But that won't be why they're asking. It never is.

I remember when Luke was training, he told me that you only ever ask a question if you already know the answer. Lawyers don't like surprises, least of all when they're on the record. So they won't be asking because they want to know the date, the time, the address, all the little details. They will have done their homework, I'm sure. They've spoken to Robert, my old boss, already. So they know when I arrived in Edinburgh, and which day I started work. They probably have a copy of my timetable. If they wanted to, they could pinpoint our first meeting to the minute.

They won't be asking because they want to know what I'll say, they'll just want to know how I say it. Will my eyes go right or left? Am I remembering, or inventing? They'll be measuring my truth against the one they've built from other witnesses. Gauging whether I can be trusted, or whether I'm a liar.

So when they ask, I'm not going to roll my eyes and tell them they're wasting my time. I'm not going to tell them that I can hardly bear to go over this again, that every time someone asks me, I have to live through it all over again. I'm not going to ask if they know what it feels like, holding up the weight of everything that happened. I won't make a fuss. It wouldn't help.

I'm going to take a small breath, look straight ahead, and tell them the truth. I can't get nervous and start rattling on about how I didn't plan to be in Edinburgh. I won't ask them to remember what had happened to me, and why I'd had to run away from London, why I was in Scotland at all. I won't remind them that I could have had no inkling of how terribly things would turn out. Besides, even if I had, I wouldn't have cared. I didn't care about anything then.

I'm just going to answer as simply as I can: I met them on the 6th of January 2011, in the basement room at 58 Rankeillor Street. And I wouldn't have believed any of them could do something so monstrous.

That isn't quite true, of course. Even by the standards of the Unit, they were a difficult group. But Robert had warned me that they would be challenging, so my expectations were low.

I went to meet Robert the day before term began, at the pupil referral unit on Rankeillor Street. The building was empty except for the two of us, but I had to pick up forms and files and registration lists, most of which were covered in Post-it notes linking children's names to medical conditions. At first glance, at least half of them were allergic to something: nuts, pollen, air pollution, gluten, mould spores.

'They don't seem very sturdy,' I pointed out, skimming the top few pages Robert had just given me. His office was a huge, high-ceilinged room whose elegant proportions had been sliced in two by a partition wall. One half had been converted into his secretary's office. It was lined with filing cabinets from the door all the way to the far wall. In front of these stood her symmetrical desk: a computer in one corner was matched in the opposite one by three wire trays balanced on top of one another and marked 'In', 'Out' and 'Pending'; all of them were empty. Next to them was a picture of two young children, dark-haired and grinning in front of a loch in the pouring rain. The frame was clearly handmade – in bright, misshapen purple clay – presumably by one of the children it contained.

Robert's office was the yin to Cynthia's yang. Bulging files were piled up on every flat surface, including the floor. Torn scraps of paper with names or initials were balanced on top of them. Where Cynthia's only light source was the greenish long-life bulb overhead, Robert's room had two huge sash windows which looked out onto Rankeillor Street. Look up to the left, and you could see Salisbury Crags, the dark cliffs which glower down over Edinburgh, reminding you that there will be no nonsense here. The windows were framed with thick, theatrical curtains, their dark crimson folds coated with a thin film of dust, through which narrow, wandering tracks of curtain showed. Someone had taken an erratic vacuum cleaner to them but had lost the will before victory could be claimed.

'Don't believe a word of it,' he panted, as he hunted around the desk, the table and the mantelpiece over the long-dead fireplace, trying to make sure he had gathered everything with 'Alex' or 'A.M.' written on or near it. 'I mean, do believe it,' he corrected himself. 'Don't test them by throwing peanuts at them, or asking an asthmatic one to run up the stairs. But rest assured, Alex, these children will not be felled by a mere allergen. These details come up when they're assessed by doctors and social workers, of course, for their specific educational needs and challenges, and we have to keep full records of everything, even if it seems trivial. I doubt,' he glanced down at the file he was holding, 'if Jenny Stratton will meet a sticky end from her lychee allergy in your classroom. You'd have to go a long way to find a lychee anywhere in this city, come to that. It makes you wonder how they found out she was allergic at all. Most of them will be fine when they get to know you. Some of them might be less keen on doing drama or dramatherapy than others. Some of them are very confident, some are, you know, shyer.'

'How many kids do you have here?' I asked him, looking at the paper chaos. There couldn't possibly be room in the building – a vast converted terraced house spread over four floors, its yellow bricks blackened with dirt – for the number of children needed to generate this many forms.

'There are about thirty of them here at any one time, but they come and go, obviously. New children will be referred here from about the second week of term, I expect. And we'll lose some of these ones as we go along.'

'Lose them?'

'Rankeillor Street is a charity. Children come here when nowhere else will take them. Thanks to our benefactors, we can take a few children out of the system which is failing them. Most of them have been expelled from at least one school, though we do take some children before that point.' He began hunting around for something under the papers on his desk. 'Their parents or guardians apply to us, and if we think we can help, genuinely help, we try and make space for them. Our admissions procedure was enshrined in the original gift of the building and the fund: we don't take children who are simply struggling academically. There are plenty of other options available to them. Not all of them are good options, I know, but they do exist.'

He eventually found what he was looking for – a battered biro, which he used to scrawl a note on the file he held in his left hand. He didn't even pause while he was writing. 'We take the ones who don't function well elsewhere, for whatever reason: they've been bullied, or they are bullies, or they don't fit in, or whatever. The ones for whom we might actually be able to make a difference. But our aim is to get these children back into mainstream schools, if we possibly can. So really, we're trying to get rid of them as soon as they get here. And sometimes it works, but not always. We also lose some because they can't function here any more successfully than they did at other schools. Even safety nets have holes in them, you know.'

I nodded, wondering what he meant. Robert had always been like this: he tended to assume you were more attuned to his thought processes than you actually were. Than I actually was, anyway.

'Not usually more than one or two each term,' he added. 'Unless it's a very bad term.'

He looked over his half-moon spectacles at the papers I was now trying to arrange into a coherent order. 'This class,' he reached over and prodded one of the pages with the wrong end of his pen, 'will probably be the most difficult for you.'

'Why?' The sheet listed only five names, a small class of fourth-years. I did the maths in my head: fifteen years old. He handed me three more files, which I slotted in to what seemed to be a sensible order. If I could control the paperwork, perhaps I could control a classroom. I now had one set of files for each class, and one class for each year-group, five in total. Looking at the lists of unfamiliar names, I wondered how long it would take to match them to children. Robert didn't answer the question.

'I think that's the last of them, Alex,' he said. 'I won't lie to you. They can be right little fuckers. But don't worry. You'll win them over in the end. I'm not giving you every sentence we have on every child: it'll just stress you out, thinking you need to read it all. You have everything you need here. If you feel like you're at sea with a particular student, come and ask for their full file; Cynthia will have a copy you can read. These children deserve to be more than their records, though, so please don't ask unless you really need to know something.'

I wanted to ask him what kind of information might be in the files which I didn't have, but he had already skipped on to talk about something else. Butterfly-brained, my mother would have called him: always lighting upon one topic, then fluttering off to another one before you could catch up. It should have been infuriating, but his enthusiasm was always so complete that he made you want to race to catch up with him instead of sulking that he'd gone off without you. He had always been like that, even when I was a student and he was teaching drama over in the University buildings on George Square, less than a mile from where I now sat perched on the balding arm of his tweed-covered chair. He was the teacher you always hope for: passionate, exciting, funny. His chubby frame gave him a cuddly appearance that he only fulfilled if you handed work in on time, fully referenced and neatly printed out. Though his reddish hair had now faded to a sandy grey, and his face had creased into a few more lines, he still looked like the actor he had been in his youth. Even today, before the Unit was officially open, he was wearing a three-piece suit with a tartan waistcoat, as though he might be a wedding baritone, temporarily missing the rest of his choir. And this was him dressed down. I looked at my jeans, which were now covered with specks of white paper, shed from the papers I held, like tiny dirty confetti.

'Let me show you your classroom,' he said. 'Leave those.' He pointed at the files, then looked round his office, trying to find an empty spot. 'Perhaps put them on Cynthia's desk,' he said more quietly, as if she might appear and berate him. 'I'm sure she wouldn't mind. Just for now.'

I dusted them off with my sleeve before placing them on her desk, then followed him out of the room. He took me down the two flights of stairs to the ground floor, then down again to the basement, and what was now my room. The stairs grew darker as we reached the hallway at the bottom. Two scratchy yellow bulbs threw a thin light onto the final steps and the industrial-green classroom door. It was like climbing down into a cold swamp. Edinburgh in the winter is dingy enough without going underground. It was barely warmer in the damp hallway than it was outside, in the sleeting rain.

'The kids like it down here,' he said, opening the door and stepping to one side so I could walk in. For a man who had once done a season at the RSC (one up from spear-carrying, darling, but it still counts), he was a terrible liar.

At least my predecessor had tried to make the place cosy. The back wall was a fiery orange, and the radiators were turned up to their highest setting, so the room itself was relatively dry. But the air smelled sourly of mildew, and as I scanned the warped doors of the cupboards which ran along the wall under the windows at the front of the building, I guessed that if I opened them, the smell would be stronger still.

The room was huge, easily bigger than the one-bedroom flat I was staying in down the road. It ran under the whole building, which had to compensate for standing on a hill. The windows at the back looked out over a yard which must have replaced the garden when the house had been converted into a pupil referral unit. Guessing from the litter, it was now mainly used for smoking. But at the front, where the ground had snuck up underneath it, the window looked out onto a whitewashed wall with a small door on one side. I noticed a large, dented keyhole and wondered if the door still opened. I had a brief vision of being locked in there by a class of jeering children who hated me, and shuddered. It had probably once been the coal-cellar, I supposed.

Way above head-height you could see the thick layer of pebbles in the space between the gate onto the street and the steps up to the front door of the building. I could just see the bottom of a few sorry shrubs in pots, which did nothing to change the Unit's unloved face. Like so many buildings in Edinburgh, it was grand but tired at the same time.

Robert flicked the light switch next to the door and three weary lamps flickered on overhead, two over the chairs and tables at the front end of the room and one more over the dingy, empty space towards the back. I blinked, wondering if bulbs came in a lower wattage than forty, and if they did, why someone would use them in a classroom.

'Carole – your predecessor – probably did most of her teaching here,' he said, pointing towards the chairs. I nodded. If she wanted to make out the kids through the gloom, she would have had to. Even in the summer, I would discover, the lights needed to be on in this room. How on earth had Carole taught art lessons in here? Why hadn't she asked for more lights to be fitted?

The chairs were old and mismatched. A battered brown leather chair stood behind the teacher's desk, my desk, and the rest were fabric-covered in grimy reds, purples and maroons. The walls were decorated with bright collages and paintings, made by the children last term, I supposed. But the corners were already peeling up from the bottom of each picture, as though the room were trying to rid itself of any signs of life.

The following afternoon I was sitting in the basement, waiting for them. I'd taught three classes that morning, which had gone relatively well, considering that it was three years since I'd finished my PGCE. I'd run quite a few theatre workshops for children in the meantime, but I hadn't taught, properly taught, a single lesson since I'd qualified. I knew perfectly well that if Robert hadn't been my friend, I would never have got a job at Rankeillor Street – on merit, or experience. How many people are given a job on the strength of a phone call? Robert had blustered something about an unexpected vacancy and short-term contracts being hard to fill, but he could easily have found someone better than me. I couldn't even bring myself to feel guilty about all the people he must have overlooked.

I'd met the rest of the Unit's staff over lunch upstairs, as they gossiped over sandwiches and microwaved pots of soup. One thing was clear: the class Robert had warned me about was indeed unpopular with almost every teacher. Eyes rolled when I asked why they were so much worse than the other kids. 'How long have you got?' snapped one irritable woman, settling herself against a cushion before she began her litany. But Robert, whose bat-like ears missed nothing, swooped in and told everyone to stop frightening me.

'If she leaves,' he hissed, 'someone's going to have to cover her classes.' He looked round at the rest of the staff. 'All her classes,' he emphasised.

So, as the classroom door opened, I was remembering the conversations that I used to have with my housemates when we were all teacher-training: one in maths, one in history, and me in drama and dramatherapy. Children are like animals, we agreed. They can sense fear. Like pack animals. Like hyenas. They know when you're afraid and they use it against you, taking advantage of their superior numbers to destroy you. We really did see our charges as interchangeable with wild dogs. No wonder I'd given up as soon as I'd qualified: no audience was ever as frightening as a classroom, and besides, the director doesn't have to face the audience. We – I should say, they – can hide behind the actors.

I could smell them before I saw them; fresh smoke clung to their clothes as they came in. Whatever else they were allergic to, it wasn't cigarettes. As the five of them slunk into the room – they were late, of course – it was a small, scrappy, red-haired boy who voiced what they were all thinking. 'Who the fuck are you?'

'Come in, sit down,' I replied, gesturing at the chairs in the middle of the room. I was leaning against the front of my desk, trying to look casual. It was the first of many things I got wrong. I didn't need to befriend them, I needed to look like an authority figure. That's why they give teachers the biggest desks.

'You know who she is,' one of the girls hissed at the red-headed boy. 'She's Robert's friend. Miss Allen's gone on maternity leave early, hasn't she?'

He shrugged and nodded. The five of them took their seats – three girls, two boys.

'I'm Alex Morris,' I said, 'and I'm very glad to meet you.' I read from the sheet Robert had given me: 'You must be Annika, Mel, Carly, Ricky and Jono.'

They stared at me. The two boys were sitting together. The one who had asked who I was looked much younger than the other four. He had to be at least fourteen, but he looked no older than the twelve-year-olds I'd taught in the morning. He was skinny, with short, almost shaved ginger hair. His pale scalp shone through in patches, as if the hair had been hacked off against his will. He wore a huge hoody over his shirt and tie; he must have borrowed it from the boy he sat next to, who was several inches taller and much bulkier.

The larger boy had greasy dark hair hanging down in front of his face. The buttons of his school shirt strained when he sat down and his shoulders were slightly hunched, either because he spent a lot of time leaning over a computer, or because the shoulders of his shirt were as tight as the chest and it was the only way he could fit into it. His cheeks were pink and freckled. The notes I'd cribbed over lunch told me they were the same age, though it didn't seem possible.

'Are you Ricky?' I asked the dark-haired one. He rolled his eyes and pointed at the scrawny redhead.

'You must be Jono, then,' I continued. He shrugged. I added them to my mental list, as I had been doing with all the other children that day. Ricky – red hair. That was easy. I couldn't think of an alliteration for Jono. I'd have to rely on his dead-eyed stare to jog my memory.

Two of the girls were also sitting together. The one who had spoken to Ricky was also a redhead, but her hair was a beautiful pale orange colour, like a pedigree cat's. I couldn't tell if it was dyed or natural, but it framed her face, curling under her jaw in neat wings. I had worked with actresses who didn't have such a perfect blow-dry. Her eyes were lined in a bright emerald green, and she had added some green eyelashes in among her own. I looked the question at her.

'I'm Carly,' she said. A small, neat voice to match her small, neat frame. 'And this is Mel.' She put her arm round the slender blonde girl next to her and squeezed her shoulders, smiling. The blonde girl said nothing, just tilted her feathery head a little and looked at me. Clear blue eyes shone out from under her fringe. I tried to remember what I'd read about Mel or Carly, but I came up blank. I had memorised as many children as I could that day, and the details were starting to get fuzzy. This was already the busiest day I'd had in weeks: meeting all the staff and students and learning all their names was beginning to overwhelm me.

'Hello,' I said to them both.

Mel waved the fingers of one hand at me. I guessed she was trying to convey that she was not hostile, but not interested either. I wished I could do the same. So the girl sitting alone was Annika, long-limbed, golden-haired and dark-eyed. She wore big glasses with thick black frames. Only a girl who knew she was beautiful would wear something so deliberately ugly. They made her look like a seventies spy. Without them, she would be only one fur hat away from a Russian novel. Annika Karenina, I thought. Another easy one to remember.

'So you must be Annika?' I asked her, smiling.

'Yes, well done. Five out of five.' She flicked her blonde mane as she turned away, like an ill-tempered racehorse. I felt the smile freeze on my face. This was what one teacher had told me earlier. Annika is a right cow, she had said, succinctly. Whatever you say or do, she will punish you for it. Don't take it personally. None of the rest of us do.'

I took a breath and began. 'I know you usually do art therapy in here. But this term, I'd like us to do some dramatherapy instead, if that's OK with you.'

'Fuck off,' said Ricky, without malice. 'Art's the only thing I like.' He picked up his bag, lifted it onto his spindly shoulder, then stood up and slouched out of the room. The remaining four stared at me. I had no idea what to say.

'Does anyone else feel that strongly about art?'

'I don't think so,' said Carly, smiling again. She and Mel made eye contact, and they both started laughing. I tried not to redden, wondering if it was a joke at my expense.

'Good,' I said, too loudly. Any fragment of authority I might have possessed had walked straight out of the room with that boy.

'Will we be putting on plays?' Carly asked, still giggling. I caught another glint of green from the outer corner of her eyes, as her false lashes caught the light.

'We can do, of course.' I looked round the vast room. We were only using about a third of it, so there was plenty of room for performing if they wanted to. Though I would have to find some way of lighting the rest of the space. 'Is that something you'd like to do?'

More shrugs.

'Maybe we should try to get to know each other a bit better?' I suggested, trying not to sound desperate. I thought of the years that had passed since my teacher-training year, and knew that I was now paying the price for never having taken it seriously enough. Teacher-training was something I'd chosen to endure so I could keep on directing student plays. I must have sat through hours of discussion about difficult students and conflict resolution, but I could remember none of it. Maybe the directing could help me instead. I cast around for a game or something to break the ice.

'Let's try this. I want each of you to tell the rest of us two truths and one lie. We'll try and work out what the lie is, and by the end of it, I hope I'll know a bit more about you all.'

They looked sceptical.

'I'll start,' I said. 'I'm from London, I have a degree in English and Drama, and this is my first time in Edinburgh.'

'You're definitely from London,' said Carly, her pale red hair tipping to and fro as she nodded. 'You sound it. What do you think's the lie?' She looked at Mel, who frowned, then shook her head.

'Why are you in our unit, then?' asked Annika. She shook loose a few hairs that had caught the edge of her pink lip-gloss. 'Are you even qualified?'

'Yes, thank you. I'm a trained teacher and I have a postgraduate qualification in dramatherapy,' I explained.

'Oooh,' she said, with contempt. She reached into her pockets and pulled out a pair of white headphones, fitting them carefully into her ears. I heard a faint, tinny sound and wondered what to do. Challenge her and risk losing another student in the first five minutes of the lesson, or ignore her and risk looking like I was scared of her? Which I was, as the whole room must have realised. I was more embarrassed than upset at this point. I looked at Carly, hoping she'd continue to play the game.

'Then it's not your first time here. That's the lie,' she guessed. 'And that's how you know Robert.'

'Yes,' I agreed. 'You got me. I did my degree here. Robert was one of my tutors. Now your turn.'

'I'm Carly Jones,' she said. 'Can that be one of my three things?'

I shook my head.

She thought for a moment and tried again. 'I'm fifteen. My favourite colour is blue. And…' She paused. People always pause before the lie. 'I like cats.'

'She hates cats,' said Jono, instantly. 'She's allergic to them.'

'Now you,' I said to Jono.

'This is fucking pathetic,' he replied. I waited, hoping he couldn't smell my desperation over the sweaty odour which was coming from his bag. Did he have a gym kit? I didn't think they did PE at the Unit.

'Fine. I'm fourteen, I wanted a PS3 for Christmas, but my parents got me an Xbox, because they're too stupid to know the difference. And I hated art therapy. If I never see another fucking collage as long as I live, that'll be fine.'

'Is an Xbox so bad?' I asked.

'It's OK,' he said. 'I suppose. But the PS3 is obviously better. They just don't listen.'

We had already passed the limits of my knowledge of games consoles. I was relieved when Carly spoke again.

'He's not fourteen, he's fifteen,' she said. 'Miss Allen brought in a cake.'

I felt a grudging respect for my predecessor. Perhaps that was how to win them over.

'So you really hated making collages?' I asked Jono.

'It's the glue,' he said. 'It stinks. I can still smell it now.' Once he said it, I realised that he had identified the chemical tang beneath the stench of damp that filled the basement, which I hadn't been able to place. 'You can't even sniff it,' he added, 'because it's safety glue.'

'Not that you would sniff glue, since it's dangerous and illegal.' I was trying to smile, but my face felt tight.

'Of course not, miss.' He didn't smile back.

'You don't have to call me miss,' I said, quickly. 'Alex is fine.'

'Alright, "Alex",' he said, as if I might be lying about my name.

I turned to Annika and raised my eyebrows. 'Perhaps you could take your headphones out and switch your music off,' I said.

'Oh, have you started to say something interesting?' she said, all mock-surprise. 'Because if you're still bleating on about getting to know us, I'm not going to waste my time.' She was flipping through screens on her phone.

'I'll do three things for her,' said Mel, the quiet blonde girl. It was the first thing she'd said since she walked through the door. Her voice was unexpected, but I couldn't work out why. Was the emphasis on the wrong word? Her accent was impossible to place. She continued. 'Her name's Annika, she's Swedish, and she's a total bitch. Wait, did you say one of them should be a lie?'

'Fuck you,' said Annika as she switched from one song to another.

'You now,' I said to Mel.

'I'm Mel Pearce,' she said. 'I'm in the Unit because I got chucked out of my old school. I'm deaf, and I wish I wasn't.'

There was another awkward silence. They were all watching, waiting to see what I might say.

'The last one's the lie? You like being deaf?' I asked her.

She nodded. 'It's everyone else who doesn't like me being deaf,' she said.

'OK, maybe that's something we could talk about later in the session.'

'Yeah, because that sounds interesting,' said Annika.

'Don't be such a fucking bitch,' said Carly, her soft Edinburgh accent blunting the force of the words only a touch.

'Shut up, you stupid cunt,' snapped Annika. She jumped out of her seat.

'Don't start on her, Carly,' said Jono, delighted to see the lesson collapsing around him. 'She might go for you with a knife.'

'Christ, I didn't go for anyone with a knife. I was slicing bread and he started pissing me off. It was the school's stupid knife.' Annika grabbed her bag and stalked towards the door. She opened it, and turned back to me. 'And next time, "Alex", maybe we could talk about something that isn't how someone feels. I am so fucking bored of talking and hearing about everyone's feelings. This is the only education we're going to get, you know.'

'It's the only education you're going to get because you got kicked out of your school for threatening someone at knife-point,' Jono muttered, but quietly.

'I mean it,' she said. 'I don't want to be… twenty, and not know more than I know now.' Twenty, it seemed, was the greatest age she could consider being. 'If you're so qualified, teach us something. Otherwise it's all just,' she looked back at Jono, 'fucking collages.'

'OK. Do you all feel that way?' I asked.

They nodded.

'We're not stupid,' Carly said. 'We can do anything they do in normal schools.'

'Alright then. We'll do that. There will have to be some feelings involved though.' I turned back to Annika, who still stood with one hand on the door handle. 'That's part of what plays are for. They should change the way you feel about things, otherwise they're not good plays.'

'Fine,' she said. 'So long as it's about something that isn't these fucking losers.' She jerked her head back at her classmates as she walked out. The door banged shut behind her.

'OK, well, this is a dramatherapy session,' I said to the remaining three. 'So, for homework, I'd like you all to start keeping a diary, if you don't do that already.' They stared at me. 'You don't have to bring it in to the Unit, you don't have to tell anyone what's in it, I just want you to write something every day, that you learned, or noticed or thought or felt. Then you can try and write scenes based on your diary entries later in the term, if we feel like it?'

'Yeah, we'll think about it, miss.' Jono was up out of his seat already. 'I'll definitely tell Annika you want her to note down her feelings in a book.' He sniggered as he lumbered past.

The two girls collected their things too. They'd simply decided the lesson was over, and I'd barely kept them in the room for twenty minutes, half of the session time.

'Don't worry,' Carly said, kindly. 'You might do better next time. What shall we tell Ricky?'

The whole thing had gone as badly as it could possibly have done, and I knew it was because I was incapable of coping with the kind of children I was supposed to be teaching here. These weren't the middle-class London children I was used to, coming to a theatre workshop on a Saturday morning because their mothers thought it sounded fun and it gave them a couple of hours to spend drinking lattes in peace.

I thought for a moment. 'Ricky said he liked art, didn't he? Tell him to draw me a picture.'

As Carly and Mel came past my chair, Mel looked at me. 'You told two lies,' she said.

'What?' I thought I'd misheard her. She spoke so softly, and when I first met her, I thought that was odd. I suppose I must have thought deaf people would be more likely to shout, because they couldn't judge their own volume. I'd never given it much thought.

'You said we had to tell two truths and one lie. But you told two. You lied about not having been in Edinburgh before, and before that, you lied about being glad to meet us.'

I wanted to correct her, but I could see it would be no use. There was no point lying to her again.

'You don't want to be here with us,' she said. 'So why would we want to be here with you?'

2

I climbed the stairs to Robert's office, tripping on a step as I went. I heard the sound of sniggering behind me, but I didn't turn round to see who it was. I walked into Cynthia's office and asked if I could see him.

'I think you better had,' she said. 'The first day is always the hardest.'

I nodded, wishing she wouldn't be nice. It's always kindness that makes me cry. I knocked on Robert's door, and went in.

'Alex,' he said, investing a single word with both pleasure and alarm. 'What happened?' He looked at the telephone receiver he was holding in one hand, and returned it to its cradle.

'They saw right through me. And they walked out. I'm really sorry. I told you this would happen. You should have hired someone who knew what they were doing.'

Robert sighed. 'They didn't see through you. They're children. They don't have psychic powers and they don't have x-ray vision.'

He got up and walked over to the corner of his office where he kept a microwave, a toaster and a kettle. Pouring hot milk and cocoa into a cup, he blitzed it for a couple of minutes while I dug through my bag for a tissue. He handed it to me and went over to the filing cabinet. The cup was so hot that I almost dropped it. Taking my burned fingertips off it, I balanced it on my knee, hoping the denim would insulate my leg. He opened the drawer marked 'B', removed a small, almost full bottle of brandy, and walked back to me. He slugged the cocoa.

'Don't give me that look, young lady,' he said. 'I'll have none of your bourgeois, no-drinking-at-three-o'clock nonsense here. It's dark out. That makes it time for a drink.'

'It's dark out between October and March in Edinburgh.'

'Which is precisely why you need to leave your puritanical teetotal ideas south of the border,' he replied. 'Alex, you are having a very difficult year. Anyone would be upset if they had been through what you have been through in the past few months. But you are a good, kind, clever person, and you will be an inspiration to these children, if you can simply resist the urge to fall apart. Can you do that? For me if not for yourself?'

'I don't know.' I had no idea what the honest answer was. I felt like I was falling apart already, and the bell hadn't even rung for the end of my first day. 'They say they don't want to talk about feelings. Apparently they're bored of therapy. Except for Ricky, who says art was the only thing he enjoyed. He walked out first.' I could feel myself losing control, and pulled a tissue from my pocket. I blew my nose, while Robert looked away and pretended I had a cold.

'Oh, let him,' he said, airily. 'He's functionally literate and mostly numerate, which, considering the skills he had when he arrived here last year, is not bad at all. He's made friends here and he is, largely, a good influence on Jono, who was – and this isn't exactly what it says on his form – a total fucking nightmare before he met Ricky. So if you want to teach drama to the others while Ricky draws or paints, that's fine. They need some creative lessons in the timetable, and they need a therapeutic outlet. Honestly, I don't care what he does so long as he's not out on the streets, and he's not in a fight anywhere.'

'Really?' I wasn't sure if he was being serious, or just trying to make me feel better. Although, after the complete failure of my last lesson, either was OK.

Robert crouched down in front of me, resting his hands on the arms of my chair to keep his balance. His eyes were level with mine.

'I gave you a lot of files to read, and you can't memorise them all in one day. Ricky lives with his grandparents. His father has never been on the scene, his mother is either in prison or in rehab, depending on which day of the week it is, and his big brother is in jail, too. He was so badly nourished when social services gave him to his grandmother that he will always be a little wee scrap. He has nothing going for him at all, except that he is actually quite a sweet boy, even if he does get in the occasional rammy, as we used to say in my youth.'

'A what?'

'A fight,' he said.

At least I'd learned something today, even if the fourth-years hadn't.

Robert looked hard at the mug of cocoa, which I was drinking as quickly as I could, relying on its volcanic heat to mask the taste of the brandy. He levered himself back to standing and made a second cup for himself.

'Don't tell Jeff,' he said, as he sipped it.

Jeff was Robert's other half, or 'the moon of my existence', as he liked to refer to him, having dismissed 'boyfriend' as being inappropriately youthful for men of their age.

'I won't.'

'I mean it, you know. Everything in Ricky's life has been chaotic. I mean everything. Let him do what makes him feel happy and safe. That's what matters most in his case.'

'But the others are so…' I gave up, before I said what I wanted to say. They were so hostile and aggressive and angry with everyone, especially me. Robert's lack of concern was disconcerting. He couldn't really think I'd done an adequate job today. But if he didn't, he was faking it beautifully.

'Your classes will all be fine. You've met most of them now, and you've got on with them perfectly well. So teach them all drama, if you think they'll enjoy it. Or let them write and perform plays or role-plays if you and they prefer. They have other teachers for literacy and numeracy; your dramatherapy class is supposed to be somewhere they can learn some different things if they're interested. They just need a space to express themselves creatively, if that doesn't sound unspeakably poncey. And even if it does, frankly, that's still what they need. They need to have a little control over their lives, and your classroom is a place where they can do that and, I hope, have some fun. They are teenagers, after all.' He looked over his glasses at me.

I held the cocoa mug higher in front of my face. 'And the fourth-years?' I asked.

'Read some plays with them,' he said. He waved a theatrical arm. 'You know a lot about plays. You were directing at the Royal Court in London six months ago, for God's sake, woman. You were one of my most promising students. And if you can inspire them to dream of being a little more than badly behaved children, you'll have done everything I hoped you would. If you don't, you don't. There are plenty of teachers and therapists with bags of experience who would find it too challenging to work with these kids, and we all know that. A few of them work in this very unit, in spite of my best efforts. The board was happy to take a punt on you because I told them you were marvellous.'

'And because it was an emergency?'

He sighed. 'Yes, of course. I had an art therapist, she got pregnant, I expected her to go on maternity leave at Easter, and suddenly she was in hospital with pre-eclampsia, and was told she should do nothing more taxing than rest in bed for the next three months. So, yes, it was an emergency. You were available with no notice, and someone is better than no-one. Especially if that someone is you.'

I nodded. It was pathetic, the way I still wanted his approval all these years after he'd finished being my teacher.

'Any expression of interest from any child in this building is gold, and you must treat it as such,' he continued, growing more expansive with the brandy. 'When they tell you they want to learn about something, take them at their word. You'll gain their respect because you listened to them, and you might accidentally end up teaching them something.'

'OK.'

'When are you next due to see them? What day is today? Thursday?'

I nodded.

'So you see them next on Monday? Tuesday? Take in some plays – let them choose one to read, and see where you end up. We don't have an extensive library here, but I have plenty of texts at home – I'll bring some in for you. Or you could go round to Blackwell's and buy a couple – was it Blackwell's when you were here? Or was it still a James Thin? I lose track of the way these bloody bookshops change names.'

'The one on South Bridge? It was Blackwell's by the time I got here.'

'Keep the receipts,' he said. I nodded. 'Now will you stop crying? You know I don't like crying.'

'I'm sorry. I just felt like a fraud.' I mopped my face one last time with the tissue and dropped it in the bin.

'But you aren't. Have you got less professional experience than your predecessor? Yes. But things being as they are, you are the best woman for the job. The children will realise that as they get to know you. Why wouldn't they? They're naughty, they're not stupid.'

I raised my eyebrows at him, feeling the weight of my puffy eyelids stretching upwards. 'Only you could describe Annika, a girl who apparently once threatened someone with a kitchen knife, as "naughty".'

'Well, I understand that he was a deeply annoying young man who had been harassing her for some time. If you will approach someone in a cookery lesson and annoy them when they're using a knife, you can't then be princessy about things. Anyway, her former school should have had a more robust bullying policy, in my opinion. Annika is impatient and rude because she's clever and no-one challenges her.'

'Perhaps that's because of the knife thing?'

Robert ignored me. 'I took this job on to make a difference, Alex. It might be a cliché, but it's still true. I could have stayed at the University until I retired, spending my days with lovely, hard-working girls like you. These children need us. I know it sounds mad when it's your first day and I've already turned you to drink, but you'll see. It feels good to be needed.'

And, of course, he was right. Everyone wants to be needed. Even me, even then.

> *Dear Diary,*
>
> *Christ, I did not write that. Is this the worst idea anyone's ever had? Keeping a diary is lame. She asked us to, so this is kind of like homework. But she said we didn't have to bring it in to the Unit, so how would she even know if I was doing it?*
>
> *I don't need a diary to keep my secret thoughts in, because I don't really have any. I do like writing though. I won a prize for creative writing at Bruntsfield, my old school. I wrote a short story about this old jakey woman you see on the Links sometimes. I used to notice her when I was heading into town. So I made up some stuff about her, and they gave me a book token for twenty quid.*
>
> *We don't get to do much of that at Rankeillor. No wonder Annika's bored. I haven't decided yet, but I think I might want to be a journalist one day. I used to write for the school paper, when I was at Bruntsfield, but we don't have anything like that now.*

It'd be a big waste of time. I mean, what would Ricky do with a school paper? Fold it into a hat?

So that's what I'll do with this diary. Practise being a journalist, and write about actual stuff I've noticed or found out.

Let's start with the new teacher, call-me-Alex. She's a state, that's for starters. We were trying to work out when she last had her hair cut. I think two years ago, minimum. She doesn't look, you know, grimy. She doesn't smell bad, or anything. I'm just saying, she doesn't make much of an effort: jeans, jumper, and not a fucking hairbrush in sight. We're trying to work out if she overslept or if that's how she usually looks. She might be pretty if she made an effort. She's probably twenty-five, or maybe thirty. She's got brown hair, which she used to dye, definitely, because the ends are a completely different brown from the roots. And she doesn't have any make-up on at all. So I guess she isn't trying to impress anyone at Rankeillor. Not that there's anyone to impress, since Robert is clearly a poof and all the other teachers are female.

She's from London, she isn't very good at teaching, and she likes plays. That's all I know at the moment.

Robert came round to my flat that evening with a pile of play texts. He looked less harassed now than he had done in the afternoon.

'You smell nice,' I told him, as he kissed me on both cheeks.

'New cologne,' he said, happily. 'Jeff chose it. Now, how are you settling in?'

He bustled past me in the narrow hallway, his shoes tapping on the pine flooring that peeped through the bright, moth-bitten rugs.

'I'm fine, thanks. It's a lovely building. Thanks for sorting it out for me.'

Robert had arranged everything about my move to Edinburgh except the train ticket. The flat I was renting belonged to an actor friend of his, currently touring South Asia with a physical-theatre production of *Crime and Punishment* – described by Robert, who had been to the press night, as 'both of the above'.

New Skinner's Close was one of those tiny secret pockets that lurk in Edinburgh's Old Town, completely hidden unless you were looking for it. You could get into it through a narrow, cobbled passage off Blackfriars Street, one of those small, steep roads that cut down the hill between the Royal Mile and the dingy bars and student haunts of the Cowgate, beneath the huge South Bridge in the Old Town. Every weekend you could hear weary clubbers shriek with horror as they sheltered from the weather while they argued about where to go next and then discovered they had swapped the rain for some unidentifiable liquid that was now dripping down on them from the bridges above. They would stay at the youth hostel opposite the entrance to New Skinner's Close, which announced its presence with a sign in the shape of a hat-wearing red cow. You could hear music pulsing through the windows at night. The rest of Blackfriars Street catered to older visitors: Highland tours could be booked a few doors up. Otherwise it was all small cafés, and shops which sold felted knitwear and silver jewellery.

You could also reach the little close from the other side, through a tiny archway which stood almost hidden between sandwich shops on the Royal Mile. Even though the street was a tourist trap, drawing visitors up to the Castle or down to Holyrood, it wasn't busy in the winter. It was lined with shops which sold cashmere, tweed, tartan, small furry toys of the Loch Ness monster, and dozens of kinds of malt whisky, all waiting for visitors to arrive later in the year. And hiding behind them was New Skinner's Close.

Whichever direction you came from, you wound down to a cobbled courtyard, with this tiny, turreted building in the middle, surrounded by washing lines and potted plants. No-one was mad enough to try drying their washing in Edinburgh in January, so the lines stood empty but for some sturdy clothes pegs. Only a few small heathers were surviving the winter in their terracotta planters, some of which had cracked open from the cold, spilling soil onto the frozen paving stones. My flat was on the second floor, and to reach it I had to climb a spiral staircase carved from old, grey Scottish stone. I was only a few missed haircuts from being Rapunzel.

It was a one-bedroom flat with a living room that opened out into a small kitchen. The bedroom was opposite the front door and looked out over another little courtyard at the back of the building. The tiny bathroom was decorated with a jaunty nautical theme: blue tiles round the bath, fish on the shower curtain, a few shells from the beach in a glass dish on a shelf. I guessed they'd come from Portobello, a couple of miles away to the east. I used to go there in the summer when I was a student, and I'd had a collection of seashells too.

The living room was a little bare. Robert's friend had left minimal furnishings: a TV, a digital radio, a gate-leg table at which I ate porridge every morning, and a small desk. I'd brought only what I could carry from London: one bag of clothes, a laptop and almost nothing else.

'Christ, Alex,' Robert said as he walked into the living room and caught sight of the empty shelves on the far wall. He squeezed my arm the way people had taken to doing in the last few months, like they needed to check I was really there. 'Are you living like a monk for a reason?'

'No.' Even as I said it I could hear how defensive I sounded. 'I just didn't want to bring more than I could carry.'

'Where are the rest of your things? I thought you'd moved out of the flat in…' He paused, trying to remember. 'Richmond, wasn't it?'

'It was, and I did. Luke's parents have the rest of it.'

'They took your things as well as his?'

'Yes. I was going to chuck it all, but they didn't want me to. I told them if it was important to them, they could have it, but I didn't have anywhere to put it. So they said they'd take it and keep it for "when I was ready".'

'Was that really what you wanted?'

'I didn't want anything. I just wanted not to be in London. And because of you, I'm not.'

Robert sighed. 'Well, it's lucky I brought you these, then,' he said as he dropped the books on the table. 'At least you'll have one shelf to keep you going.' He looked down at the pile and back at the shelves. 'I'll bring you some more tomorrow. Don't for God's sake let me bring Jeff here, or you'll have to move in with me for a week while he decorates the place.'

'Thank you.' I took the books.

'Do you just watch TV every evening, Alex?' He was still looking around the room, as if he were expecting hobbies or magazines to leap from the walls.

'Yes,' I said. 'I come home and I turn on the news and make dinner. Then I watch silly costume dramas which sometimes have someone I know in them, playing a housemaid or the third daughter of a duke or something, and I think how funny it is that I used to be part of that world and now I'm not. Then I go to bed with the radio on, and I listen to it as I fall asleep. Sometimes I fit some ironing into the mix.'

'Fun, fun, fun,' he said. 'What will you do at weekends?'

'I'll swim, and walk, and go to the National Gallery. What do you do at the weekend?'

'Drink, mainly,' he replied. 'They're long weeks.'

'These are great.' I was looking at the spines of the books he'd brought. A complete Shakespeare in four volumes, and *A Man For All Seasons* that was losing some of its pages as the glue on its spine had splintered away. A dilapidated copy of *The Caretaker*, a dog-eared

Candide, with the part of Pangloss underlined in pencil, and at the bottom of the pile, Lorca's *Blood Wedding*.

'We'd better go out for dinner,' he said, looking around again. 'So I don't feel like I'm in prison all evening.'

'OK, OK. I'll buy a picture, or something, if it'll cheer you up.'

He looked at me. 'Will it cheer you up?'

'No.'

'Then I'll buy you one. A nice poster of a Highland coo or the Loch Ness monster, if you're lucky.'

'Promises, promises.'

His eye suddenly caught the small wooden box on the bottom of the bookshelves.

'What's that?' he asked. 'Alex, it isn't…? You haven't brought…?'

'It's nothing,' I told him. 'I mean, it isn't nothing. It's my engagement ring.'

'Oh God, I'm sorry,' he said. 'I'm so sorry. I thought you'd brought his ashes up here in an ornamental tin, like some demented Russian widow.'

'No. It's just the ring.'

'Don't you want to wear it?'

'No. Not really.'

'I suppose it would remind you every time you looked at your hand,' he said.

I didn't cry now when I talked about Luke. For the first few months, I cried all the time. I don't mean that metaphorically. I mean that the tears were ever-present in my eyes and required no provocation to make them flow. I don't know what I expected grief to be like, even though I'd lost my father a few years before. When that was still a fresh wound, I used to cry suddenly and copiously, when something made me think of him or someone used some stupid phrase he used to say. Missing him would hit me like a well-aimed punch, so I would cry because it hurt.

But with Luke, it was different. I was never reminded of Luke because I never stopped thinking about him. All the time I was teaching, I would guess I was giving the kids, at best, seventy per cent of my attention. It wasn't that I didn't care about them. I wanted them to like me, wanted them to learn. I wanted to do the job well, or at least as well as I could. But the children never once had my undivided attention, until it all went wrong. And I do still wonder if that was — at least in part — why it all went wrong.

At the time, I didn't know any of this, of course. And while I know that no-one can see the future, when I look back at that time, I realise I couldn't even see the present. I listened to them talk, but I only heard part of what they were saying, because I was so consumed with carrying the weight of Luke. My lungs felt tight with it sometimes. The world was heavier without him in it, and slower, and darker, and it took energy, actual physical energy to move through it. And I didn't want to let go of it, either. What other way did I have to keep him real? Carrying his dead weight was better than forgetting him. Grieving was better than waking up to realise I couldn't remember which of his eyes had the brown fleck in it.

3

I took Robert's advice and stopped in at Blackwell's before I next saw the fourth-years. I bought a few more books – a collected Sophocles, *The Seagull* – trying to think what I would have liked to read when I was fifteen. My father was the theatre fan in our family, always booking tickets to every new play or revival. His shelves bowed under the weight of glossy theatre programmes and scripts. I couldn't now remember how I'd chosen which ones I liked the look of: the titles, probably. But that was eleven years ago, and anyway, when I was their age, I was nothing like them – never in trouble with a teacher, let alone kicked out of a school. But there had to be one thing we could all connect to. I found myself scanning the shelves, trying to guess which one might be the charm.

One of the things I'd liked least about Edinburgh when I first moved there was how straight, ordinary roads kept changing their names, like a criminal with a roster of alibis. North Bridge became South Bridge, South Bridge became Nicolson Street, Nicolson Street became Clerk Street. I could never quite remember the points of conversion, so even a major bus route felt slippery and uncertain. I'd reached Clerk Street now, and felt my spirits drop as the empty shop fronts increased and even the charity shops thinned out. I turned left onto Rankeillor Street, and walked to the very end, gazing up at Arthur's Seat, which sulked ahead of me, clouds shrouding its peak.

The volcano was long dead, but its sullenness remained. The Unit was the last building before the end of the road, next to a tiny newsagent's that must have made most of its money selling crisps and cigarettes to our kids.

I was relieved and surprised when all five of the fourth-years turned up.

'Hello again.'

They mumbled and took the same seats as before.

'As Annika suggested, I've brought you some plays,' I said. Ricky gave a huge sigh, his tiny frame swamped today by a green football shirt which flattened onto his chest as he exhaled. He was hunched into it, clearly cold. His scabby elbows were raw and red.

'I'm sorry, Ricky. I know you'd prefer to do art, but we're going to have to do some drama. That's what the majority of the group would prefer, and it is what I came here to teach.'

He looked around at his classmates, trying to work out who had stitched him up.

'If you want to draw or paint, you're very welcome to do that. We'll be discussing plays in class, but you'll do some work in your own time as well, I hope.'

Jono's eyebrows shot up, and I realised that hope was extremely slender.

I carried on talking to Ricky. 'You can draw your homework for me. That would be brilliant, actually.'

'Brilliant, actually…' Though Ricky seemed placated, Jono was mimicking me under his breath. This would be the most difficult part of dealing with these kids, I was discovering. In order to gain ground with one, I inevitably antagonised another. Even when they were ostensibly friends. My other classes were the same, though they were usually easier to cope with than this one. Someone always felt things were unfair.

Ricky settled back into his seat, and began doodling on the back page of his exercise book.

'We'll pick a play and read it together. What do you fancy? Shakespeare? Molière? Chekhov?' I held the books up to the room, one after another.

'Those are just words,' Ricky said. 'Not even words, to be honest. Noises. What's the difference?'

'Are they hard?' asked Jono. 'We should do the easiest one.'

'Why?'

'Because it'll be the easiest one,' he said. He shook his head like I was an idiot. I bet he did that to his parents. I must be at least ten years younger than his parents, and it made me feel old. I tried to explain myself.

'What's wrong with something hard? You're smart. Everyone's told me how clever you five are. Why would difficult be a bad thing?'

He stared at me blankly. I stared back. I was beginning to see that this was the way the kids in Edinburgh communicated. I'd come into Rankeillor expecting them to talk in slang, like London kids – a whole special patois, with no distinction between class or wealth, based entirely on their desire to speak in a language their elders couldn't penetrate. But here, teenagers spoke so much more formally, it was like travelling back in time. I wondered if they spoke this way when there was no teacher in the room, or if the act of observing them made a difference. Either way, they seemed to have only two settings: adult speech, or staring and grunts.

'It's just common sense,' he sighed. 'Difficult means boring.'

'Since when? Do you choose a video game because it's the easiest?'

'Obviously not. I'd have finished it in a day. They cost forty pounds, you know.' This provoked a snigger from Ricky. Later, I would discover from the basic skills teacher that both boys were barred from the St

James Centre, the dilapidated shopping mall over in the New Town, for shoplifting.

'Well, let's treat plays like that. Let's assume that difficult doesn't mean boring, it means something you have to work at a bit, which you'll like better.'

'Video games and work aren't the same,' he said. 'Obviously.'

'Humour me, and pretend they are, will you? Just for a while.'

I wondered if the lesson's first walk-out was about to happen. But Jono stayed in his seat, pitying me, and Mel broke the awkward silence that had fallen. I wondered if she could sense the difference between good and bad silences, or if she just spoke when she was ready.

'Not Shakespeare,' she said, shaking her head. 'We did *Romeo and Juliet* at my old school. The hot guy dies halfway through.'

'The hot guy is Mercutio?' I wanted to be sure.

'Yeah. Shakespeare just kills him off so that Romeo doesn't look like such a loser in comparison.'

'Is he the black guy?' asked Carly. 'He is hot.'

'The black guy?' I asked.

'In the film. With Leonardo DiCaprio in it?'

'Oh, yes. Mercutio is the black guy.' Finally, they seemed to be interested in something, even if it was only the film adaptation.

'I don't want to do Shakespeare either,' said Ricky.

'OK, not Shakespeare.' Of course they wouldn't want to do Shakespeare. They'd probably been bored to tears trying to get through *Macbeth* at school. 'Then how about someone modern?'

'Like who?'

'We could do *Jerusalem*.' I picked up the newest play I'd brought for them. 'It's full of swearing. You might like it.'

'What's it about?' asked Jono.

'It's about a man who lives in a caravan. The council wants to evict him.'

Jono reached over and took the book from me, lured by the red cover and the picture of a man smoking a joint.

'Looks alright,' he said as he flipped it over to read the back. 'Wait,' he continued. 'It says, "A dark comedy about contemporary life in rural England."' His chubby finger jabbed at the words.

'Yes,' I replied, not seeing the man-trap opening up beneath my feet.

'And, "A bold and often hilarious State-of-England play."'

'It got very good reviews,' I agreed. 'Is that the one you'd like to do?'

'Why would I want to read a play about England?' he spat. 'It wouldn't have anything to do with us.'

'Oh my God,' said Annika, slamming her hand down on her desk. 'Could you be any more pathetic?'

His face was glowing bright red. 'Yeah, it doesn't matter to you because you're not fucking Scottish. So you wouldn't understand, would you?'

'Christ, could you stop being such a victim!' she shrieked. 'This poor-wee-Scotland-the-Brave mentality.' For a girl whose first language was Swedish, she could parody the Edinburgh accent unnervingly well. 'It's just so…' She cast around for the word. 'Boring.'

She reached down to her bag. Ricky was doodling with increasing fervour, drawing himself out of the conflict.

'Let's not make a big deal out of it,' I said, and their two furious faces both turned in my direction. I had to fight not to raise my hands. I had half a memory of a weeping supply teacher at my old school, and I knew I was heading that way myself. 'It's not life and death. It's just a play. I thought you might like it, but it's OK if you don't, because we have plenty more to choose from. Mel, Carly – you've gone very quiet. Do you have any thoughts?'

I passed two more books to them. Mel leaned forward to take one. Her sleeves were much too long, I noticed. Even as she reached forward, her hand was half-covered by the pale blue cuff of her sweater.

'This one,' said Carly, as she looked at the jacket of a new version of *The Misanthrope.*

'No,' said Mel. 'I can't stand her.' She pointed her thumb at the film star who had appeared in the recent London revival.

'OK.' My patience had worn through. 'Which one are you holding?'

'Sophocles, *The Theban Plays*,' she replied.

'Then shall we do one of those?' I snapped. 'It's not set in England, it doesn't have a hot guy dying halfway through, Keira Knightley has never appeared in it, and there are several scenes in it which I imagine Ricky would be able to draw. Will that do?'

Ricky jumped as I said his name, then continued cross-hatching whatever he was drawing when he realised he wasn't in trouble. The others looked blank.

'What's it about?' asked Carly, quietly.

'We'll read *Oedipus the King.* That's the first play in the book. It's about a man who's destined to do something terrible and tries to escape his fate.'

'What's his fate?' she asked.

'He's destined to kill his father and marry his mother.'

'That's disgusting,' Ricky said, starting to laugh. The tension in the room relaxed very slightly. I felt my shoulders drop an inch.

'It was even more disgusting to the ancient Greeks than it is to us,' I said, trying to remember my first year as an undergraduate, when we'd read all these Greek plays: it must have been Robert's way of weeding out the students he didn't think were serious enough about his art. I had written piles of essays on the reception of Greek tragedy and its historical context, silently thanking my father for having dragged me to see some of them when I was at school. It was all in my head somewhere.

Annika was glaring through the window at the white wall outside, and Jono was still breathing heavily, though his cheeks were fading back to normal.

'I don't think so. They couldn't think it was more disgusting than I do,' Ricky said.

'Honestly. Incest was a really big taboo in their world. And they didn't care about loads of things we think are taboo, so it counts double, at least.'

'What's a taboo?' he asked, still holding his pencil but no longer scribbling with it.

'It's something forbidden. Like incest or paedophilia or something like that.'

Ricky was giggling properly now. Even Jono smiled briefly.

'The Greeks didn't have a problem with paedophilia at all,' I said, hoping this was the right way to go. 'But having sex with your mother was very bad indeed.'

'That's fucking bizarre,' said Jono.

'Your mum's not so bad,' said Ricky. Jono turned to look at him. 'Sorry, man, I didn't mean that.'

'Let's not over-relate, shall we?' I realised that this lesson could be about to go wrong in a whole new direction.

'Sorry, miss.' He picked his pencil up again.

'So we're going to read *Oedipus*, then. I'll make sure I have five copies by the end of today. You can pick them up from my desk before you leave.'

'How do you know about all this stuff?' asked Mel. She was rocking on her chair, leaning back to the furthest point she could go before it tipped up.

'It's what she did at college, isn't it?' Carly answered for me. She loved to gossip, about pupils and teachers alike. Learning was just an interlude from her real interest at Rankeillor. 'You studied here, didn't you? In Edinburgh? With Robert?'

'Yes, I did. I came here in 2002, and I graduated five years ago. Then I did some postgraduate studying for a couple of years here and in London.'

She counted back. 'So you left college in 2008?'

'That's right.' In another world, I wanted to say.

'Was Robert a good teacher?' asked Mel.

'Of course he was. He knows everything about acting and perform-ance, because he used to be an actor.'

'Didn't you want to be an actor, miss?'

'No, I suppose I didn't, Carly. I'm not very comfortable in another person's skin – does that make sense?'

She looked at me, and I wondered if she might point out that I didn't look very comfortable in my own, either. But she thought for a moment and nodded. 'So why did you leave Edinburgh then?'

'Well, I suppose I wanted to go back to London.'

'Is that where your family is?'

'It's near where my mother is, yes.' I realised that I had fallen into another trap that we'd discussed when we were training – if you don't give kids enough to do, their curiosity turns inevitably onto you. When I was at school, I remember, we were so fixated on a glamorous French teacher that we spent months trying to find out her first name. The Rankeillor kids were a lot more ambitious.

'And what about your dad?' she asked.

'My dad died a few years ago.'

'I'm sorry, miss.' Carly flushed.

'That's OK.'

'Doesn't your mum miss you, though?' She pressed on.

'I don't know.' I could feel sweat starting to prickle on the back of my neck. I needed to move her back into safer territory.

'You should ring her, miss. Tell her how you're getting on.' She nodded at me encouragingly, like you might do to a dog.

'Thank you, Carly. I'm sure she'd agree with you. Shall we get back to Oedipus and his mum?'

'OK,' she said, happily. She only needed a small fix to sustain her.

'First of all, you should know where this story happens. It's in a city called Thebes.'

'And when is this?' asked Annika. She pulled off her glasses and cleaned them with the hem of her t-shirt, before returning them to her perfect nose.

'Half twelve,' Jono snapped.

She sighed loudly, and began to rearrange the pens and books on her desk into ever more perfect straight lines. 'I mean what year or what century or whatever. Obviously.'

'It's the Bronze Age,' I said.

'And when's that?' she asked, just before I realised I didn't entirely know.

'Are there dinosaurs?' Ricky asked.

'Don't be an idiot.' Jono twitched, like he was trying to shake the words out of his head.

'I was just asking.'

'No, it's later than dinosaurs,' I told him. 'Sophocles is writing in the fifth century BC, two and a half thousand years ago. And the time when this play is set is the mythic past to him, right? Like Robin Hood, or…' I saw Jono's eyebrows contract. 'Or maybe William Wallace would be to us. So this play is set in the past, and it's set in Thebes, which is where Oedipus was born. His father, Laius, and his mother, Jocasta, were delighted to have a baby son. But then they were told that Oedipus had this terrible fate predicted for him.'

'Who by?' asked Annika.

I couldn't remember. 'An oracle,' I said, hoping this was true.

'What's an oracle?' she said.

I was definitely going to need to do more reading before their next class. 'It's like a horoscope,' I said. 'And it predicts that he'll commit two terrible crimes.'

'He'll kill his dad and shag his mum?'

'Exactly, Jono. And, as you might expect, his parents didn't want that to happen on several counts. So they tried to get around it. When Oedipus was still a baby, they sent him away with a servant who'd been ordered to leave him out on a hillside to die.'

'Oh my God,' said Carly, her pale red hair swinging as she also started tipping back in her chair. I could feel my jaw tense as I waited for the chair legs to come back to the floor. It was like watching a glass that someone had left balanced on the edge of a table, waiting for it to crash to the ground. 'Isn't that illegal?'

'It is now, yes. So don't get any ideas. But no, it wasn't then. Besides, Laius was the king of Thebes, and Jocasta was the queen, so they could pretty much do what they wanted. And that isn't all. Do you know what Oedipus means?'

They all shook their heads.

'It means swollen foot. Because his feet were pinned together when he was taken out to the mountainside, so he wouldn't be able to move.'

'Jesus,' said Jono. 'How did they do that?'

'I don't know, exactly. I suppose the pins must have gone through the soft part of his feet.'

'That's horrible.' Carly looked appalled.

'Yes. But the servant who was sent to abandon him there couldn't bring himself to leave a baby to die like that, so he gave him to a kindly shepherd instead.'

'He wasn't a paedophile, was he, miss?' asked Ricky.

'Not in Sophocles' version, no. Or in any other version,' I added, seeing his mouth begin to form another question. I wished he had a jumper or something. Pale red hairs were standing up on his bare arms.

'The kindly shepherd and his wife took the child to Corinth, which is another town in Greece. It's the skinny bit in the middle between the north, where Athens is, and the south, in case you've been to Greece.'

'I've been to Chios,' said Mel. 'I went with my dad two years ago.'

'Well, maybe if he takes you again, you could go to the mainland, instead of one of the islands. Or as well, if he's feeling generous.'

She smiled at me. 'Maybe I'll ask him,' she said, nodding.

'Now, the king and queen of Corinth didn't have any children, and they really wanted one. So they adopted this baby that the shepherd had brought to their city. But they never told him he was adopted. So when Oedipus grew up and heard rumours about his fate – that he was going to kill his father and marry his mother – he was horrified. He loved the people he thought were his parents and didn't want to harm them in any way. He wanted to protect them, so he ran away from Corinth. Which way do you think he headed?'

'Where you said the play was set,' said Jono. He was biting the skin next to his thumb nail until a tiny globe of blood appeared and he stopped, apparently satisfied.

'Thebes?' asked Mel.

'Exactly. And on his way there, at a crossroads, he was pushed aside by a rude old man and his servants. The rude old man hit Oedipus with his stick. In anger, Oedipus struck him back and killed him. He killed all but one of the servants, too. Five or six of them, I think.'

'How did the other one escape?' said Ricky. He was drawing a brontosaurus, grazing next to a caveman. At least I wasn't supposed to be teaching him history.

'He ran away. He turns up later, as the only witness to the fight that killed Laius. But that's not till later. This is still all the background stuff which has happened before the action of the play starts.'

'We're not even at the beginning yet?' Carly sounded faintly panicked.

'Remember what I said about difficult and boring?' Jono muttered.

'When Oedipus got to Thebes, he found them living under the curse of the Sphinx.'

'Like in Egypt?' Mel asked. 'I've always wanted to go there.'

'Exactly like in Egypt, except this Sphinx isn't made of stone. It's real.'

'It isn't real.' Jono rolled his eyes, as though he had to deal with this kind of nonsense every day. Looking at Ricky's dinosaur, I guessed he might.

'In the world of the play, the Sphinx is real. Like a dragon might be real in a story, right? Or a unicorn?'

He shrugged. Or perhaps his hunched shoulders just rebelled sometimes of their own accord.

'Now, the Sphinx had set a riddle, and no-one could pass her until he could answer it. The riddle was this: what has four legs in the morning, two legs in the afternoon, and three legs in the evening?'

'And what's the answer?' Annika asked. She was holding a pen poised above her notebook, midway between chewing it and writing with it. I realised she might be taking notes.

'Maybe you could try and work it out,' I suggested.

'Nothing has a different number of legs at different times of the day,' she said, tapping the end of her pen quickly and softly on her book.

'OK, I'll give you a clue. The morning in the riddle means when something is young. The evening is when that thing is old.'

All five of them stared at me.

'None of you can guess? OK, well the answer is a person. We all used four limbs to get around as babies, when we could only crawl, right? Then we learned to walk and so we're on two legs for most of our lives. Then when we get old, we might need a walking stick, right? So we become three-legged in the end. Kind of.'

'And Oedipus worked that out?' Jono snorted.

'He did. And the people of Thebes were so glad that they let him marry the queen, who had been recently widowed. Guess who her husband had been.'

'The old man at the crossroads?' asked Mel.

'Exactly right.'

She smiled again.

'So Oedipus has killed his father and married his mother. And when they find out what they've done, Jocasta hangs herself, and Oedipus puts his eyes out with her brooch pins.'

'Brooch pins? What the fuck?'

'People did wear jewellery in the ancient world, Jono.'

'They didn't use it to stab themselves in the eye, though. Did they?' he said.

'Well, Oedipus does. And I think there's another play where some-one gets stabbed in the eye with brooch pins, now you mention it.'

'But that's not fair,' Carly said. 'Oedipus didn't mean to marry his mother.'

'You think something's only a crime if you mean to do it?'

'Yes,' she said.

'Well, what about a car accident?' I asked them. 'If you ran someone over but didn't mean to, they'd still be dead.'

'But he didn't know she was his mum.' Carly wasn't persuaded. 'And she thought he was just some guy.'

'If someone's told you you're going to marry your son, wouldn't you avoid men young enough to be your son?'

'But she thought her son was dead,' said Mel.

'That's true. And maybe she had no choice?' I suggested. 'If she was fated to marry her son, and even sending him away to die on a hillside wasn't enough to change that fate, maybe nothing could, and she had no free will at all.'

'That's really fucking bleak,' said Jono, leaning onto the arm of his chair, which gave a quiet creak.

'But no-one would believe that,' said Annika.

'Really? Do you read your horoscope?' I asked her.

'Sometimes,' she said, frowning. Annika saw potential tricks and humiliations everywhere.

'Then aren't you agreeing to a world where your destiny for that day or week or whatever is dictated by your birthday?'

She shrugged.

'So that's what I want you all to think about before I see you again. Free will, and how much of it you think you have. Do you believe in destiny? Or do you think what happens in your life is entirely up to you? Try to read the first act of the play, or some of it at least. Then write me a side of paper.'

They groaned as they put their things into their bags and headed out, but they had all stayed to the end. Maybe Robert had been right, I thought. Maybe I would be alright at this. Maybe I would even like it.

4

DD,

Everything's changed, after Annika made her big scene last week. I don't like her at all, most of the time. She's such a bitch, and no-one ever calls her on it except Jono and me. Last week, when she stormed out of our first lesson with Alex, she called her a cunt. As she was leaving, I mean. She was walking right past her desk when she said it, and it was loud enough for me to hear even though she was facing away from me. Alex didn't react at all, though. She just sat there like she couldn't believe what she'd heard.

By the time we were out of the classroom, Annika had gone, left the Unit, I mean. I wanted to go after her and talk to her, because it just isn't OK to speak to someone like that on their first day. But Carly wouldn't let me, so we wrote an anonymous note and left it in Robert's pigeonhole. I wonder if Alex noticed how much nicer Annika was being today? She doesn't want to get kicked out of Rankeillor any more than the rest of us do, even though she's always saying she does. She says she hates her mum and she doesn't care what happens, but I bet that's not really true.

Still, Annika being a bitch paid off in some ways. I've been at Rankeillor for three months now, and all we've done is basic skills and key skills and the rest of it has all been music therapy, art therapy, personal development, anger management. It's been bothering me – aren't we going to be behind when we go back to proper school, or to college or whatever? But now we're reading a play by Sophocles, who I hadn't even heard of last week. Alex wants us to think about whether we have a destiny. So is it my destiny that I can't hear? Or can I just not hear?

Since I've decided I might want to be a journalist, I've been reading more blogs and stuff. And here's what I've noticed: they're all about the writer. I mean, they seem to be about something else – something the writer is, or likes, or cares about – but those are just ways for the writers to talk about themselves. It's a bit fake, I think. I'm not going to pretend I'm talking about something else when I'm talking about me. I'll just talk about me when I want to.

So here are ten things you might not know about being deaf:

1) I can't hear you if we're outside and there is a lot of traffic. The traffic is always louder than your voice, and because it's lower-pitched, I can hear it more easily than I can hear your voice.

2) I can't hear you if you don't enunciate properly. Mumbling at a deaf person is really fucking rude.

3) I can't always hear you if you don't face me. I know it's weird talking to a deaf person, because hearing people look at your eyes, while deaf people mostly look at your mouth. But if you look away, I can't read your lips, and even though I have hearing aids, I lip-read too. My audiologist says that everyone lip-reads a bit, even people with perfect hearing, but most people don't realise they're doing it.

4) I can hear music, but I need to adjust my aids for it, and it needs to have the bass turned up.

5) When my mum asks me to do something for the third time, she can't say, 'Are you listening to me?' And I can't say, 'I'm not deaf.' Usually, she goes with, 'Why aren't you paying attention to me?' And I go with, 'I'm not stupid.' A lot of people think that deaf and stupid are the same thing. That's because they are stupid.

6) I wasn't born deaf. If I had been, I would probably use sign language as well as lip-reading, and I might not be able to speak properly. I know some sign language, but only the basic stuff.

7) Sometimes I get tired from the effort of listening. My head starts to ache from concentrating on your mouth, and blocking out the interference from everywhere else. When this happens, I take my aids out so I can just forget about hearing for a while. If I close my eyes, you could all be on another planet. You just disappear. You're gone so completely that I wonder if you were ever really there.

8) I'd rather be deaf than blind. Have you ever noticed how much people use seeing words in normal speech? I see what you mean, I'll look into it. Whereas hearing words are used for when people are arguing: listen, I hear what you're saying. I don't mind being deaf, but I would really hate to be blind. I've never met a blind person, but I'd like to know if they feel the same way as me, or the opposite.

9) I sleep with an alarm next to my pillow. If the fire alarm goes off, I won't hear it, because obviously I take my aids out to sleep. So I have a special alarm that vibrates and strobes to wake me up. It's connected to the fire alarm wirelessly, so it goes off if the main alarm goes off. This is so I don't burn to death, because we live on the first floor, and it's a long way down to the street, and also there are railings. I have to take it with me when I go to stay with my dad.

10) I'll think of a tenth thing for next time.

It was a filthy day outside. The wind was up, so the sleet was falling diagonally, stinging and vicious. I had two routes to Rankeillor: I could either walk out of New Skinner's Close onto Blackfriars Street, turn left onto the Royal Mile and left again onto the South Bridge. Then half a mile past all the bus stops and left onto Rankeillor Street. Or

I could go the other way, out of the close at the bottom, turn left past the big Catholic church, then right up the hill, past the student union buildings on the Pleasance, then eventually turn right onto Rankeillor Street just before St Leonard's police station. On wet days, I usually went for the former. Climbing into the rain was somehow worse than walking into it.

As I walked up Nicolson Street, sharp pinpricks of cold found the few exposed inches of my skin. I bunched my hands into my coat pockets. The buildings were dulled by the rain and even the cars driving past me were losing their colour, the sleet and dirt and road salt rendering them interchangeable with the road. The pavement was greasy underfoot with frost and salt; the broken paving stones were booby-traps, poised to spray freezing water on the feet of the unwary. Even wearing a sweater and a thick coat, I was bone cold. It was only just past seven a.m., but I'd woken at five and hadn't been able to get back to sleep. And if I wasn't going to sleep, I'd decided, I might as well swim.

I used to go to the Commonwealth Pool all the time when I was a student, until a zealous week in my final year when I went there three days in a row, and saw the same brightly coloured M&M carcasses ground into the changing room floor every day. After that, I couldn't quite convince myself that the rest of the pool was any cleaner than the floors, and it put me off going back. But when I moved to London and swam in the tiny pool at my local gym, I found that I missed those fifty-metre lengths. And since returning to Edinburgh, I'd been thinking about going there again. I hadn't swum for months. When Robert asked me what I was doing with my spare time, I'd told him I would be swimming, because it didn't feel like a lie. I used to swim and maybe I would again.

And as soon as the doors swung open and I smelled the chlorine in the air, I knew I'd made the right choice. It was so quiet in there on cold mornings: only the most committed swimmers could face getting out of bed before six in the winter. And the water was cool, unlike my old London pool, where it felt like swimming in a bath. Here, it was all about long distance, and distance swimmers could keep themselves warm. I walked through from the changing room to the lanes, stopping under the showers on the way to get my goggles wet. I clocked the speed of the five swimmers using the lanes already. I didn't trust myself to the fast lane when I hadn't been in the water for months. So I splashed down into the middle lane and swam two freestyle lengths. My muscles hurt a little, but it was a clean pain. I checked the clock and began to swim again. I probably had time for twenty lengths before I needed to shower and head to the Unit.

Everything was quiet. My goggles and hat covered my ears so completely that they blocked out almost all the noise of the pool. The city outside seemed completely unreal in there. Just the taste of chlorine and the occasional splashing of another swimmer in the next lane over. I cut through the water, staying under the surface for as long as my lungs could bear it each time I pushed off from the wall. You move more quickly through water than over it. And the only thing that matters is the next breath.

I showered and dried my hair before I left the pool. It was far too cold to go outside with wet hair, and it would be for weeks. I still had the imprint of my goggles on my face, I realised, as I caught my reflection by the hairdryers, and I hoped it would fade by the time I got to the Unit.

The weather made a big difference to the mood at Rankeillor. The kids were always on edge on these cold wet days – Luke would have called them 'baity' – because they had to stay indoors all day. Even the Unit's keenest smokers didn't want to drown or freeze. And the basement itself was swampier than usual – I could smell the damp creeping into it as I climbed down the stairs. The earth wanted to reclaim Rankeillor Street. I wedged the door open, to try and reduce the mildewed smell. One of my second-years – who I was teaching that morning – had, I remembered reading, an allergy to mould spores. I wasn't sure how the allergy manifested itself, but I worried that he would start coughing and scratching if he came into the basement in its present condition.

I saw the pile of plays which the kids had rejected on my desk, where I'd left them, and thought I should tidy up. I opened one of the cupboards under the front windows and blanched. The smell was coming from there. The wooden skirting boards curved away from the wall, the plaster was blistered, and all of it was covered in a thin layer of black mould. I looked at the small round clock behind my desk. I still had forty minutes before my first lesson, which was surely enough time.

I walked out to the hall and tried the door under the stairs. It was locked, but I had a pile of keys which Robert had given me on my first day, including a spindly brass one which opened the cupboard. As I'd expected, there was a bucket, mops and brooms next to a tiny sink. Under it was an industrial container of bleach. I filled the bucket with bleach and water, took rubber gloves and a mop, and scrubbed the mould away from the walls and the floor. The knots in the wood made it impossible to remove every trace, but at least I could get rid of the worst of it.

'It smells horrible in here,' said Carly as she walked in at the end of the morning. 'Has someone been sick?' Today, her shiny orange hair had a dark blue streak down one side, like a technicolour badger. She'd matched it with a blue bangle and blue Perspex earrings.

'It's just bleach,' I said, as three more of them trudged in. 'Where's Ricky?'

Annika shrugged. It seemed that she spoke for them all.

'Hasn't anyone seen him?'

'He's not here,' snapped Jono.

'Is he ill?'

He didn't reply.

'How did you get on with reading the play?' I said. More shrugging.

'We don't feel like working today,' said Carly.

'Maybe you should make collages, then,' I suggested. 'You were the ones who said you wanted to do something more challenging.'

'I know,' she sighed. 'But today it all just seems too high-maintenance.'

'You must have spent an hour doing that eye make-up this morning,' I replied. Carly blushed happily, and turned her face from one side to the other, so I could fully appreciate the light glinting off her gleaming turquoise brow-bone and blue-glittered lashes. 'So I don't think you're afraid of being high-maintenance. But I take your point. Edinburgh isn't much fun on days like today, is it?' I said.

I had clearly learned nothing. Did I want them to get side-tracked so we could talk about me instead of doing any work? I've thought about it hard, and I honestly don't think so. But I did want them to like me, and perhaps that's the same thing. I can only really be sure that I kept giving them openings like this, which they were incredibly good at exploiting – Carly especially.

'So why did you come back to Edinburgh, then?' she asked. 'It wasn't for the weather.'

'I like the smell of yeast,' I said, which was an obvious lie. Edinburgh isn't as reekie as its nickname suggests it once was, but you can still smell yeast in the air on some days. It always reminds me of over-cooked food, of baked potatoes kept warm for so long that they've become nothing but thick, blackened skins.

'No, but really?' she said.

'Robert asked me to come and teach you lot, when Miss Allen fell ill. And it's impossible to say no to him.'

'But what were you doing before?' she asked.

'I was directing plays.'

'Really? Who was in them? Anyone famous?'

'No, no-one famous. They don't let you have a go on the famous people till you've practised on the ones no-one's heard of.'

'So why aren't you doing that any more?' asked Jono. 'Were you rubbish at it?' He was always like this, I was beginning to realise. I tried not to take it personally. And besides, when I was up in the staffroom yesterday, one of their other teachers had told me that he'd lobbed a brick through her car windscreen a couple of months ago, after she'd kept him behind for swearing at her. So if the worst I got from him was this default assumption of my incompetence, I'd take it.

'I don't think so. I just didn't want to be in London any more. I wanted to come back to Scotland. And this job seemed like the right one. Maybe I'll direct another play sometime. But not at the moment. I don't have the time.'

'Why not?'

'Because I'm using all of it to find plays for you to read, so you can tell me you don't feel like it because the weather's bad.'

'When you say it like that, it sounds like you're cross with us,' Jono said.

'I'm not cross with you. I just think we should do what we set out to do today, which is to talk about Oedipus.'

'Alright, if you insist,' he sighed and reached down to his bag to find the book, still muttering. 'If it makes you happy.'

'I might try to make my happiness dependent on something other than what you read in the average week, Jono.'

'But, are you happy?' It was Mel who asked. It was such an unexpected question that I felt a reflex answer coming. Then I remembered that she'd called me out for lying to her the first day I met her. I thought for a moment and told her the truth.

'Not really,' I said.

She nodded, her blue eyes fixed on mine. 'Me either.'

'Aw, babe,' said Carly, and reached over to her. Mel leaned into the hug, and patted Carly's arm as she did so, but she didn't break eye contact with me.

'Oh God, really?' said Annika. Her whole body was taut with annoyance. 'Could you just not?'

'Fuck you,' said Mel, finally turning her head to look at her. Annika paid no attention.

'Seriously, I'm asking.' Annika took off her glasses to glare at me. 'Are we bleating on about you and Mel being a bit sad today, or are we talking about something I might give a shit about?' She began flipping her pen in her hand. 'Because if it's the first one, say so now and I'll go and do something else. I've only just met you, so I don't really give a fuck how you feel, to be honest.'

'We're talking about Oedipus.' I was growing tired of Annika. 'Whether you give a shit about it or not is entirely up to you. Now, are you staying or going?' She shrugged again. 'Then I'll assume you're staying. Have you read the first act?'

No-one said anything. Jono drummed his fingers on the back cover of his book. Carly smoothed invisible stray hairs back into place.

I'd had some awkward scenes in my other classes, but I was beginning to feel like I could set my watch by Annika's temper, and this was only the third time I'd met her.

'OK, so, where did we get to last time?'

'We were talking about fate, and destiny. Are they the same thing?' Mel asked.

'I think they are, really. The ancient Greeks had three Fates, called the Moirae – the singular is Moira.'

'I have an Aunt Moira,' said Jono. I didn't know if he was trying to ease the tension in the room, or just offering up information. 'She lives near Berwick.'

'Is she a sinister old crone who spins the thread of men's lives and is feared by the gods themselves?' I asked.

'Pretty much.' He grinned. He had a chipped tooth, I noticed, like a fang. Was it a new injury or had I just not seen him smile before?

'And the Moirae are a sort of triple incarnation of Fate: three women, like the witches in *Macbeth*, who see the future as it will be. Which is why *Oedipus* is such a difficult story – does he deserve his fate? Does anyone?'

'Some people are just born unlucky,' said Mel.

'Really?' I asked her. 'That's what you believe?'

'Of course,' she replied. 'None of us has any control over most of what's happened to us. We don't have a say in anything. Annika doesn't want to live here, you see, but her parents make her, and that's why she's such a bitch.'

'Fuck off,' said Annika as she stretched her arms over her head to elongate her spine. The age-softened chairs at Rankeillor wanted you to sit on them forever, and eventually your back rebelled. She didn't disagree, however.

'Where would you prefer to live?' I asked her.

'Back in Stockholm,' she replied instantly, as though she was in a perpetual state of readiness to answer this question. 'We lived there till I was twelve. It's so much better than Edinburgh.'

'Why did you move here?' Even though she was permanently hostile, I didn't want to give up on the idea of having any kind of civil relationship with her.

'My dad works for an oil company. He was transferred to Aberdeen, so my mum decided we had to move there with him.'

'Aberdeen,' said Carly. 'Can you imagine?'

'I don't have to imagine,' she snapped. 'We lived there for six months before my mum couldn't stand it and we moved here.'

'Do you still see your dad at weekends, then?' I asked her.

'We could see him as often if we were in Sweden. He'd have to take one extra flight each way. He's just being selfish.'

'Well, I hope you can visit Stockholm soon, at least,' I said.

She shrugged, immune to ingratiation.

'Ricky isn't lucky either,' said Carly. 'He didn't choose to be living with his grandparents, did he? No-one would. You'd rather live with your parents, even if they're intensely annoying, like mine. But that's still where he is.'

'Do you think that's why he hasn't come in today?' I asked.

It was Jono who replied, without looking up from his desk. He was fiddling with something shiny and black. I couldn't tell if it was a phone or a console. 'He comes in when he feels like it. They're old. They don't really notice what he does.'

'And some people don't even get that,' Mel added. 'My brother was three when he died. He wasn't being punished for being bad, he just got ill and then he died.'

The room fell silent. Even Jono stopped fidgeting. All I could hear were the distant sirens from the main road.

'Are you OK talking about this?' I asked her.

She gave a small smile. 'I wouldn't have brought it up otherwise. Anyway, it was ten years ago. Nearly eleven, actually. I got measles at school. Or maybe Jamie caught them at nursery. I can't remember who got sick first. We were both ill at the same time, anyway, and I was only five. But we both got really bad, and had to go to hospital. Jamie died, and I went deaf. But I didn't mind that so much, once my ears stopped hurting. That bit was terrible.'

'I didn't think you could die of the measles,' Annika said. Her usual fuck-you tone was missing.

'You can't if you've been vaccinated,' Mel explained. 'You have the MMR jab when you're little, and then if you do catch measles or whatever, you don't get it so badly. But me and Jamie hadn't been vaccinated. My mum blamed my dad for that. He thought the injection was dangerous. She said he talked her out of us having it. She's never forgiven him. That's why they got divorced.'

Carly was watching her friend intently. Her left arm was hovering, ready to hug.

'God, Mel, that is awful,' said Jono, turning back to look at her. 'I didn't know you went deaf, I thought you were born that way.'

'No.' She shook her head. 'I could hear fine till the measles. That's why I can talk properly now.'

And it was true: she didn't sound deaf. At least, not to me. Her consonants had a slight thickening to them, which people might easily attribute to a cold, if they didn't notice her hearing aids. And since she had shoulder-length blonde hair which fell into layered waves over her ears, her tiny hearing aids were easily missed. I didn't even realise they were hearing aids when I first saw them: they were so small and silver, I thought they were ear buds.

'So, what do you think about your destiny, Mel? Do you think you were fated to be deaf?'

'Maybe.' She shrugged. 'I don't know. I'm not, like, politically deaf. Deaf with a capital D, I mean. Some deaf people are really hard core. But I don't want to be part of Deaf culture, do I?'

'Don't you?' I asked. 'Why not?'

'They only hang out with other deaf people and only talk with sign language and stuff. I want to live like the rest of you, but I have to do it with hearing aids. It's not terrible. It's not like missing a leg or something. I don't really think about what it would be like to hear properly. I can't remember what that felt like, to be honest. So I don't know. Maybe I was destined for deafness, and that's why I'm not upset by it.'

'And do you think your brother was destined to die?' Annika leaned forward past Carly so she could see Mel more clearly.

I flinched, but Mel's expression didn't change at all.

'I don't know,' she said. 'It seems kind of a waste, doesn't it? Being born just to get to three and then die. People kept telling us we should be glad of the time we had with him, like he'd just wandered off to the shops or something. Got a better offer than hanging out with us losers. Or they went all Goddy about it. I remember one card my mum got after the funeral, from complete strangers. I guess they'd read about it in the paper. It was quite a big story, you know? A boy dying of measles. It was the first time it had happened for a while, I think. And the card had a cherub on it – a little fat baby with gold wings. I remember it really well. They wanted her to think that Jamie was like that now. Not dead, just feathery and fat. But who the fuck really believes in angels? I was five and even I could tell the difference between what you get on Christmas cards and my kid brother. Jamie wasn't even chubby.'

Carly reached over and squeezed Mel's hand, just like Robert had done to me a few days earlier.

'Thanks for talking to us about that, Mel,' I said. 'I hope it wasn't too upsetting for you, but you have brought an incredible perspective to the discussion.' I sounded so condescending, I could have slapped myself. But the other three began to clap, and she looked genuinely pleased.

'For next time, I'd like you to read the second half of the play, please,' I said. 'I want us to look at what kind of person Oedipus is, and what makes him the play's hero. Think about how he behaves, and if you would do things differently. I want you to think about how angry he is. And I also want you to think about whether it's better to know something or whether ignorance is bliss. OK? Thanks again, Mel especially. I'll see you next week.'

DD,

Today is the first time I have ever talked about Jamie. Well, that's not quite true. I told Carly about him before, way back when we were at Bruntsfield High. Before we got kicked out, I mean. And sometimes I talk about him with my mum. I don't bring him up if she doesn't, though, as it's guaranteed to make her start crying, and that can go on for hours.

The strange thing is, I had literally no idea I was going to mention him until his name came out of my mouth. I haven't thought about him in ages. I never say this to my mum (because of the crying thing), but I don't really remember him. I remember the idea of him, if that makes sense. I remember having a kid brother. I remember that he used to scream a lot. I remember him saying my name, eventually, after I spent ages teaching him. I remember him screeching when he first had the measles and me telling him to shut up because my ears hurt. And that's it. It was too long ago, and I was too little. Almost everything I remember about him is noise, and that's the opposite of what I remember about people now.

I remember what came after Jamie much better than I remember Jamie: the fighting and the crying. Not the funeral, because I didn't go to it. I suppose I was still in hospital, learning how to be deaf. That's not as easy as I make it look. You've got to get the right hearing aids that don't blare what Doctor Meikle calls ambient noise right into the middle of your head. You've got to adjust them when you go from one place to another, so you can still hear people talking even if they're to one side of you. You've got to find ones that fit and aren't massive and, more importantly, aren't that disgusting fleshy colour like old ladies' tights. You've got to wear your hair long and forwards, so that people talk to you like a person. You've got to learn to lip-read.

My mum just came barging in. Why she can't knock, like normal people, I have no idea. She said she did. But people say that kind of thing all the time when you're deaf. I mean, you would, wouldn't you? She's going on about the music I'm playing. She says it's because the neighbours have complained, but I bet it's just because she doesn't like it. Can't I hear them, she said, banging on the walls. I told her of course I can't, I'm fucking deaf. And if the bass isn't turned right up, I can't hear that either. Jesus. I told her I'd turn it off, if it was upsetting everyone so much. She said, you don't have to do that, just turn it down a bit. I swear to God, sometimes, there is literally no point talking to her at all.

So, here are two things I have noticed. One is that we all talk a lot more now Alex is our whatever she is. Teacher? Therapist? Responsible adult? Especially me. I don't think I have ever said as much since I got to Rankeillor as I did today. Which is OK. The second thing is that Alex doesn't come in on Fridays. I thought she just didn't have our group that day, but she isn't there at all. Does she just not feel like working five days a week? Or does she have another job to go to? Miss Allen used to be there on Fridays, though, so something's changed.

And before I sign off for today, I said I'd come up with a tenth fact about being deaf. So here it is: I have to watch TV with the subtitles on, because the sound mix of pretty much every programme and film is so fucking bad. If I turned my aids up high enough to hear people talking, I'd be almost bleeding from the ears when something blows up, or a plane takes off, or the music kicks in. It's the same at the cinema. I have to go to screenings with subtitles, because the sound at the top end is way too loud. And the surround sound they have at some cinemas is even worse. My hearing aids don't work very well when noise comes from lots of different directions at once. It's like they're not expecting it. I don't ever watch the news. If you want to know why, turn the sound off, and put the subtitles on. It's literally gibberish half the time.

The next time I saw that group I wasn't feeling well at all. I'd made my first trip back to London the previous Friday. Wait a minute, the lawyers will say. You said before that you didn't want to be in London. That you were hoping never to go back there again. It's in our notes. That's what you said. So, Miss Morris, why did you return to London only a couple of weeks after you'd left the city, of your own volition? I don't know if they'll use words like volition, obviously. But my guess is that they will. I'd almost be disappointed if they didn't. There's really no point going into Law if you aren't going to say 'volition' from time to time.

And as with everything else, I'll have to tell them the truth. Though it will be hard to explain in a way that makes sense to anyone else. Once a fortnight, or sometimes once a week, depending on how much money I had going spare and how much I needed to do it, I would sit on a train for four and a half hours to go somewhere I didn't want to be. I never contacted any of my friends in the city, nor my mother in the suburbs. I never spent the night; I always caught the five-thirty train back. Why that one? Because the six o'clock is the last train, and it's always too busy. So the five thirty is better.

And what did I do when I got to London? Went for a walk. Always the same route, always the same time, then back onto the train and back to Edinburgh. I realise that at no point in this process do I think of, or describe, either London or Edinburgh as home. I spent three hours in London each time, and then left. And if they ask me why I did this every week, or every fortnight, I will have no better answer than this: because I had to.

'Hello there.' Three of them came in and sat in their usual seats. Ricky had barely sat down before he restarted his campaign to colour in the cover of every book he owned. This time, Annika and Carly were missing. 'Where are the others?'

'I don't know about Annika, but Carly has the flu. She'll be off for a couple of days,' said Mel, quickly.

'You look tired, miss,' said Jono. 'No offence.'

'I feel tired, so none taken. I have a headache, truthfully.'

He frowned, then began rootling through his blue school bag, producing three small brown bottles of prescription medicines.

'Do I want to know where you got these from?' I asked.

'The doctor.' He shrugged. 'Two painkillers, one anti-anxiety. What d'you fancy?' He waved the bottles at me.

'I'm pretty sure you shouldn't have all those with you,' I said. 'And why did anyone prescribe you Valium?'

'Nerves,' he said.

'Is that right? Is it your name on that bottle?'

'Absolutely,' he said, pocketing it. 'Would you prefer codeine?'

'Thank you, but I think I have some aspirin somewhere.' I hunted through my own bag until I found a battered cardboard packet, crushed at one end. I dug around for a bottle of water and took two pills, wincing at the acrid taste. 'Well, even though we're missing the other two, I think we'd better get back to Oedipus.'

'He probably had a headache, too. What with the eye-gouging,' Jono said. Was it possible he was trying to be nice? Jono's moods were spoken of in hushed tones by the other staff, since you could never predict them. Mostly, I found him sullen, but every now and then I saw a glimpse of someone funny, engaged, almost kind. Then he would clam up again and the sulkiness returned.

'You're right, of course. Nothing like the pain of another to distract us from our own ills. But what I really wanted to discuss was whether Oedipus is better off at the end of the play or at the beginning.'

'At the beginning,' said Ricky. 'At the end he hasn't got any eyes, miss.' I wondered how much of the book he'd read, or whether he'd just asked Jono what happened. But then, if even one of them was reading even a few pages of Sophocles, Robert would be pleased. So perhaps I should be too.

'But at the beginning,' said Mel, 'Thebes has the plague, doesn't it? And the plague is a punishment for the city because Oedipus is the king. But he doesn't know that. So he's got all the bad news to come, hasn't he? There's no way he could just not find out. He has to deal with the plague, and that means finding out what he's done – all the stuff you told us about before.'

'So the plague is a collective punishment for the whole city?' I asked her.

She nodded, curling her hair into the neck of the reddish-orange sweater she wore. Rankeillor had a relaxed uniform policy. So long as the kids looked presentable, that was enough. Some of the girls, like Carly, were peacock perfect every day. But Mel mostly wore her own version of a uniform, much like I did: jeans, vests, t-shirts and a thick jumper. Sometimes two jumpers.

'Yes, because he's…' She paused. 'They keep saying "unclean".'

'Yes, you're quite right. I'm impressed.' She looked a little embarrassed. 'He's polluted the city because he's a criminal who hasn't been punished. Does that make sense to you? I know it's a strange concept to us.'

'No, it sort of makes sense,' she replied.

Jono nodded slowly. 'But is it all criminals?' he asked. 'I mean, if the city gets the plague every time someone does something bad and doesn't get punished, it would have plague all the time.'

'It's because the crime of killing a parent – and marrying one –' I ignored the look of disgust that passed over his face, 'is so much more terrible than a regular crime,' I said. 'Do you want some paper, Ricky?' Having covered his book, he had begun biroing the desk. He twitched guiltily. I passed him a few sheets of A4 from my desk. He was under-dressed for the weather again. I could see goose-bumps covering his forearms. Did his grandparents not notice?

'Thanks.' He reached over to take them, and began drawing a man bleeding from his ruined eye sockets. I hoped he wouldn't show it around when he got home.

'What do you think?' I asked him.

'I don't know,' he replied, without hesitation.

'You thought he was better off not knowing what he'd done,' I reminded him.

'Yeah, he should have just ignored that,' Ricky said. 'It's only plague.'

'But if he'd ignored it, then there would have been a revolution or something. People panic when they're getting ill and dying. And it's his job, isn't it, as king, to sort this stuff out?'

He shrugged. 'If you say so. I'd've left it.'

'He's better off at the end,' Mel said. 'He's been living a lie, hasn't he? And now he knows the truth. That bit about him being able to see clearly only when he's blind – it's right.'

'So you think he's better off knowing the depths of his crime rather than being ignorant of them?'

'Yes.'

'And do you think he's a hero?'

'Yes.' She was quite certain.

'Why?'

'Because he steps up. I mean, when all the bad stuff is going on at the start, he tries to uncover the truth. And when the story comes out, he takes it. His dad, his mum, all of it. It keeps coming.'

'Yes, you're right. And everyone else who has responsibility for it is dead. There's just him left, isn't there? And he doesn't kill himself like Jocasta does. He decides to live with what he's done, which is much braver.' I could hear the weight of each one of the words as it crashed from my mouth. Mel and Jono were both staring at me. Ricky was still scribbling away. I swallowed. 'And I think maybe that's important, for a hero?'

Jono shrugged. He'd lost interest again. Mel looked down at her nails as she thought before she answered.

'Everyone has to live the life they have, don't they? It doesn't matter if it's fated to be that way or if it just happens. You can't say you have no responsibility for doing what you do. Even if you have no control over your life, you should live like you have a choice.'

I smiled at her. The star pupil.

And of course I agreed with her. I still do.

I don't imagine it's a question they will ask me. They're not going to put a heading on the page and start making notes on whether destiny has any impact on how things work out. But that doesn't change the fact that this is the very crux of it all: of what I did, of what happened in the end, and before all of that, of what Luke did. Because I really do believe we control how we live. I can't believe that some people are fated to live and die as they do.

We're all responsible for our actions, and that includes me. In retrospect, I did everything wrong, almost from the moment I arrived in Edinburgh. I was weak, thoughtless and self-centred. I believed I was helping them, or at least I persuaded myself that I was. But the undeniable truth is that if I had made even the slightest effort to look outwards at these children, instead of inwards, I could have changed everything that happened. No-one was destined to die at this point.

6

DD,

What I would like to be able to report today is that I got a good mark for the Oedipus homework I did. I spent ages on it. Nearly an hour, actually. But I don't know if Alex thought it was good, because she hasn't given it back yet. And I can't even look forward to getting it back, because I feel too guilty.

Yes, you read that right: I feel guilty. Because we gave our work in on Thursday morning. And I asked her when we would get it back. No-one else seemed interested, but I wanted to know. And Alex said she'd try to read them that evening and we could pick them up from her classroom the next day, even though we didn't have a lesson.

So I thought she must be coming in on Fridays now. I figured whatever it was she used to do on Fridays was done, and now she would be at Rankeillor Street every day like the rest of us are. And so me and Carly went down to her room on the Friday — even though Carly had skipped the last lesson so didn't have any work to get back — and she wasn't there. It was weird being in there without her, actually. It looks exactly like it did last term. I mean, exactly: Alex hasn't put up any posters or pictures, or anything. She doesn't even have stuff on the desk or in the drawers or anything. Maybe I shouldn't have been looking. But we wanted to know where she was, and we thought maybe she'd left the books in there or something. Besides, if I'm completely honest, I just wanted to see what she keeps in there. Here's the answer: nothing at all. If she's not in the room herself, it's like she was never in it at all. Most of us leave traces of ourselves, don't we? Even if it's only a dip in the cushions. But not Alex. She's like a ghost.

So we went upstairs to Robert's office and asked if he had our books. He didn't, and he didn't seem even slightly worried that Alex wasn't there, even though she'd said she'd give us our work today.

She doesn't come in on Fridays, Melody, he said. She just made a mistake. She must have meant Monday.

But she said today.

She doesn't come in on Fridays. I'm sure you'll have your work on Monday. Who'd have ever thought you lot would be so desperate for your homework back? Alex is working miracles with you. I thought I'd be lucky if she could get you to stop fighting with each other, and ideally encourage you not to set anything or each other on fire. And now here you are, desperate for marked books. Amazing.

He's only half paying attention to us as he says all this. He's reading letters at the same time.

Why doesn't she come in on Fridays, Robert? Miss Allen used to.

Miss Allen used to, yes. But Alex has other commitments on a Friday, so she can't, I'm afraid.

But what other commitments? Does she have another job?

Of course she doesn't have another job, Melody. She just has other commitments which are none of your business.

He's smiling all the time he's saying this. His eyebrows are way up in his hairline, and he's looking at me over his reading glasses. He looks like a fat old fox. I mostly like Robert, but he can be really annoying. Patronising, I mean. Like it's just adorable that

*we worry about her and wonder where she is. It makes me want
to slap him till he tells me what I want to know.*

Is she seeing someone, Robert? Is it her boyfriend?

No, it isn't her boyfriend.

*Doesn't she have one? Why not? Someone must like her. If she
did her hair properly. Carly's trying to be nice. But that's when he
flips. Robert never shouts, I mean not properly. He does this actor
thing of going all low and breathy and formal.*

*She is not seeing a boyfriend, and I would thank you both
very kindly – he looks at Carly here. He's seriously unimpressed
that she mentioned Alex's hair – not to say such cruel things about
her. If it got back to Alex that you were gossiping and speculating
about her, her feelings would be dreadfully hurt.*

We only asked if she had a boyfriend.

*I am aware of what you 'only asked'. Robert does those air
commas as he says that. I think that's for my benefit, in case I can't
read his tone from his body language, from his face. Which obviously
I can, because I'm not stupid.*

*I'm annoyed by him doing it, so I say, Then you don't need to
be so histrionic, do you?*

*And that's what provokes him into telling us the truth. His
face has gone dark red, like he's about to have a heart attack, and
he's almost hissing out the words now.*

*Alex doesn't have a boyfriend because she was engaged to be
married until last year, to a man she loved very much. And then
he died.*

He takes a huge breath, like he's been underwater.

I don't say anything. The voice comes from next to me.

Died?

*Yes, Carly, he died. Alex has come to teach you and to make
your lives a little better. Perhaps you might return that courtesy by*

trying just a tiny bit not to make her regret that decision profoundly because she finds you've been prying into her personal life. Could you, please?

And it's then that we realise, that I realise: he isn't telling us off any more. He's pleading with us. He knows he shouldn't have told us about Alex's boyfriend, no matter how angry we made him, and now he's worried that we'll tell Alex and make things worse. So of course we tell him yes.

We don't want to upset Alex, because she's ours now. She has been for almost three weeks. And she's sad, and we didn't see. And so now I feel guilty, really guilty. Because we weren't all that nice to her when she first came to Rankeillor. And she's only ever been nice to us, even though she must want to cry all the time.

That's what I remember most about Jamie, you see. Not Jamie himself, just my mum crying every day for what seemed like forever. And my dad locking himself in the bathroom, so I wouldn't see him cry, then coming out with big fat eyes that wouldn't fool anyone. That's what Jamie meant to me, in the end: everyone I loved crying. And the shouting. People think when you're deaf that you can't hear arguments. But it's not like that at all. I can't hear some sounds. But I could always hear the shouting, right up till my dad moved out.

The next time I saw them, they were eerily well behaved, at least at first. All five turned up on time. They unpacked books and pencil cases and placed them neatly on their desks. They faced the front, in total silence. No pushing, no muttering, not even Jono drumming on the desk. I wanted to enjoy it, but I was having a tough day: I'd slept badly the night before, and my morning lessons had been filled with squabbles and ill will which had, in turn, made it impossible to achieve anything. I wanted to go home, and I was clock-watching through this last hour till I could head back and get some sleep. I tried to focus on the final lesson of the day, then remembered that two of them had been missing from our last session.

'Are you all alright?' I looked at Carly.

'Yes,' she replied. 'Why do you ask?'

'Well, you weren't well last week, were you?'

I realised as I asked this question that I had no idea if it was actually true. I'd reached my fourth week at the school, and I was beginning to see that many of the children at Rankeillor considered lessons to be largely optional. You were as likely to be missing a few of them as to have the full set, like I did today. This wasn't merely true for my lessons, but for every class. Some children were persistent truants from the Unit, like Ricky and a couple of kids in the year below. Some were in the building somewhere, but not always in lessons. All of them could pull a sickie: there were days when someone was visibly hung-over, and days when they just didn't make it in at all. Carly was so amenable, I didn't know which category she fitted into. But I only had Mel's word for it that Carly had had the flu. She might have spent the day shopping on Princes Street for all I knew.

'Yes, I'm fine now,' she said, dipping into her pink pencil case and choosing a pen, which she then held poised in one hand, as though about to take dictation in an old film.

'I'm glad to hear it. Now, I have books for a couple of you. Perhaps the rest of you might write something for me tonight, since you missed the deadline on this one.'

Jono nodded awkwardly. His big frame made small gestures look odd, almost spasmodic. I was wondering how long it would be before one of them told me what all the good behaviour was for.

'So in today's lesson, I thought we could look at the defining characteristic of Oedipus. What would you say that was?'

'He fucked his mum,' said Jono.

'That's maybe his defining behaviour, but it's not really a characteristic, is it?' He reddened and looked away. I tried not to sigh, knowing
I'd upset him. He wouldn't make eye contact for the rest of the lesson
now. 'If you had to describe him to someone – I mean, what kind of
person he is – what would you say?'

'That isn't motherfucker?' he said, his gaze firmly on the patch
of floor between us.

'Let's go for adjectives, shall we? Clever or stupid?'

'Clever,' said Annika. 'I mean, it takes him a while to catch on,
but that's because he doesn't want it to be true.' She volunteered
information like a disinterested spy: her chin on her hand, her mouth
barely opening.

'You're absolutely right,' I told her. Where another child would
smile, she nodded, grateful to discover I had finally come round to
the correct way of thinking.

'What else?' I said. Ricky was blinking fast, desperate not to be
called on. 'Is he patient or impatient?'

'Impatient,' said Mel. 'He's got a really short fuse. He yells at
everyone.'

'Right. And it actually slows down the process of finding stuff out,
doesn't it? Because people are too scared to tell him things which
they think he won't want to hear. What else?'

They had run out. I couldn't leave it any longer.

'Ricky?'

'I don't know,' he replied.

'Do you think he's a nice person?' I asked him.

'I don't know.'

'Does anybody else have an idea?'

They all looked blank.

'Maybe if you gave us more options?' said Carly, ever helpful.
'Clever or stupid, patient or impatient, like that.'

I felt myself deflating. I could deal with their frequent lack of enthusiasm most of the time, but today I was tired and running low on patience. 'This isn't supposed to be a quiz, Carly. I don't want you to guess at the answers, I want you to have an opinion, based on what you've read. It doesn't matter if you feel the same way about the characters as I do, or if you agree with each other. It just matters that you have a response of your own.'

She put her pen back down on the desk, and looked at it, hard.

'So my question was, what do you think about Oedipus as a human being? Would you like to talk to him, or do you think he'd be obnoxious or boring or rude or aggressive or what?'

'I don't know,' she said, refusing to look back up at me. 'I'm sorry. I was ill, so I didn't read as much as you asked us to.'

I wanted to bang my head on my desk. 'Remember how you all said you wanted to study drama? Has anyone done any actual reading? Because it's going to be difficult for us to discuss anything if none of you bothers to read any of the books. Though it isn't none of you, is it? Annika, you've read to the end – yes?' She shrugged a vague assent. 'And Mel, you read it too?'

'Yes,' she said, uncertain. 'But I haven't been ill.'

I ignored the defence of her friend. 'And Ricky, you don't know, so that just leaves Jono. Did you read it, Jono? What do you think?'

He ignored me.

'Jono? Hello?'

'Christ, does it matter?' he yelled, kicking the frame of his desk so hard it leapt to one side. It came out of nowhere, and I felt myself jump. I smelled something sweet and familiar on his breath. He'd been drinking cider, at a guess, during the lunch break. The one time I'd lost patience with a class since I'd started teaching there, and I'd managed to pick a fight with a boy who was drunk.

'Ricky doesn't know. I don't know. And it doesn't matter

because it's just a fucking play. What difference does it make if he's nice, for fuck's sake? It's not like we're going to meet him, is it? Even if he wasn't fictional, he would have been dead thousands of years ago.'

'Don't shout at her.' Mel was on her feet. She shoved Jono, but his bulk didn't move. He swatted behind him as though she were an insect. 'It's not her fault you're retarded.'

I wanted to remonstrate with her for using such a vile word, but found myself oddly touched by her decision to defend me. I said nothing.

Jono turned to her. 'Fuck you, you little cunt,' he said, spittle dripping onto his chin with the force of the words.

'I'm not taking sides or anything,' said Annika. 'But just for the record, that,' she pointed at Jono's face, 'is gross.'

He spun round to swear at her, and sweat beaded off him, landing on her desk.

'Oh my God, you fucking freak. Who sweats like that?' she shrieked, leaping away from the shiny discs of water. Then she spat at him, her beautiful mouth twisting to give it momentum. Her saliva landed on his left cheek, and he raised a disbelieving hand to touch it.

There was a moment of silence. Then Jono barged past his chair, spinning it across the floor, his fist pulled back to punch her.

I started to get up, but found myself completely frozen. The staff-room was always full of stories about fights between students, but no-one ever seemed to take them very seriously. Did the other teachers just step in between the kids and hope for the best? Would I be assaulting Jono if I grabbed him? He was nearer than Annika: I couldn't get to her without going past him, and her desk. Or did everyone else on the staff just have more authority than I did? Perhaps they could simply raise their voices and order would be restored. I opened my mouth, but no sound came out.

THE FURIES

Of course it should have been me and I knew it, but as I stood immobile, it was Ricky who jumped up in front of his friend, grabbing his arms without thinking. He looked like a mouse intervening with a bear. A mouse doing his teacher's job.

'Could we all take a moment and breathe?' I asked. 'And try to calm down. Please.' I meant it for me as much as for them. I was so ashamed of myself, doing nothing while Ricky – a child – didn't hesitate to act.

But it was too late. Jono pushed past me, so close I had to shift to the side to avoid getting hit by his bag. He turned to look back at Ricky, who was sitting down again.

'Are you coming?' Jono asked.

Ricky was hunched over behind his desk. 'I might just sit here for a bit and do some drawing,' he said, quietly. 'I'll see you in a bit.'

'Fuck's sake.' Jono slammed the door behind him. This time, we all jumped.

'Where the hell did that come from?' Carly asked Ricky.

He was almost doubled over, desperate not to have to answer.

'It's alright,' I told him. 'You aren't responsible for your friends. You're only responsible for yourself, OK?'

He nodded.

'Is there anything more disgusting than an angry fat kid, though?' said Annika.

Mel began to giggle. 'Spitting at one?' she asked.

'I'm serious,' Annika said. 'Oedipus couldn't be fat. We'd just laugh at him.'

'There's no need to be unkind,' I told her. 'And there's never any need to spit at someone.'

'Whatever,' she sighed.

I knew I needed to send Annika to Robert's office, but I didn't want to run the risk of her bumping into Jono on the stairs. I looked out of the window, and saw the problem disappear: his bulky frame was running out of the front gate.

'Annika, could you go up and see Robert, please?'

She glared at me. For a moment, I thought she was going to refuse. And what would I do then? I gazed back at her, hoping like hell that she would give in.

She rolled her eyes, picked up her bag, and stalked out without speaking.

I looked back at the remaining three.

'I don't think we can really carry on with this lesson now, do you?'

No-one spoke.

'OK, I'll see you next time.' I turned away, and followed Annika out of the room. I was back in my flat, a mile away, before I stopped shaking.

DD,

So, today was awful. Carly told the other three what Robert had told us about Alex. I don't know why. We should have kept it to ourselves. It's OK for us to know about Alex, but I didn't really want everyone else to, because obviously Alex doesn't want everyone to know. And telling them made everything go weird.

Alex could tell there was something wrong. We were all way too polite. Then Jono went off on one for no reason, because that's the kind of self-centred prick he is. Carly thinks he's OK, because about three months ago he told her she looked pretty, and she thinks that's a sign that he's a good person. I said at the time, she is pretty, so it just means Jono isn't blind. I asked her how good he can be when he's so obnoxious to me, and to basically everyone at Rankeillor except for Ricky and her. She said he's misunderstood. By her, is what I wanted to say, but I didn't.

Anyway, even she didn't defend him today, after he started screaming at Alex. He's always like that: completely fine one minute, bug-fuck mental the next. He was drinking with some other kids at lunchtime and he was fucking stocious by the time we had Alex's lesson. Ricky was pished as well, but it doesn't turn him nasty like it does Jono. It's easy to see how he ended up at Rankeillor.

But here's the worst thing about today: when Annika spat on him, and he went for her, Alex went completely white. I mean it, she looked like a statue. She just sat there, completely still, drained of colour. If Ricky hadn't stepped in, I honestly don't know what would have happened. Jono would have pasted Annika, I think. It only lasted a second — Alex disappearing, I mean — and then she was back asking everyone to calm down. But it was really, really strange.

And the fight fucked everything up. I was hoping we'd be able to ask her about why she moved here. And then she might have told us about her fiancé. We'd have that in common, you see — me and Alex — because my mum and I moved to Edinburgh after Jamie died. When we first moved here, my dad was going to be joining us in a few weeks, and then after a while he wasn't meant to be joining us any more. So we stayed here, and he stayed in Leeds, and now I hardly ever see him.

My mum has always blamed him for what happened to me and Jamie. She told me she didn't, but she did. And every time there's another story on the news about how the MMR vaccine was safe all along, and how it was stupid not to get your kids inoculated, she blames him all over again. Now she thinks that even if the injection had been dangerous, she should have had it done anyway. An autistic kid would have been a lot better than a dead one.

This is why I like the play we're reading. It's about the things which can't be forgiven, even if no-one meant to do the wrong thing.

My mother would ring, invariably, on Monday evenings, and this week was no different. After a day at Rankeillor, the last thing I felt like doing was talking to her.

'You sound tired,' she said, as I answered.

'I'm sure you can't deduce that from two syllables.' I don't know why I was always so tetchy with her, except that my mother is someone whose entire life philosophy could be summarised with the words 'I was only trying to help', and there are few things more irritating.

'Well, you do,' she replied, defensively.

'I'm just trying to do two things at once.'

'What are you doing?'

'Making dinner.' This was true. I had the phone sandwiched between my head and my shoulder, at an uncomfortable angle. Luke had been the keen cook, always trying to track down a place which sold tamarind paste or palm sugar. I just heated things up.

The kettle was boiling noisily, and I was about to pour water over half a packet of tortellini. I had no idea what they were filled with. They all tasted identical, orange, brown or green. I had half a jar of pesto open on the side.

'Oh,' she said. 'I had mine already. Shall I call back when you're done?'

'No, it's fine,' I said, as the pasta bubbled to the top of the pan.

'I would have called yesterday,' she said, 'but we had a parish meeting and a fund-raising committee brainstorm and—'

'It's OK,' I repeated. 'I know Sunday is your busy day.'

'And I couldn't call on Saturday because I still had my sermon to write for yesterday, and there was a rumour that the bishop might drop by, so I wanted it to be a good one. And then he didn't come, so I could have just recycled an old one.' She sighed.

'Blah blah, thou shalt not kill?' I suggested.

My mother laughed to fill time. Then she asked, 'Have you found a church in Edinburgh?'

I could feel my jaw setting as I drained the pasta. 'Edinburgh is full of churches. I live behind one, actually, but not your kind.'

'I wouldn't mind if you went to a Catholic church,' she said, her voice rising to a pitch which suggested she would probably prefer it if I joined a Satanic cult.

'Well, I would. I don't go to church. You know that.'

'You used to.'

'I used to do a lot of things.'

There was a long pause, which I ignored, because I was stirring the sauce through the pasta and grinding pepper onto the top. I might not be cooking, but at least I was seasoning.

'Well, I thought you might be ready...' she said. My mother never knowingly ended a difficult sentence.

'Really?' I snapped. 'Ready to go to church and accept the love of a God who let my father die, and then my fiancé? You thought I might want to bathe in his warm embrace, did you?'

'I know you're angry,' she said. 'But Luke...'

'Don't even say it,' I told her. 'Don't even try to tell me his death has meaning, because you know it doesn't. You know it.' I could hear my voice growing harsh and ragged. 'If you want to find consolation in the trite words of idiots, be my guest. But don't tell me he's gone to a better place, because he hasn't. I know he hasn't and so do you. This was the better place. Here, with me. And now he's gone, and you want me to just accept that. To move on.'

'I had to,' she said, quietly.

'Dad was fifty-four.' I was shouting now. I wondered if the woman downstairs could hear. 'I know he wasn't old, but he had cancer. You had time to prepare, and so did he. So did I, for that matter. Don't compare what we went through with him to what happened with

Luke, because they aren't remotely comparable. I can't believe you could even suggest that they are.'

'I didn't mean to upset you,' she said.

'And yet, you've succeeded.'

'I'm sorry. I only want to help you.'

'I'm sorry too. I have to go.'

I could hear the muffled sounds of her crying as she said goodbye. I was too angry to cry, but I could feel the tears building up behind my eyes. I looked at the food, which was developing an opaque sheen as it cooled. I took a fork from the cutlery drawer, and slid the pasta into the bin.

7

'Where's Ricky?' I asked Jono when they arrived in the basement for the next lesson a couple of days later. Jono had written a terse apology to me in Robert's office the previous afternoon. The letters were pressed so hard onto the page that it had ripped in two places.

'I'm not his keeper.'

'OK.' I tried not to sound martyred; I knew how annoying that was. 'Does anyone know where Ricky is?'

'He's not in for the rest of this week,' said Carly. 'He punched a kid on the stairs this morning.'

'Oh no. Really?' I don't know why I was surprised. Keeping track of these kids was like spinning plates: it was always the one you weren't watching that hit the floor.

'Get to fuck,' Jono said, turning round to Carly. 'Donnie Brooks isn't a kid. He's a wee scrote.'

'So the punching is uncontested? He definitely hit another child?' I wanted to be sure of the facts. Ricky was so spindly and quiet, I couldn't see him as an aggressor.

'Donnie Brooks has been asking for it since last term,' Jono said. 'Eventually he was going to get a crack. And now he has, and Ricky's the bad guy who gets sent home for a week.' He looked furious, again. Robert always reminded us, his teachers, that the children didn't enjoy being angry. Jono had purple shadows under his eyes: maintaining this level of rage must be exhausting.

'Wait. Is Donnie Brooks that tiny boy with the runny nose?' I asked. I remembered seeing a cluster of third-years gossiping on the stairs when I'd come down to the basement earlier.

'Don't be fooled by appearances,' said Jono. 'He's a little cunt. He's been going after Ricky for weeks. Asking for a slapping. His brother knows Ricky's brother. They've been fighting for years. Ricky tries to ignore him, but eventually it gets to him.'

'OK. So Ricky finally cracked and punched him?'

'Yeah.'

'And now he's not here till next week?'

'Donnie's parents complained to Robert,' said Carly. 'It was probably the trip to A&E that clinched it.'

'That's it,' said Jono, his face darkening as they recounted the injustice. 'Donnie's parents don't like hospitals. It must remind them of all the people their fucking kids have put in there. Anyway, it was only a broken nose. And only a fucking woman goes to hospital with a broken nose.'

'Because women are...?'

'You know what I mean, miss.'

'I think I do. What a horrible situation. Poor Ricky. Has anyone spoken to him? Do you know if he's OK?'

'He'll be fine,' said Carly. 'It isn't the first time he's been suspended.'

'Could you be more of a fucking grass?' Jono snapped.

'Alex can see our forms anytime she wants,' she replied. 'Do you think she doesn't know this stuff?'

'Could we redirect this analytical zeal to Sophocles, please?' I didn't really care how this lesson went now. I just wanted to get through it without anyone punching anyone else, or storming out, or getting suspended, or, in my case, fired. I wondered if they were all making the same choice. Only Annika looked like she was actually enjoying herself. She loved a fight.

'I'll take that silence as a yes. We've mainly focussed on Oedipus up till now. So today, I'd like us to think about Jocasta. Do you think she suffers a worse fate than her son?'

There was a long pause. Jono was clenching and unclenching his hands. I looked over at the girls, hoping he'd calm down if I left him alone.

'Yes,' said Mel.

'Because…?'

'Because she lives with it for longer,' she said. 'She knows from the minute he's born that something terrible is going to happen. She tries to get around it by getting rid of him, and that must have been awful. She must spend her whole life thinking about him, and what she and Laius have done. And then, when they find out what really happened, she kills herself. She can't live with it.'

Carly shot her a look, which I couldn't read. Mel didn't notice, or if she did, she didn't respond.

'And her husband died,' Annika added. 'And she thinks her son's dead, too. So she might be lonely?'

'Those are really good answers,' I said. 'Both of you. Well done. Since there are four of you, and since we're all in need of a bit of empathy today, I'd like you to each take on a different character. You can make notes for ten minutes, and then we'll do it as a debate. Annika – you be Oedipus. Try to think about why he's so angry and how his pride causes him harm, yes? Mel, be Jocasta. Jono, you can be Laius, and Carly, you be the shepherd. Work out why you're the most tragic figure in the play, and be ready to argue your case. OK?'

They settled down to work without too much fuss. I could feel my bunched shoulders relaxing again. It was almost impossible not to have a physical response to the fury that spun between them most of the time. I wondered how the hell their former teachers had coped with them when they were in classes with thirty other kids.

DD,

Is it just because it's February that everything is so awful? Maybe I've got that SAD thing, where you don't see enough sunlight and you get depressed. It's virtually dark when I leave home in the morning. And even if it isn't raining, which it usually is, it's not a nice walk across the Meadows from Bruntsfield to Rankeillor in the winter. The paths are frozen, so you have to walk on the grass and that's all muddy and horrible.

And when we have Alex's lessons, we have to sit underground, like trolls. And by the time we get out and I walk home, it's nearly dark again. I can't remember what the sun looks like. And this is something no-one tells you about being deaf: you need light more than other people, so you can read them. This time of year, if Carly comes back to mine for tea, I can feel my head starting to ache from trying to read what she's saying on the way home.

And it was horrible in class today without Ricky, even though he's usually a waste of space. I felt like Alex was disappointed in us somehow. Like we'd all let her down because one of us got in trouble. Not that she said that. She just looked sad today. Sadder than usual. I don't know if Jono's apologised to her for shouting at her the other day. He had a go at Carly today, too.

Alex really believes we'd be better people if we read more Greek tragedy. She thinks it has these big truths in it, you know. And when we were doing this debate today – it was kind of lame, but fun at the same time – I thought she might actually have a point. The four of us were trying to work out who is the most tragic person in the play, and I realised this is exactly how my parents used to behave with each other. Who's the most bereaved? Who's the saddest? Who can make everyone else feel guiltiest? Who can run away the furthest? I wonder if she asked me to be Jocasta because I said she suffered the most, in the play. No wonder she let Annika be Oedipus when she has the shortest fuse in the world, apart from Jono. And he played Laius, who is so obnoxious that Oedipus kills him as soon as he meets him. Perfect casting, I reckon.

Though my mum is being nice at the moment, actually. She bought me this big illustrated book of Greek myths. I don't know why. She said she could see I was really passionate about something at school (she always calls Rankeillor Street 'school', she never calls it the Unit), and she wanted to encourage me. It sounds a bit young for me, doesn't it? But it isn't. It's not drawings, it's pictures from vases and stuff: Jason and the golden fleece, Odysseus and the Cyclops, Theseus and the Minotaur.

It was nice of her, anyway. It's because she's going away this weekend (she says with friends, but I'm pretty certain it's with this guy from work she's been seeing) and she feels bad about it. I was supposed to be going down to see my dad, but now he's busy, so I can't. She worries if I'm here on my own, especially overnight. So Carly said I could spend the weekend at hers.

Her mum pretends to like me, but she secretly hates me, I think. She wishes Carly wasn't friends with me, and she totally blames me for us getting chucked out of Bruntsfield and dumped in the Unit. She never believed Carly — she knew it was my fault and that Carly was just covering for me. But she can't actually say that, because she's posh, and she doesn't want to discriminate against someone disabled. I think she's worried they won't serve her in Jenners if they hear she was mean to a deaf girl. Last time I went to stay, she took us to a signed performance of some fuck-awful play. I have literally never spoken to her in sign. I hardly know any, because most deaf people don't use sign. They lip-read and have hearing aids, like I do.

The next morning, I stopped off to see Robert before I went down to the basement. I wasn't able to shake off my concern about the fourth-years. Yes, there were other difficult children on the Unit. There were other personality clashes, fights and disagreements. But somehow the fourth-years seemed less happy than the other kids, and it was making me uneasy. They antagonised each other so much and they were targets for troublemakers, as Ricky's suspension proved. I'd started the term thinking they had a problem with me. But now I was beginning to think something had been wrong with this group long before I arrived. I needed to do something, before a broken nose was the least of their misdemeanours.

'Does he have a few minutes?' I asked Cynthia, who was brushing dust from her trousers.

'He does,' she replied. Her usually neat hair was ruffled, and when I walked into Robert's office, I could see why. Cynthia must have cracked and forced him to deal with the piles of paper that towered over him from every flat surface. His office had never been emptier, though two drawers in his filing cabinet now didn't close. He was sitting over the shredder, with his tie clamped inside his waistcoat, filling a fourth bin bag with shreds. His hair was damp with sweat and annoyance.

'Wow,' I said. 'It looks amazing.'

'Thank you,' he replied, looking around the room with grim pride. 'We've been here since seven. How can I help?'

'I'm worried about my group.'

'I don't need to ask which one, do I?' he groaned. 'Here.' He shunted a second shredder in my direction, and thrust a pile of documents into my hand. 'Slice while you talk.'

'I wonder if I should break them into two groups.' I'd been thinking about this since the previous lesson. It was the only solution I'd come up with. 'They really don't get on well, and I think—'

'Let me stop you right there.' Robert ran his hand across his forehead. 'It can't happen. The timetable takes a week to devise at the start of each term. They don't have much space structured into their days, because when we tried that, their behaviour deteriorated considerably. You'll have to keep them as they are.'

'It wouldn't be possible to—'

'Alex…' He shredded a page to emphasise his dramatic pause. 'It can't be done. Fitting your classes into four days nearly broke me. I can't do any more. I'm sorry.'

I acknowledged the guilt trip, but I couldn't let it slide. I tried again. 'I'm just worried that—'

He waved the sheaf of papers he was about to shred. 'You'll be fine. They'll be fine.'

'But they aren't fine. Ricky's been suspended, hasn't he? Fighting on the stairwell isn't a sign that he's coping well, is it?' I could hear my voice becoming shrill, but I couldn't help it. I didn't think Robert was listening to any of my concerns.

He sighed. 'Ricky, as I'm sure you've noticed, has some problems when he's provoked. He isn't unique among the children here. We're trying to teach him negotiation skills, and he's improved a great deal. A very great deal. Sometimes he falls off the wagon. It happens.'

'But Jono—' Surely we could both agree that Jono was getting nothing out of lessons with me. He could barely stay in his seat.

'Jono is a very difficult boy. He was thrown out of school for caus-ing criminal damage. If he isn't setting fire to the basement, you're doing fine.'

He wasn't taking this anywhere near as seriously as I'd anticipated he would. 'The basement is too damp to burn,' I pointed out, but he ignored me. I tried a different tack. 'He has a very antagonistic attitude to the girls.'

'Well, he knows better than to pick on Carly,' he said.

'What does that mean?'

'Carly was bullied very badly at her previous school: malicious texts and pictures and so on. One day she was in a classroom on her own. Another girl, whom she'd accused of bullying her before, entered the classroom. A few moments later so did Melody. Next thing anyone knew, the nameless bully was semi-conscious on the classroom floor. She was never prepared to say who had done what, but in the school's estimation, someone had slammed a desk lid on her head several times. Hard enough to fracture her skull in two places.'

'Seriously? Mel and Carly did this? I had them down as the well-behaved ones.' Well, them and Ricky, until he'd been suspended.

'The school interviewed Carly and Mel separately. Mel took her hearing aids out and refused to answer any questions. Carly said Mel had done nothing. The girl, as I say, refused to give any statement other than that she couldn't remember and might have fallen. Carly and Mel were handed over to my custody, or care, or whatever it is we provide here, after one of the teachers at Bruntsfield – was it Bruntsfield they were at?' I shrugged. I was catching it from the kids. 'Yes, Bruntsfield,' he continued. 'One of their teachers is friends with one of the Rankeillor Charity trustees, and she – rightly – thought they might benefit from coming here.'

I was shocked. I'd begun to think of Mel and Carly as – for want of a better word – my allies in the group. I liked them. They didn't have much time for Annika, for a start, which made a big difference to our lessons. If either of them had gone along with her bitching, Annika would have undermined my authority completely by now. Mel stood up to Jono, without deliberately baiting him, which I admired. I found it hard to imagine either of them doing anything even close to what Robert had described. But then, perhaps bullying could provoke anyone into extreme behaviour. I shouldn't judge them when I only knew half of the story.

The pile of forms and photocopies which Robert had given me before I started at Rankeillor covered only the most basic information on each child. He had more detailed paperwork in his office, but you had to apply with a good reason to read any of it. The Unit had stern views on data protection, which Robert was happy to enforce, determined that the children shouldn't become prisoners of their files and of the low expectations that accompanied them. Only a child's pastoral supervisor or social worker had full access to Robert's filing cabinet. Mostly people simply swapped gossip in the staffroom instead. I supposed this story must have been old news before I arrived here.

I wasn't sure what I wanted to say. I blurted, 'But Mel seems so normal. They both do.'

'And that's because she is normal. She's certainly normal for here. She has, like all of them, some difficulty controlling her temper. But she likes you. She's behaving well in lessons, isn't she?'

'She turns up every day. She seems engaged.'

'Then don't worry. Please don't. Meet me after work and we'll have a drink somewhere nice.' His face crumpled as he pleaded with me. I knew when I was beaten.

The following Monday, Ricky was first into the classroom. He was almost bouncing: I guessed he had returned to the Unit a hero. Donnie Brooks, I now knew from the building grapevine, was not a popular boy.

'Ricky, I'm glad you're back.'

'Hello, miss.' He grinned. 'Sorry about that.'

'I understand you were conducting your own epic battles on the stairs?'

'Not really. Donnie went down after one punch. I can't wait till he gets bigger. It'll make it so much easier—'

'Ricky, I feel sure that if I don't know what the end of that sentence is, I won't ever have to admit it to the police.'

'Yes, miss. Sorry.' He smiled again and sat down.

The others straggled in behind him. Having them for the first lesson of the day always meant that the first ten minutes were a bust. Carly and Mel turned up together, Annika was late and Jono later still. When he finally arrived, he was sweaty and harassed.

'Nice to see you, Jono.'

'Sorry.' He was panting.

'Is everything OK?'

'Not really, I can't find... It doesn't matter.'

He sat down heavily and there was a small cracking sound. I hoped his chair wasn't going to collapse. Annika sniggered, but said nothing.

Jono looked down at his feet, and let out a cry of anger. 'It's here. I...'

'What is it?'

'Which one of you fucking cunts did this?' He was on his feet, and turned away from me to the girls.

Annika was smirking, Mel was reading the back of her book. Carly cracked first.

'What exactly is it you think we've done?' she asked.

'This.' He reached down and lifted the chair leg. A shattered plastic games console was beneath it. 'My PSP. That's why I was late. I couldn't find it and that's because one of you took it and left it here so it would get broken.'

'It's hardly our fault you're so heavy,' said Annika.

'That isn't either helpful or pleasant, Annika.' I had to step in. I'd never seen him so upset. 'The weight of anyone would have cracked it. I'm so sorry, Jono. Let me take it to Robert's office at break. I'll see if it's covered on the Unit's insurance.'

'It won't be,' said Annika. 'We're not supposed to bring that stuff to school.'

Jono's darkening face was now plastered with his damp hair, the sweat was dripping onto his shoulders.

Ricky pawed at Jono's arm. 'Leave it, pal. It wasn't any of them. Why would they do something like that?'

'Who else would have done it?' Jono turned his fury on Ricky, who didn't reply.

I answered him. 'None of us knows who did it, Jono. I'm really sorry it's broken. But I don't think you can just fling accusations at everyone. Let me take it to Robert. I'll see what I can do.' I reached over and touched his arm. He flinched and so did I. For a moment, I thought he might hit me. I looked up into his eyes: I hadn't really noticed before that he was taller than me. 'Please.'

His face suddenly morphed from almost-adult to child. In a second you could see what he must have looked like when he was a toddler, all round face and screwed-up eyes, trying so hard not to cry.

He opened his hand, and I took the broken plastic from him. The screen was completely shattered. It was someone's perfect revenge.

DD,

Today, I have two things to report. The first is that I've found out something else about Alex. I spent the weekend at Carly's. Which was brilliant, actually. Her mum was less weird than usual. Maybe she's getting used to me. We went there together on Friday, after we finished at Rankeillor.

It's a nice walk over to Carly's: across the North Bridge, then over to Princes Street, to the shops so Carly could buy some hair extensions and I could get some nail varnish, even though I've broken three nails so they look like shit at the moment. Then we head down Dundas Street, which is all fancy little shops with ornaments and stuff. For rich old people. At the bottom of Dundas

Street the shops run out and we get to Inverleith Row, which is where Carly lives, in one of those big terraces. It must be amazing living right by the Botanics. I love going there. They're the most beautiful gardens in Scotland, Carly's mum says, and she might be right. I haven't been to any others, so I don't know for sure.

The other thing that's good about them is that it's always so quiet there. They're so big that you can wander round for hours and not hear anything. But everywhere's quiet to me, right? That's another myth about deaf people I can put right. Hearing aids mean that I spend a lot of my time hearing too much. Sirens are the worst thing. It's like someone drilling into my head when a police car comes past. And they're not even emergencies half the time. I once saw an ambulance driver, all guns blazing, going up Nicolson Street eating a doughnut. If it's a real emergency, you don't have time to stop and buy a cake. They just like using the siren. But I would honestly rather get run over than have to hear them coming.

So on Saturday we went to the Botanic Gardens and walked round the hothouses and the rock garden. That's the best part – it's so high up there. You can see all the way over Edinburgh. I love that.

But I'm getting ahead of the story, because it was Friday when we saw her. On Friday night, we went out for pizza in the Old Town. There's a new place that Carly's mum had been to with some people from work and she thought we'd like it there. And we did, actually: the garlic bread was all crispy and oily. It was really good.

Then on the way home we went down curly little Cockburn Street so we could look in the windows. They have loads of cool stuff there – proper shops, you know, where you can buy clothes and bags and those cute little Japanese dolls that Carly loves. I bought her two of them for Christmas. Then we walked up past Waverley Station. I don't like going down a hill and then up one if you don't have to, but the North Bridge was rammed with people on Friday evening: hen nights, stag nights, the lot. All with their matching t-shirts and hilarious Jimmy wigs. Carly's mum doesn't like crowds, so we went the hilly way instead.

And it was lucky we did, because as we went past the station we saw Alex coming out of there. If it had been even a few seconds earlier, we'd have missed her: the airport buses all wait there, so you can't usually see across the road. But the bus had just pulled away, and the next bus hadn't pulled up into the space yet, and there she was. She didn't see us, though. Carly wanted to go and say hello, but I stopped her. Alex looked really tired and really sad, so I thought we should leave her alone.

But still, this means we know where she goes on a Friday. Actually, it doesn't. As Carly pointed out, it means we sort-of know where she went on one Friday. And since no-one would go to Waverley for a look round the shops, all we really know is that she goes somewhere by train on Fridays. Or on one Friday.

But that's more than we knew before, isn't it? Carly thinks she goes to London to visit the grave of her fiancé. That's a bit lame, I admit, but it is romantic. And I reckon Alex is the romantic kind. Or why does she like all those plays so much? I know they're not romantic like I-pine-away-for-the-love-of-you bollocks. But I don't think that's all that romantic, actually. You know who pined away for the love of someone who died? Greyfriars Bobby, and he's a fucking dog.

Tragedies are romantic because they're about people fucking up their own and other people's lives even though they're often trying really hard not to. And happy endings are much less romantic than fuck-ups, aren't they? Carly thinks I'm mental for believing this. We talked about it in her room that night. She wants everyone to kiss and live happily-ever-after. I bet she does that, actually. I bet she meets a boy who really loves her and they do just fall in love *and be happy forever. He'd better not be a dick, is all I can say. I've seen enough of that with my mum.*

I wonder if any of the others have started writing like I have. Alex mentions it sometimes – we could make notes about the text we're reading in our diaries, that kind of thing. No-one ever says they don't have one. But then she never asks to see the notes. So maybe it's just me doing it. But I'm the one who wants to be a journalist. I'm the one who's going to make things happen.

And the second thing I have to report is this: Jono is sorry now that he was so vile to Alex. I hope she saw how clever I was. All this term we've been reading about Oedipus being, as Alex says, the architect of his own misfortune, and that's just what Jono was. He's always angry and obnoxious, exactly like Oedipus. What's the word Alex uses? Hubris. Jono has a lot of that. So I made the story happen in the real world, sort of. And even if Alex doesn't guess it was me, I still know.

It's this side of things that I think I will struggle to explain to the lawyers when we eventually meet. Why wasn't I afraid of these children? And did I really think that I was helping them by asking them to read Sophocles or Aeschylus? In which case, was I naïve, or actually stupid? I suppose I was both, and that's what I will have to tell them.

Yes, I thought that the tragedies we were reading were better for them than other therapeutic stuff we could have done. I didn't mind playing therapy games with the younger children. They loved acting and it was good for them, I think, the role-plays and so on. But this group, the group Mel was in, was different. They wanted to feel like grown-ups, and playing games would have been just another type of collage: the very thing they said they didn't want to do any more. So, yes, studying serious plays by real writers was better.

Besides, I had lost patience with therapy after Luke died. I was referred to a grief counsellor who was every kind of idiot. Her capacity for trying to look on the bright side made my mother look like Sartre. I tried not to hate her and everything she stood for, but it was one struggle too many. I didn't want to be cured of my grief, I wanted to wrap myself up in it like a comfortable old coat which I'd first put on when my father died.

I wanted to wear it every minute of the day, to sleep in it and wake in it, and never to be rid of it because it was the only thing keeping me warm. I gave up talking to my friends, to Luke's friends, because everyone wanted to try to make me feel better, to talk about the healing qualities of time and what Luke would have wanted. But what Luke wanted didn't matter any more. That's what happens when you die. And I didn't want time to heal my wounds. I wanted to pick at them until fat bubbles of dark blood formed on my skin, and then I wanted to watch them scab over and pick at them again.

'Are there any Greek plays where everyone doesn't die?' Carly asked. I had brought in a pile of Penguin Classics for them to choose from.

'Yes, of course. I don't think anyone dies in Sophocles' *Philoctetes*.'

'What's it about?'

'It's about a man who has a bad foot, after he got bitten by a snake,' I said.

'Nah, we did a play with a bloke who had a sore foot already,' said Jono.

He had calmed down after the last disastrous lesson. I had taken his broken console to Robert's office and explained there had been an accident. Robert had called his parents, and Jono's mother couldn't have been nicer, apparently. She was happy to claim the console on her insurance, and had promised Robert that her son wouldn't bring the replacement to the Unit. Jono still looked at Mel and Annika with thinly veiled suspicion, but he seemed to have accepted that whoever had set him up had done so too efficiently to get caught. I hoped he wasn't biding his time to exact revenge.

'It's a different kind of sore foot. It won't ever heal up, and his friends abandon him on an island so they don't have to put up with him any longer.'

'Jesus. Did Sophocles have more than one idea?' he asked. 'Or did he only write about a bloke with a bad foot getting abandoned?'

'He wrote *Antigone*. I think you'd like that.' I looked at Carly. 'But lots of people do die in it, so maybe we should leave that one for now. We could do Euripides' *Helen*. That's a fun one. It turns out that Helen didn't go to Troy after all, but to Egypt.'

'Isn't she called Helen of Troy?' Annika said.

'She often is, yes.'

'Well, someone's telling fibs, then,' said Jono. 'Let's give that one a miss.'

'What about *Alcestis*?' asked Mel. She was reading the back cover of the collected Euripides plays.

'We can certainly do that next, if you like. It's a different playwright, so the foot obsession shouldn't be a problem. And it has a happy ending.'

'It's a tragedy and no-one dies?' Annika asked, suspiciously.

'Someone does die. But it isn't permanent.'

'How can you die and it not be permanent?'

'You'll have to read the play to find out.'

'Can't you give us the background? So that when we read it, we know what's going on?' asked Jono.

They were, in this regard, exactly like every other child in lessons anywhere in the country. They would seize any opportunity for me to do the work so they didn't have to.

Mel read the back cover aloud. '"*Alcestis*, an early play in which a queen agrees to die to save her husband's life, is cast in a tragic vein, although it contains passages of satire and even comedy." That sounds alright, doesn't it?'

Carly nodded. 'So she doesn't die? She just agrees to die?'

'She's dying at the start of the play,' I said. 'Her husband, Admetus, was supposed to get ill and die. But the god Apollo owes him a favour, and so he makes a bargain with the Fates. Admetus can live, if he can persuade someone else to die in his place. That's where we are at the start of the play: Alcestis is dying because she wants to save her husband from dying.'

'God, that is devoted,' said Jono. 'Would any of you die for me?' He looked over his shoulder at the girls. 'Anyone?'

'I'd be as likely to die for you as to marry you,' said Annika.

'Great.'

'Not really,' she said.

'You'll come around.' Perhaps he had decided she wasn't the guilty one.

'Dying to save the life of someone you love is a good reason to die, though, isn't it?' I asked them. I wanted to know if it was an idea that was meaningful to them, I suppose. There would have been no point doing the play at all if self-sacrifice didn't seem like a potent motivator. After all, the first time I met them, they told me that dying for love, in *Romeo and Juliet*, seemed kind of lame.

'I wouldn't die to save anyone,' said Jono. 'Would you, miss?'

There was total silence. Carly blushed a deep maroon colour, clashing horribly with her hair. I had no idea how they had found out about Luke, but in that moment I knew that they had. Was Jono trying to hurt me, or did the words just come out that way? I thought about the question for a moment.

'I don't know, Jono.' I wasn't angry. I wasn't even shocked that they'd somehow uncovered something I didn't want them to know.

Would I have died to save Luke? I don't know. I would have died to save me and Luke, the combination of us and our future together, but that was a logical impossibility, obviously.

I shook my head. 'I don't know.'

'But if you could have stopped him from dying?' Mel asked, leaning forward to be certain she would hear what I said.

And I knew, I knew as I answered her that I was breaking a rule of conduct which was there to protect them and me equally. Therapists, teachers, doctors, nurses: none of them should share their personal lives with their charges. It isn't appropriate or fair. They aren't friends, even if they take your advice, even if they rely on it, even when they share their darkest thoughts and deepest wishes with you. You must never reciprocate and share your feelings, hopes and fears, because in doing so you damage your respective roles in each other's lives beyond repair.

I had never spoken to anyone about Luke's death. Not my mother, not his parents, not our friends. Not even the useless grief counsellor: I would have rather shared my confidences with my mother's dog. At least Pickle looked like she understood when you spoke to her. That was why I had come away to Edinburgh, because Robert didn't ask any questions. He knew all he needed to from the newspapers, and he never mentioned it. It was the most precious thing which he, or anyone else, could have given me.

And yet now, months after it had happened, I found I wanted to tell someone. And not just anyone, but children for whom I was responsible. I was stepping over a boundary, and I knew as I did it that it was wrong. I didn't realise afterwards, I knew right then, just before I opened my mouth.

'Luke didn't die. He was killed.'

ACT TWO

1

The first meeting with the lawyers did not go well. They called me in for an hour this morning, and it turns out that I had been, as so often, worrying about the wrong thing. Because when I first heard that they wanted to speak to me, my main concern was that they wouldn't be any good. Not good enough, I mean, to keep their client out of jail. How could they be focussing properly on their case, if they'd waited all these weeks before asking to speak to me? Besides, I was worried they'd have read the newspapers, and formed their initial judgements from there.

Luke used to hate going to parties, facing the questions people always asked. They would ask me what it was like directing someone famous, and they would ask him what it was like to defend someone you knew to be guilty. The last party we ever went to was no exception. I got cornered by a man who was quite certain that he had a great play in him, or that he would have, if only I would agree to meet him every week to help him write it. As I tried to explain that I was busy directing a play someone had already written, unassisted, I was also eavesdropping on Luke. I often did this at parties. I never really knew why we went to them when the person I most wanted to talk to was the person I already lived with. A small, stocky woman with dark hair and a top so low-cut that Luke was looking over her head to avoid eyeballing her cleavage was pointing at the air. Lawyers get a lot of those pointing talkers. I couldn't hear her question, but I heard him say, if I have evidence they're guilty, I submit it to the police. Otherwise I'd be breaking the law.

No, but you know what I mean. She was speaking more loudly now, jabbing the air with enthusiasm, smiling in a manner I imagine she thought was impish, the dim lights glinting in her dark eyes. From where I was standing, she looked too predatory for an imp. Luke was looking over at me and pointing at his watch, but she was too animated to notice.

If you had to defend a murderer, and you didn't have evidence but you knew he'd done it, then how would you sleep at night?

Luke gave a tiny sigh and explained that he slept better knowing a mistrial wouldn't be declared because he didn't feel like doing his job that day.

But what if a guilty man walks free? The money shot.

He knocked back the last of his drink, and with it the last drops of his patience, and said, it's better than an innocent man going to jail. That's the price you pay. No system of justice is foolproof. Only God knows who's guilty or innocent. I don't, and neither does a jury and neither does a judge and nor do you. I do my job, which is to represent anyone who needs to be represented and try to keep them from being convicted. Because the other option is that someone makes you king and you decide. And I'm not comfortable with that.

He leaned down, kissed the air near her face, swung across the room to tell the man I was talking to that he should really send me a first draft when it was done, and then steered me out of the hall and into the night. We went to some cheap Indonesian place for dinner, where he railed about how tiresome he found that kind of person at that kind of party. I agreed, because I loved him too much to tell him what was then the truth, which is that I hoped only the innocent people got him, and I didn't really care if the guilty ones got some shambles with a briefcase.

And then it was now, and I know that sometimes I do care, very much, that guilty people have good lawyers. At least, I care that one guilty person has a good lawyer. I finally see what Luke always knew, which is that guilt and blame and responsibility aren't the same things at all. They're not even close.

So, I was worrying that the lawyers would be incompetent. And because I was worrying about that, I didn't even consider the alternative, which is that they'd be the kind who would do literally anything to make sure their client got off, no matter how unethical it was, and no matter which innocent people they tried to implicate on the way. That didn't occur to me.

It used to baffle Luke how I had a superstitious belief in the preventative power of worrying. You're worrying about something that might never happen, he would say. He never understood that I believed that there was every point in worrying about things which wouldn't happen because, somewhere deep in my DNA, I believed that it was precisely by worrying about them that I prevented them from happening. It wasn't a pejorative belief: I don't think that people whose houses are swept away in floods or who succumb to a mysterious wasting disease weren't worrying hard enough. The ones like me – the fretful and the fearful – were trying incredibly hard. But they focussed so hard on averting one disaster that another one snuck up on them anyway. The flooded house wasn't caused by no-one caring, it was caused by someone caring too much about the wrong thing – an exam, a test result, whatever. They were worrying so hard about what didn't happen that they weren't even facing the same direction as the trouble which was coming for them all along.

I know because I did it all the time with Luke: take care, I would say, whenever he left me. And I meant, take care crossing the road because there are so many idiots driving while texting, take care when you get on the Tube that no-one looks too bomby and get off the damn train if they do. Take care of jostling crowds by busy roads, take care of slippery stairs on frozen mornings, take care of falling stowaways landing on west London from the flight path overhead. I never once meant, take care not to walk into the malice of a stranger, so that, of course, is what he did. And I was facing the wrong way.

There were two lawyers. The important one was a man in a suit which looked like it cost more than my mother's car. He was in his mid-thirties, I suppose: short dark hair with tiny flecks of grey round the edges, to match his tie. His tan spoke of a man who, if he had been to Edinburgh to interview his client, had done so only very briefly, en route to some winter ski resort.

When actors are training, they're often asked to think animalistic-ally: which animal are you, how can you convey that without words, and so on. Much leaping about the room channelling an inner rabbit ensues. But on that cold, damp morning, when I walked into his Gray's Inn Road office, Charles Brayford made me think that if he had ever decided to search for his inner bunny, he would have eaten it. Any actor playing him would have realised he was a great white: a born predator who would die if he ever stopped moving, able to smell blood at homeopathic levels of dilution.

We talked for nearly an hour, and by the end of it my jaw hurt from clenching it. I didn't know if I'd been grinding my teeth or trying to stop them from chattering. I was shivery but not cold. He was never rude, at least not quite. His eyebrows conveyed an easy scepticism at every answer I gave, which I presumed was his equivalent of a poker face. If you treat everything someone says as though it is probably a lie, even when you've only asked them the time, you leave them with no idea whether you believe anything they've said, or not. It was quite clever. I wondered if Luke ever made people feel like this, and hoped that he didn't.

It was a slow process. After an hour of my talking and his scornful eyebrows we had only discussed the first few times I'd met the children, and what I had said or done on each of those occasions. No-one but a fantasist or a liar remembers exactly what they said on a particular day over a year ago. Yet my failure to do so was somehow suspect in his eyes, something he might be able to use against me. When the clock reached eleven, he glanced at his colleague: a man in his twenties, not much younger than Luke. I guessed it was probably considered a privilege in this legal practice to assist Charles Brayford in his pageant of self-delight. Geeky, bespectacled Adam must be a favoured son here, even if he looked like he might shatter into pieces if you shouted at him. Perhaps his father was a partner.

I have another meeting, Charles Brayford declared, jerking his head back as he stood up to tell me that I should do the same. We'll have to speak again, Miss Morris. My client's case is obviously complex, and we'll need to ask you a few more questions. The same time next week? I nodded. Adam will see you out, he said, and strode past me. Adam pushed his glasses up his nose, more from habit than necessity, as they scarcely shifted. This way, he said, holding the door and standing to one side, before walking me back to the lifts. Every time we came to a junction I would have to wait for him to tell me which way to go, because every corridor looked identical, like in an anxiety dream. He would then slide back to walking just behind me, having clearly been told this was polite. It made me want to yell that since he knew where we were going and I didn't, chivalry was not really a priority, but as no-one spoke above a hushed whisper in this office, I didn't dare. No-one made eye contact with us at all: no secretary at her desk, no assistant hurrying past with a messenger envelope under his arm.

In the lobby, a bored receptionist was signing for a parcel from a motorbike courier, whose helmet was pushed back onto the top of his head. Adam pressed the lift button for me and waited till it pinged to announce its imminent arrival. Here you are, Ms Morris, he said, carefully correct, as I stepped past him. He looked back up the corridor to the main office and then over to the reception desk where the courier was still talking, in no rush to share the lift with me. Adam looked back at me. You need to get a lawyer, he said, quietly, as the lift doors sliced shut between us.

2

Everything changed after that lesson, when I'd told them about Luke. The children hummed with curiosity, though a realisation that it would be tactless to ask me any more seemed to keep them in check for a while. But the next time we met they were, as so often, in no mood to work.

It must have been mid-February by then, and the weather was still testing my resolve. There are days when Edinburgh completely loses its skyline: craggy Arthur's Seat no longer looms over you but disappears from view, covered in the same heartless grey as the sky. The Firth of Forth – glittering in the distance on a sunny day – is obliterated as you look north, and even the Castle, right in the middle of the city, becomes invisible. The city has no colour at all on those days. The buildings, the sky, the rain, the pavement, the faces, everything is grey. It can go on for days, sometimes for weeks.

When I couldn't take it any more, I would walk around the corner from my flat down to the art galleries on Market Street. I'd wander round the rooms for half an hour or so, just to regain the rest of the spectrum by looking at bright colours on white walls. Still, on that day, by the time I'd walked back up Cockburn Street and down the South Bridge to get to work, the memory of colour had ebbed away again. At one point, the rain transformed into hailstones, so I stopped off at one of the charity shops to wait it out. The storm's endurance was greater than mine, though, so I ran the last part of the journey. As I turned down Rankeillor Street the sky was like a headache, and I guessed the children would be jittery, as they always were on these dingy, oppressive days.

'Let's do something different today, before we start working on the next play.'

I was keen to move the focus back onto them, but it was becoming easier to work out which days were salvageable for learning purposes, and which ones were lost before they'd even arrived in the basement. Today was one of the latter. I was trying not to fight them when they were in this kind of mood: what would be the point? Rankeillor wasn't a normal school, and it wasn't like they had to sit an exam on Sophocles at the end of the year. Robert's advice was starting to make sense to me. If I caught them on a day like this, I would just use the opportunity to get them to open up in a different way. This is what it meant to be doing a reasonable job at the Unit.

'Remember when I first met you and you told me truths and lies about yourselves?' They all nodded. 'Tell me something else today, then.'

'Like what?' asked Ricky, rubbing his arms together as he spoke. He was happier when he didn't think there could be a wrong answer. Education was something to be endured, for him. And once he'd been kicked out of school, the Unit simply filled its place, and he endured that instead. But even if his handwriting was that of a much younger child and his spelling was atrocious, he knew enough to cope with the outside world.

'It's freezing down here today, isn't it?' I said.

'It's always freezing down here, miss.'

'Why don't you take this?' I offered him the hoody I had bought from the charity shop on my way in to work. I didn't know if I was

allowed to give things to the children, and I didn't want to be seen
to have favourites. But I couldn't bear seeing him shivering at his
desk every day, or dressed in Jono's coat because he didn't seem to
have one of his own.

'Thanks.' He took it off me and put it on. It was a large size and
he wrapped himself in its navy folds. 'Did someone leave it in here?'

'I think they must have,' I said. I saw Mel looking at me. I hoped
her lie-detectors were turned down today.

'Does this sound OK to the rest of you? And we'll start the new
play next time?'

Annika shrugged. It was already, after only six weeks at Rankeillor,
my fervent wish that no-one would answer a question with their
shoulders ever again.

'Then why don't you tell me what you want to do when you
grow up,' I said. 'Or when you leave school, I mean, since you're quite
grown up already.'

They all looked at the floor. No-one ever wants to go first. I raised
my eyebrows at Carly.

'Me?' she said, entirely betraying that she was desperate to answer.
'I want to be a make-up artist. I'm going to go to college when I'm
seventeen and train as a beautician and then specialise in make-up.
Then I'm going to go through to Glasgow and work in television
there.'

I was impressed, not by the ambition itself so much as by the
precision of her plan.

I tried to remember if I had been so self-possessed when I was their
age, eleven years ago. I had left school knowing I wanted to work in
theatre. And I knew I didn't want to be an actor. But I didn't know I
wanted to direct: at my school, the plays were directed by the drama
teacher. She chose the plays, she cast them, and she directed them. If
anyone had even a hint of the sniffles, she would pack them off to

the nurse and take the lead role too. If you wanted to get involved, you either had to act or paint the set.

So it was here in Edinburgh, only a few hundred yards from where I was standing now, in fact, when I had first realised that I could direct a play if I wanted. I started out with a small studio piece in my second term – Sartre's *Huis Clos* – and built up to doing a huge version of *A Midsummer Night's Dream* in the Botanic Gardens in the summer of my final year. I stayed on to do a PGCE just so I could keep doing more plays.

The List pegged me as a talent to watch, and *The Scotsman* ran a piece on my rosy future after the Royal Court picked me for their Young Directors programme. In other words, everything was working out brilliantly. I moved to London with Luke; he did his law conversion course, and I got a bursary to do a dramatherapy course part-time while I worked at the Royal Court. I was living exactly the way I had dreamed I would: completely broke, but certain it wouldn't last and that success would follow potential just like it does in a feel-good film. I was so stupidly, smugly happy that I used to give money to every beggar who asked, to try and avert the evil eye. I wanted to be sure no malevolent ill-wisher could ever say I didn't know how lucky I was.

I knew exactly how lucky I was, right up until the whole thing was destroyed in three minutes. That's how long it took Luke to die, they told me. One hundred and eighty seconds of increasing pain and fear before the blackness overwhelmed him. People used to say, as though I might be consoled, that at least he didn't suffer. As though I needed their fucking consolation. As though you couldn't suffer a lifetime in three minutes.

'Really, a make-up artist? I didn't know you were interested in that, Carly.' How had I missed it? She turned up at Rankeillor every day looking more glamorous than I would have done at a black-tie event. She didn't reply, merely held up one perfectly manicured hand with nails which looked like tiny paintings – dark, inky purple with silver stars on each one. 'Wow. Those are really good. Did you do them yourself?'

'Of course,' she said. 'I could do yours, if you like.'

I looked down. The nails were chewed and uneven, and there were biro marks on two of my fingers. 'You might have to give me a few weeks to grow my nails out. And my cuticles back,' I said.

'She could do your hair too,' said Annika. Her eyes glittered behind her glasses.

I resisted the sudden temptation to reach up and smooth it down.

'What's wrong with her hair?' asked Jono.

'Nothing,' said Carly, quickly. 'It might just be nice to get it done.'

'OK, well perhaps we could schedule my makeover for another day. Why do you want to do make-up for television, particularly?'

'It's a stepping-stone to film,' she said. 'I'm going to make sure I can do monster make-up – you know, zombies and stuff. Then you get to do the cool stuff.'

'Do you know where you'll study?'

'Stevenson College,' she said. 'In Sighthill.' I looked blank. Like too many students in Edinburgh, I had lived there for years without learning about the areas which undergraduates didn't inhabit. Most of the suburbs and outskirts were just words. She kept trying. 'Near Heriot-Watt? They do a diploma in theatrical and media make-up. I'm going to do that.'

'You've certainly done your research,' I said.

'Yes, Alex,' she replied. 'It's what I want to do.'

'Mel – what about you?' I asked.

'I don't know yet,' she said, looking rather embarrassed. 'I haven't decided. I like lots of things, so it depends, really.'

'What's your dream job?'

'I'd be a journalist,' she said. 'And if that went well, perhaps I'd write books.'

'Really? What kind of books?'

'You know,' she said. 'Good ones.'

Unlike Carly, she didn't seem comfortable discussing it, so I moved on. 'Annika? How about you?'

'Me?' she said, blinking three times in rapid succession. It was one of the many mechanisms she used to convey irritation. 'I'm going to be a designer.'

'What kind of designer?'

'Do you know anything about design?' she asked.

'No. I know about set design and that's it. But you could tell us about it, and then I'd know more.'

She dug around in her bag and produced a sketchbook which she passed forward to me. It was filled with intricate pen-and-ink drawings of owls, swallows and starlings. On the later pages, she'd been converting the birds into geometric patterns.

'Textile design,' she replied.

'These are amazing,' I told her.

She smiled. 'I know.' She reached over to get her book back. 'I'll study in Stockholm. They're very strong on graphic design and textiles there. I was thinking of London, but it'll be too expensive.'

I nodded. That was two of the girls with the next five years of their lives fully mapped out. I was beginning to wish we'd talked about something else. Only Mel seemed to be as vague about her future as I felt.

'What about you, Jono?'

'I want to work for a video game company,' he replied.

'You'll have to stop killing everyone else first,' said Ricky, laughing.

'What do you mean?' I asked him.

'He's a flamer.' This was self-explanatory to them, but foreign to me.

'And a flamer does what?'

Jono grinned. 'Kills other players.'

'In the game, yes?'

'Yes, Alex.' He rolled his eyes. 'Obviously.'

'I'm missing something. So you kill the other characters?'

'Yes,' he sighed. 'But the characters are avatars for real people. In *Black Ops*,' he clocked my confusion, 'I mean, in the game *Call of Duty: Black Ops*, lots of people can play online at the same time.'

'Right.'

'And he kills loads of them,' said Ricky.

'Because you're on different sides?' I asked.

'No,' Jono answered. 'Because it's funny.'

'Then they start again.' Ricky was laughing harder. 'And he does it again.'

'You keep killing the same person? So they can't really play until you stop?'

'Yeah. That's what flaming is,' he said.

'So the plan is to convert this nihilism into creativity at some point, then?'

'If you say so.'

'And Ricky? What do you plan to do?' I had half an idea what his answer would be. Artist, perhaps? Something visual, anyway.

'I'm going to be a soldier, miss,' he said, as if he thought it should have been obvious.

'You want to join the army?' I was horrified, though I don't know why. It never occurred to me that anyone would want to join the army, I suppose, when there were soldiers dying on the news every week. 'Why is that?'

'My uncles were both in the army,' he said. 'It's what Mal is going to do when he gets out of prison.'

'And you aren't afraid of…' I trailed off.

'Of dying? No, not really,' he said. 'I might die in Edinburgh, if I stayed, mightn't I?'

He was right, of course. You can die anywhere. 'What kind of soldier would you be?'

'I dunno,' he said. 'My grandparents took me to that recruitment office on Shandwick Place. There's a few things I could do. They help you choose when you apply.'

He didn't seem old enough to join the army. He wasn't even old enough to drive. Well, not legally. The thought of him in a combat uniform made me feel awful. How could he lift a gun? How could he kill someone? In he came every week in that huge green Hibs t-shirt, his red hair giving it an oddly festive look. He was so small. But he was still old enough to sign up.

When the lesson came to an end, he peeled off the hoody and offered it back to me.

'Why don't you keep it?' I said. 'No-one's asked for it, so I think it might be going spare.'

He thought for a moment. 'I'll leave it down here,' he said. 'Then if someone does come looking for it, I won't have taken it.'

'OK,' I said. 'And if no-one claims it by the end of the week, it's yours if you want it.'

DD,

Alex was just like normal today. How weird is that? She tells us that Luke – the love of her life – was killed, I mean killed, and then she just turns up to teach us like nothing had happened.

I suppose she's used to it now. I mean, it's not news to her, is it? Just to us. No wonder she always looks sad. She's one of those people whose face changes completely when she speaks. Do you know the kind of face I mean? Her eyes almost shut when she smiles — it takes up her whole face. She doesn't just smile from the mouth, I mean. It goes right across her.

But when she's not talking, when she's just listening, or thinking, she looks sadder than anyone I've ever seen. Sadder than my mum, even, when Jamie died. I think it's because she wears it all the time. She doesn't have anyone she needs to be brave for, like my mum did. She couldn't cry all the time, because there was me and I needed her to be my mum, even if she wanted to just curl up and cry for a year.

But Alex doesn't have to hide her feelings, so she doesn't. I felt kind of bad when Carly agreed with Annika about Alex getting her hair done. We all expect Annika to say something obnoxious, but then Carly went along with it. I mean, they had a point. You can't even see what it was supposed to look like when it was cut. Carly says she's done her fringe with kitchen scissors, which is why it's so uneven. I bet she just cut it when she couldn't see any more.

I don't think Alex was offended when Carly said it, though. She just shrugged, like she was agreeing, but she was never in a million years actually going to walk round the corner to Cheynes and get a cut and blow-dry. The same with her hands — when Carly said she'd do her nails, Alex was looking for a way to say no that sounded like she was saying yes. You can't just give up biting your nails when they look like that — she must have been doing it her whole life. So she seems to agree that Carly can do them, but it won't ever actually happen.

I liked finding out what everyone's going to do when they leave school. I almost felt bad that I didn't have a proper answer. What I should have said is that I'll have to try harder than they will when we leave, because lots of people won't employ someone who's deaf. My audiologist gives me a lecture about this every time I see him.

About a fifth of deaf people are unemployed, because employers think they're stupid, or they think it's too expensive to fit out their offices for a deaf person. Even though installing an induction loop doesn't cost that much.

That's why it would be good if I could be a journalist. I wouldn't need an office to do that, really. I'd be out doing interviews and stuff, and then I could write those up anywhere. And I'm good at thinking of stories. My mum says I get that from my dad. He used to be brilliant at telling stories, ones he'd made up, I mean. He used to write them down in a book for me, when I was little, and do little drawings at the side of each page. They were really good. Then he said I'd got too old for them, so he stopped. But I still have all the old ones on my shelf.

He emailed earlier. He's wondering if I can go down to see him in a couple of weeks, because he was away when I was supposed to go before. I bet I can skive off a day from Rankeillor – Robert won't mind if it's just this once, to see my dad. Then I can go early, on a Friday.

I wonder what she meant when she said 'killed'.

3

I finally gave in and bought new boots when my first paycheque came through from Rankeillor. I had made that mistake that southerners always make about Scotland, even when they know better, like I should have. London barely has seasons, and even in the few years I'd been away, I'd forgotten what winter really means in Edinburgh. In London I was warm enough anywhere with a coat, boots, scarf and a hat.

Once I moved back to Edinburgh, I remembered what it's like when a pair of boots gets so wet that they take two days to dry, even if you fill them with balled-up newspaper and park them next to a radiator. Edinburgh is a city where you need two of everything – two coats, two pairs of boots, two umbrellas. One to wear and one to dry out, while your whole flat smells like a wet dog, and you hope it's from the wet clothes, not you.

When I walked into class, Carly noticed straight away. 'You've got new boots,' she said. 'They're lovely.'

Annika and Mel both looked over to check.

'Thank you. I think they're giving me blisters, though.' They were black with a buckle on the side – biker boots for the bikeless. I could feel the pressure on my toes as well as my heel.

'Where are they from?' she asked, scrutinising my feet.

'Russell and Bromley,' I said.

Annika shook her head, sadly.

'Too expensive?' I guessed.

'Too old for you. Seriously, you must have been the youngest person in that shop by about fifty years. But better you bought them than some old woman, I suppose. You could get some new jeans to go with them.'

'Not from Gap, though,' said Carly. They looked at each other. Maybe Gap was too old for me as well. Or too young. Or too something.

'We could take you shopping,' said Carly. 'After school one day. If you like, I mean.' Then she went red.

'Maybe next time I get paid,' I said. 'Now, shall we move on to *Alcestis*? Has anyone started reading it yet? Just Mel? OK. Thank you, Mel.'

'I like it,' she said.

'How far have the rest of you got?'

'Nowhere,' said Jono. 'Sorry, I forgot we had to read ahead.'

'Me too,' said Ricky. He was wearing the giant blue hoody, which I'd left on his chair.

'Admetus was going to die, wasn't he?' Annika had remembered something from when we'd first discussed the play.

'Oh yeah, that's right. But then he doesn't have to because his wife offers to die in his place,' said Jono.

Between the two of them, they had now reconstructed what I had already told them. But I didn't feel like having a row. At least they'd remembered one thing each.

'OK. Let's take it from there. Do you think Admetus will be pleased about that? Annika?'

Before she could reply, Ricky asked a question. 'How do you remember all their names? They all begin with "a" and end in "s".'

'I suppose I've known the plays for longer than you,' I said. 'So the names are more attached to the characters for me. Anyway, Alcestis is the wife, and Admetus is the husband.'

'Well, he must be made up,' said Ricky. 'If he thought he was going to die and now he isn't.'

'Yes, but his wife is. He'll be a one-parent family,' Carly pointed out. 'Do they have children?'

I nodded.

'Could he get someone else to die for him?' Annika asked.

'Like who?'

'I don't know. Who else is in it?' She flicked to the cast list and scanned it. 'His dad, Pheres,' she said. 'He'd do.'

'He does ask his parents if either of them would be willing to die in his place,' I told her. 'But they both refuse.'

'Seriously?' said Ricky. 'That's harsh.'

'Is it? That's certainly what Admetus thinks.'

'Yeah, of course it is. They're old. They've had a kid, now he's got kids. They could easily die and no-one would miss them,' he said.

'Wow. I hope they never let you run an old people's home,' said Jono. 'You're like Harold Shipman.'

'Who?'

'He killed a bunch of old people. He was a serial killer. Like Burke and Hare.'

'I'm not saying they should all be killed,' Ricky said, slowly enough to suggest he was certainly considering it. 'Just that one of them could take one for the team.'

'What does Pheres say when Admetus suggests that?' I asked Mel.

She flipped pages. '"You want to live. Do you think your father doesn't?"'

'That's your answer.' I looked at Ricky. 'His dad doesn't see himself as old and about to die. He sees himself as deserving to live, just as much as his son.'

Ricky shrugged.

'Who do you think is in the right?' I asked Mel.

She thought for a moment. 'None of them, really,' she said. 'Admetus is a selfish prick who thinks he's more worthy of being alive than his family, the people he's supposed to love. Pheres is just as selfish – all pleased with himself and coming to mourn for Alcestis when he could have sacrificed himself to save her, if he really meant what he was saying. And Alcestis is a bit pathetic, isn't she? She agrees to die for him, but then she's all poor-me about it. No-one made her offer to die, did they?'

'She's certainly not a great feminist figurehead – I agree with you there. But it's a good question, isn't it? Admetus is offered something we would assume everyone wants: a chance to escape an early death. But the price is to find someone else to die in his place, and the catch is that anyone who cares that much for him is someone he doesn't want to lose.'

'And he finds out that some people don't care about him as much as he thought,' Mel added.

'That's a good point. Would we really want to know how much the people we love value us? What if we don't like the answer? Admetus clearly doesn't. He's saved from dying, but he loses his wife and he pretty much loses his parents, too, because he can't forgive them for not being willing to sacrifice themselves to save him. Will you each write something about this for the next time I see you, please?'

They groaned, in unison.

'It's no good moaning. You all want to do something big with your lives – you told me so. And you should, because you're all very smart. But you can't expect to get places at college if you can't write a short essay. Not even to do a course in something practical, Carly. Any college will want to know that you like to learn, and that you're good at it. And for that to happen, you need to practise. So how about if you write me two sides of paper on sacrifice. It can be about the play or about yourself, or both, or neither. Think about who you might ask to die in your stead, if you were in Admetus' position. Think about what's at stake and what problems you might encounter. No live re-enactments, please. And I'll take them in on Monday.'

DD,

I have news. I got back last night from seeing my dad. It was too late to write then, but I had a good time. He seems really happy, and he's seeing someone but I didn't have to meet her. That was a massive relief because my parents usually both think that if they like someone, I'm going to like them too, which is insane. For a start, why would I like someone whose only connection to me is that they're having sex with one of my parents? You don't need to be Oedipus to find that bizarre.

Also, my parents obviously describe me to people as their troubled, deaf daughter, which means meeting anyone they know is always a fucking nightmare. My dad's girlfriends are always the same. They always have a special sad face they keep for when they meet someone disabled. And you can feel their saintliness from a mile away: they're storing up how good they're being by talking to a deaf girl. There was one last year who was absolutely toxic. She talked so slowly that I honestly thought she was taking the piss at first. It took ages before I worked out that she just couldn't imagine I was cleverer than her. I thought I was going to have to break them up, for sure, but luckily he chucked her. Or maybe she chucked him. People don't always tell the truth, after all.

The last one was awful too. She kept being really over-nice about my clothes and my stuff, like it was amazing that I didn't just dress in a uniform from a care home, which is clearly where all deaf people live, in her world. There's a limit to how much pity I can take from someone I've just met. So it was good to spend the weekend just with my dad.

But that's not the big news. I mean, obviously it isn't. The big news is that to get to Leeds, I have to get the East Coast train from Waverley Station. It's the train that goes to London King's Cross. But I get off at York, a couple of hours before it gets to London, and change trains there. Except this time I didn't. I got on the train and found my seat in coach B. I like coach B. It's not the quiet coach, so I can use my headphones without some uptight old bitch telling me off.

And it's near the buffet. I never understand why people make jokes about the food on trains being bad. They have three flavours of crisps on that train. So I got up to go to the buffet car before we got to Berwick. And sitting at the other end of coach B is Alex. Yes, really. Sitting in a double seat, staring out of the window.

There's no-one with her, and she doesn't have any luggage on the seat next to her, or overhead. Just the small bag that she always has, like a mini messenger bag, crossed over her body, like she'd just sat down with it on and hadn't thought to take it off.

I was so surprised that I didn't say anything. I just walked by her like I was going that way anyway, which I was, and on the way back I said hi as I went past. And here's the weirdest bit – she didn't react at all. She didn't move a muscle when I said her name, she didn't reply, she didn't do anything.

At first I thought maybe she had headphones in that I couldn't see under her hair, but she didn't. She wasn't reading a book. She didn't even have a book. She was just gazing at the sea out of the window. And that's fair enough, because it's beautiful between Edinburgh and Berwick, where the train goes along the coast. But she didn't ever stop looking out of the window, all the way to Peterborough. And most of that bit of the journey isn't beautiful at all.

And she didn't eat or drink or use the loo or anything. She just sat there, like she was made of marble. I know, because I stayed on the train at York. My dad was at work anyway, and I was just going to go to the shops for a bit when I got to Leeds, before I got the bus out to his house. So I stayed on the train instead. The next stop is Peterborough, and I got out there, because Alex didn't, which meant she must be going to London, because there aren't any more stops after Peterborough. I really wanted to stay on and see where she went when she got there. Maybe she's visiting her mum at last? Or maybe she was going somewhere else, and that's where she goes every Friday. I'm going to find out.

But I didn't want to go all the way to London this time, because I wouldn't have made it back to Leeds in time to beat my dad home, and then he would have worried. As it was, I got some shitty conductor telling me I'd stayed on too far and trying to charge me a penalty fare. Cheeky fucker. Then the guy opposite me – wearing a suit and kind of a dick, I thought, up till then – stepped in. Told the conductor that it wasn't my fault I couldn't hear the station announcements when they were 'so wilfully indistinct' and, if anything, he should be apologising to me for the fact that I'd missed my stop. His sister was deaf, he said. He knew how hard it was to adjust your aids to hear something which is loud but muffled. It was brilliant. The conductor went red and started grovelling about how he hadn't meant to be insensitive and all that bollocks.

And even though this was happening in the same coach as Alex was in, she didn't seem to notice anything. It was fucking bizarre. So I got off at Peterborough and the conductor explained to a guy at the station that I needed to go back to York, and they put me in First Class, which was amazing. You get free Coke and everything. But Alex stayed on. I texted Carly to tell her to go to Waverley that night and check if Alex came off a London train at around the same time we saw her the other week. She said I was being mental, but she still went.

And guess what? Carly saw Alex get off the train at ten fifteen, just like before. She goes to London and comes back in the same day. She must only be there for, what, three hours. It's a really long way to go for such a short time. Is she going all that way just to see her mum for a couple of hours?

Rage appeared in unexpected quarters after Luke died. Unexpected to me, at least. People sprang up all over the net, demanding that his killer be killed in turn, advocating all kind of torments for the person who had taken Luke from us. No-one had taken Luke from them, of course. These were complete strangers: not Luke's friends, and not mine. Yet they were a more virulent lynch mob than everyone who had known Luke could possibly have been. They united around their sincere desire to punish wrong-doers with death, ideally from torture. He was so innocent, you see. People were as angry as if a child had died.

When it had only just happened, when his body was yet to be released to his parents, the internet was filled with these hate-fuelled, terrifying semi-literates howling for blood and retribution. I was too numb to howl for anything. I just used to wonder how they could possibly be so angry. They couldn't have been more outraged if Luke had been their own son or brother or husband. Though, of course, Luke's parents had been calm and restrained on the news, his mother weeping wordlessly as his father made the obligatory plea for witnesses, his hands and voice shaking as he read out the police statement.

I would say that I feared for the safety of Luke's killer in the days before he was arrested. But I didn't. At that point, I would have killed the man who killed Luke with my bare hands. I wouldn't have hesitated. And if someone else decided to do that on my behalf, I would have cheered them on.

One of the things that most frightened my mother, in the aftermath of Luke's death, was how quickly her daughter changed into a Fury.

In her world-view, that's not what's supposed to happen when disaster befalls you. When my father died, my mother sought consolation from God. That path to redemption, she understood. But as I became angry, unforgiving and withdrawn, it rendered me incomprehensible to her.

If faith could save her, why couldn't it save me? It seemed obvious to me. I was younger than my mother, and Luke and I had lost our future more than our past. Of course, she might well have felt the same way about losing my father in his mid-fifties. Fifty-four is not old. But Luke wasn't even twenty-six when he died. We weren't yet married, we didn't yet have children. We had barely even been on holiday together, thanks to a perpetual combination of work and no money. We believed everything was still ahead of us, because it was. And then suddenly, it wasn't.

And that was what made me so angry. My mother had time to come to terms with what was happening to my father before he died. I did too, of course. It didn't make it anything other than terrible, and his final weeks were a long, sad march of painkillers, palliative care and hopelessness. But we knew that he would die, and there was at least time, amongst everything else, to be reconciled to that idea.

With Luke, it was different. He was alive, complete, mine, and then he was gone. He was dead before I even knew he was hurt. And when the phone rang to tell me what had happened, it was his phone, only it wasn't his voice: it was the voice of a passer-by, one of the three people who had run to help him, but could do nothing to stop the blood which flowed relentless from his chest.

They called an ambulance and then they called me, because mine was the last number Luke had dialled. If Luke had put a security lock on his phone, like I did, it would have been hours before I even found out what had happened. But of course he didn't. He could never be bothered with things like that. He would give you his debit card and PIN number if you were going out and he wanted some cash. So I answered the phone thinking it was him. And it was never going to be him again.

My overriding emotion, for months, was disbelief. I kept thinking there must have been a mistake, and that someone would rectify it, embarrassed by the error. Once that had passed, I couldn't be helped. I couldn't get to the person I wanted to hurt, so I hurt whoever was nearest. I rejected kindness and understanding and sympathy, because I wanted none of it. The only thing I wanted was not to need their pity, and it was too late for that.

I didn't care who I hurt, because I knew that whatever I did, they would still be less injured than me, so what could they possibly complain about? And when I finally realised that neither my friends nor my family deserved this, I walked away, so I wouldn't hurt them any more. I'd arrived in Edinburgh full of intentions to do something good, to make up for my cruelty. I didn't manage that either.

4

In spite of their complaints, I was delighted to see all five of them had left their essays on my desk. Carly had written a story about two girls who are prepared to die for one another but end up surviving and living happily ever after. Romeo and Juliet would have married and lived to a happy retirement in Carly's world. Annika proposed that Alcestis would have been better off as a single mother than married to Admetus, whom she considered a leech. I felt a rush of sympathy for Annika's father, wondering if he knew how much contempt she had for him.

Mel wrote about her brother, wondering if she would have sacrificed her life as well as her hearing to keep him alive. Jono, of all people, produced a really good piece about the act of sacrifice in *Halo*, a video game I half-remembered Luke playing. The hero has to give up his life at the end of the game to save the universe. Mel and Jono's essays were good, and not just for kids at Rankeillor, but for kids anywhere. Ricky, meanwhile, had pursued his belief in euthanasia for the over-fifties, which at least made it clear that he was thinking for himself, I decided, trying to look at it positively.

When I gave back their work, the kids were excited. They resisted any threat of homework, but they were thirsty for approval in the comments I wrote on the bottom of each essay. They read their own, and then leaned over to read each other's.

'Don't we get a grade?' asked Carly, turning her paper over to check I hadn't hidden the mark.

'No, you don't. I wanted you to write about something which is meaningful to you, not to pass a test. I didn't think marks would be appropriate. That's why I wrote you quite a long comment at the bottom,' I explained.

Mel's face was glowing as she read hers, and Jono was trying to conceal the fact that he had gone bright pink.

'Can I take this home, though?' asked Ricky.

'Of course, it's your work.'

'I want my grandparents to see that someone thinks I can do "a daring and original argument",' he said. I hoped they didn't read the essay itself. Or, if they did, that they wouldn't take it personally.

'Well you can. I'm proud of you all.'

I meant it too. I hadn't gone into the Unit expecting to like the job. I took it because I didn't know what else to do. But even though things still went wrong, often, I felt I was beginning to make a difference. Robert was right about the kids at Rankeillor: as much as anything, they just wanted to be treated like normal kids, instead of unexploded hand-grenades. Everyone skirted round them: you only had to see them walking up the street on their way home at the end of the day. People would cross the road to avoid their squawky, swearing, unpredictable mass. I could understand the road-crossers – the kids often progressed from shouting to shoving and occasionally all-out fighting in the street, and we had several convicted muggers on the Unit, too – but it doesn't take a leap of empathy to see that it isn't much fun being feared by everyone.

I haven't really mentioned the other kids I worked with at Rankeillor. I've focussed on the older group because they were, to me, the most interesting. The younger ones were a mixed bunch, and I had a small older group, who were halfway out of the Unit already – their minds more on where they were going next than where they were now. I took five groups in total. Some were more articulate than others, some were nicer. Some were bullies and some were victims. Many were both. I didn't discuss tragedy with any other group: either they weren't old enough, or they weren't interested. It never came up.

The younger ones liked making up stories and acting them out. They enjoyed swapping roles partway through the performance, changing perspective. They had no problem with doing the drama equivalent of collages, in other words. They would commit plenty of energy to writing a short play, or a scene about a situation they had found challenging or upsetting, and then they would design costumes and sets that they could make or build in the basement room.

I wanted our sessions to be fun as well as therapeutic. I had placed limitations on the amount of glue they could use, because even if they could inhale large quantities with no apparent loss of brain function, I couldn't. But that was pretty much my only rule. I wanted them to feel safe and to leave the room happier than they'd arrived. I worked hard to make that happen, and for the most part, I think it did.

Like most ostensibly bad children, as Robert had long maintained, they didn't want to be bad. They were keen to learn how to relate better to each other, to their families and friends. They wanted to be happier and less angry. They didn't enjoy the tantrums they nonetheless felt compelled to throw so frequently. They could usually understand that just as they didn't like being shouted and screamed at, other people didn't either. And if they couldn't always make the extra step from recognising that fact to acting on it, that didn't make them desperately unusual, for teenagers.

The real difference between the youngest kids and the older ones was that they had more time. They didn't have that sell-by date which the older kids felt: if they didn't hurry up and learn something soon, it would be too late. Too late shouldn't really exist when you're a teenager. You shouldn't feel like your options are closing off so soon. But for Annika, Carly, Mel, Jono and Ricky, the career clock was already ticking. Their lives would soon need to fit onto application forms, and they knew it.

My relationship with the older class, as the lawyers have been quick to emphasise, wasn't normal. Our sessions were unusual. But I keep clinging to this in the face of everything that has been said since: that wasn't my intention. I didn't go to Scotland to teach Greek tragedy to impressionable and emotional teenagers – another phrase the lawyers use, as if there is any other kind. I went there to try to make my life better, because I thought I could make their lives better, and I believed doing that would help me to recover something I'd lost when Luke died. And with every other group on the Unit, that is what happened. I don't deny for a moment that it is my fault that things went catastrophically wrong. I wouldn't consider denying it. But I didn't fail all of them, and that should count for something.

DD,

We did it. Me and Carly skived off on Friday and followed Alex to London. I knew that's where she was going. I am a genius. OK, maybe not a genius. Like I said before, once you don't get off at Peterborough, you have to go to London. But still, I knew it. Here's what she did.

She got on the exact same train that I was on last Friday. She sat in the same seat. And, again, she didn't have an overnight bag with her or anything to read or eat or drink. We sat in the next carriage. That was Carly's idea – she was panicking that we'd get caught when we were supposed to be at the Unit that day. She was panicking we'd get caught for fare-dodging too.

She said it was different when I'd gone the week before, because I'd had Robert's permission. Which was true, I guess. Except I don't think Alex would have noticed if we'd been sitting right next to her. Carly didn't see how she was that day. Totally impervious, you know. That's the word. I looked it up.

So we sat on the train all the way to London. Having Carly there was way more fun. We read magazines and listened to music and she did my nails a really nice dark red with blue glitter in it. These two old women opposite got all huffy about the smell and moved tables. I offered to do hers back, but she did them herself instead. She's got much steadier hands than me, even on a moving train, so you can't blame her.

We pulled into London after about a million years. Carly had never been there before. Not once. She's never actually been south of Bamburgh Castle. She said her parents never fancied taking them: they prefer Spain for their holidays, because when you get there it's definitely warm and sunny.

When we got off the train, I thought Carly was going to have a seizure at the noise and the crowds and everything. Everyone walks too fast. They're all so busy and cross all the time. Makes you wonder why they're so keen to live there. We followed Alex, but she looks like a zombie when she's in London. I thought she hated being in Edinburgh, and was just there because London makes her sad now her boyfriend's dead. But I had it the wrong way round.

Sometimes in Edinburgh she smiles. She even laughs every now and then, when one of us says something she likes. In London she's like the walking dead. But still, she knows where she is and where she's going, she's not like us. She walks like she's got to get somewhere. There's a difference, isn't there, in the way people move when they are going somewhere compared with when they're just going for a walk? And Alex is definitely doing the first one. But, even though she has somewhere to be, everything about her is sad: her shoulders are hunched over, even when she's not standing in the cold. She wears these wristwarmers, pulled up over her hands, holding them shut like mittens. And she looks at the ground all the time. You'd think she'd walk into people, but they sort of flow around her, because they can't make eye contact with her, so they move instead of expecting her to.

She came out of King's Cross and turned right. We followed her over the road and past the Harry Potter station, which I thought was supposed to be King's Cross, but it isn't, it's next door. And then we went past the British Library, which looks pretty fucking massive for a library. There's this huge statue of a man drawing something with a compass outside. And loads of posters up for an exhibition about beings from another world. I wouldn't mind seeing that. Aliens in a library.

But she walked past there, and then over this massive road junction with about ten lanes of traffic from about six different directions. Carly had stopped talking, because she knows that when there's this much stuff going on, I have to concentrate on the traffic. Then past more offices and some cafés and then we got to some fancy gates and she turned right and we went past these big white terraced houses that were fucking immense.

She crossed the road and we went into a little green park. We walked past a sign with a big map on it, and it turns out this is The Regent's Park. It's not a little park at all, even, it's massive. We were just in the bottom bit. The Avenue Gardens, it said on the sign. No dogs allowed, next to a picture of a dog who looked all sad because he wasn't allowed. Alex was still ahead of us. Even Carly had stopped flapping that she would turn around and see us. Alex barely stops for traffic. She just keeps going and going.

She crossed over a little road with a big fancy black and gold gate at one end. I wanted to see where that went, but we didn't want to lose track of Alex. She walked past this tiny café, the Cow and Coffee Bean, and the toilets. Carly had to stop to use the loos, I waited outside to make sure Alex didn't disappear. She walked up till we got to this big — actually, I don't know what it was. It looked like a fountain, but it didn't have any water in it. And then she took a path to the left and curled round this corner and suddenly we were walking alongside a zoo.

We could see some porcupines and sheep and goats. No lions and tigers and giraffes, but we saw some camels and a small kangaroo. There's a fence between the path and the zoo, but it isn't that high. We could have climbed in, easy. Then Alex turned left again, and she walked up to this big square building with huge windows around the sides.

We didn't want to follow her inside, in case she saw us. That was Carly's idea. So we hid behind a tree for a bit, and then I saw a bench and we sat on there, even though it was freezing now we'd stopped walking. It was windy in the park: the noise was really messing with my aids. I can still hear when it's windy, but there's just this really loud rumbling noise underneath everything, which I have to tune out to hear anything else. After a while it gives me a headache. I pulled my hat down over my ears, which made it harder to hear Carly, but at least I could think about something other than how loud the fucking wind was.

Carly was still worrying that Alex would notice us, but she was too far away, unless she had binoculars. Then Carly looked really worried, and I said there was no way that Alex had binoculars because who has binoculars for Christ's sake? Bird-watchers and stalkers and that's it. We sat there for ages. And it must be the most boring bit of the park. There's loads of playing fields — all flat and empty. No-one was playing football on Friday, though. You couldn't blame them, either. It started to drizzle, and then sleet.

In the end I walked round the side of the building so I could try and see what Alex was doing. It took me a while to make her out, but there she was, sitting at a table. I think it's another café, this glass-sided box. It's much bigger than the one by the toilets, though. She sat there with a cup for an hour. I walked back round to Carly and told her Alex was just sitting in this place on her own. She didn't believe me, so I made her come with me to look. We went back to the bench in the end, and an hour after Alex had walked in, pretty much exactly, she walked out again.

She didn't go back the way she'd come, though. She carried on down past the playing fields, and eventually she reaches a bridge over a tiny lake. There are these weird whirlpool things in the water, I don't know what they are. Drains or something, I guess. It looks like sea monsters from above, anyway. Loads of fancy ducks, too. Not just the regular kind. Different-coloured ones. Ones with brown hair. Well, with brown feathers that look like hair in a quiff. Pretty cute. And loads of swans.

Then the park runs out, and she walks along this little road that curves right back round until she's at the bottom of the park again. Then she walks along the park road, and then back onto the main road and all the way to King's Cross. She gets back on the train at half past five, and that's her whole trip.

It was fucking bizarre. She sits on a train for four and a half hours, and then walks miles to sit in a café on her own for an hour, and then goes all the way home again. Carly reckons she was waiting for someone who didn't show up. Actually, Carly really thinks that this is where Alex and Luke used to come every Friday for romantic afternoons in the park. And she thinks Alex is coming back to re-live them on her own.

But then her next favourite idea is that Alex was waiting for someone – a man – who she likes. I said, didn't it look kind of bad that he didn't show up? Catch me waiting an hour for some no-show. But Carly thinks he got stuck somewhere and that he rang Alex and said sorry and that when she got back to Edinburgh he'd probably sent her flowers.

But I don't think she looked like she was waiting. I watched her for about thirty minutes, and she didn't check her watch, or look at her phone or do anything people usually do when they're waiting for someone. She just sat there, dead-eyed, like when she was on the train. I don't know what she was doing, but I don't think she was there to meet somebody. She goes there because she needs something, but whatever it is, it doesn't work. Actually, it makes her emptier, like she's hungry and eating cotton wool, expecting to feel full. Does that even make sense?

5

'So, what? Alcestis dies, but then she comes back from the dead?'
Ricky hadn't managed to read to the end of *Alcestis* and was piecing
it together from the others' descriptions.

'Yup,' said Jono. 'Hercules turns up and mugs Death to get her
back.'

Ricky looked mutely at me. I nodded. That summed things up
pretty well.

'So they bury her? Alcestis? Because she's dead?'

'Yes,' I told him.

'And then Death comes to get her, and he's like a person?'

'Pluto, the god of the dead, yes.'

'And Hercules is who?'

'He's a superhero,' said Annika. 'But he doesn't have a cape.'

'He sort of does, actually,' said Mel.

We all turned to her.

'Does he really?' I felt guilty. My students shouldn't know more
about a subject than I did.

'Yes. It's like a lion skin or something. It's in pictures of him, on
Greek vases and things.'

'You're absolutely right. Well done. You know, we should go to
the Museum of Scotland one day and look at the Greek pots they
have there.'

'Lame.' I should have known Annika wouldn't be keen.

'So, he's a superhero?' Ricky was still waiting to hear the end of the story.

'Yeah. He hides behind a tombstone and then jumps out and chokes Pluto till he gives in and lets Alcestis come back to be alive again.' So Jono had read the whole play. It wasn't just Mel who was interested in this stuff.

'Oh. OK.' Ricky nodded.

'Do you think it's a good ending to the play?' I asked Jono, since he'd had more time to think about it than Ricky.

'Kind of.'

'You'd like it better if she stayed dead?'

'No,' said Carly.

'Yes.' Jono and Mel disagreed.

'Why?'

'It's cheap,' Mel said. 'If someone kills themselves to save someone else, and then they come back a few pages later, it spoils it.'

'It reduces the value of her sacrifice, you mean?'

'Yes. What's the point in dying for someone if they get you back again? And anyway, she might not have wanted to come back.'

'You think she'd rather be dead?' I asked. 'Even after the big speech she gives before she dies about her children and how they'll grow up without a mother?'

'Yes,' Jono agreed. 'Maybe. I mean, she might not want to go back to Admetus. He was happy enough for her to die in his place, wasn't he? She might prefer someone else now.'

'And no-one asks her, do they?' Mel added. 'She makes this big sacrifice, and everyone's talking about how amazing she is and how sad it is that she's died. And then Hercules decides that because the servants are sad about her dying, and because Admetus is miserable, that it's the right thing to go and get her back. Which is fine and everything, but no-one asks if it's what she wants. They just sort of assume it is, don't they? Because that's what they would want if they'd sacrificed themselves – to be alive again. But they weren't the kind of people who'd be prepared to die for someone else, so they aren't the same kind of person as she is. They don't know what she would want. Hercules gets her back to make his friend feel better. But no-one asks Alcestis.'

I was impressed, and a little smug. She was learning a lot from me, I thought.

'You're completely right, Mel. Alcestis is treated like an object, isn't she, in this part of the play? Hercules goes to get her back, as though she were a glove that Admetus had dropped or something. What do you notice about her when she returns?'

They all looked at each other, clearly hoping one of the others knew.

'She gives that great speech in the first half of the play, doesn't she? And then what does she say when she comes back?'

'Nothing,' said Annika, skimming through the pages to check. 'She doesn't say anything at all.'

'Why is that?' asked Mel. 'Hercules says it's some religious thing – that she can't talk till she's been back for three days or something?'

'That's right. She's still sacred to the gods of the underworld. There has to be a ritual of some kind to allow her to re-enter our world fully, and that takes a few days. Till then, she can't speak. So why does Euripides say this, about the ritual?' I asked them all.

'So we never know what Alcestis thought about what happened to her?' guessed Mel.

'Yes, exactly. So we're left to decide for ourselves how she must have felt, and whether she was happy with it or not.'

'I think she'd have preferred to stay dead,' Mel said.

'Of course she wouldn't.' We all jumped. I'd seen temper from a lot of the Rankeillor kids, but never from Carly. Her face had flushed a dark pink, clashing with the amethyst purple she'd put on her eyes. She was driving her green nails into the palms of her hands, trying not to cry. 'Everyone wants to be alive instead of dead. Everyone.' The tears were coming anyway, falling in dirty indigo streams down her cheeks. 'Who wouldn't rather be with their friends instead of lying in the ground? All this stuff you're saying,' she looked around at us, 'it's complete rubbish.'

'Really? You're doing this now?' Annika asked. 'Are you going to storm out and slam the door like he does?' She jerked her head at Jono, but since he'd turned the other way to look at Carly, he didn't notice.

'Thank you, Annika. Ever helpful. Carly, are you alright? I'm sure none of us meant to upset you.'

She nodded and snuffled, and dug in her pockets to find a tissue.

'I'm sorry, Alex,' she said. 'I don't like this play at all. I think it's horrible.'

'OK. Would you like to talk about that, or would you prefer to take a few minutes on your own? Or something else?' I was running out of ideas.

'I'll take a minute, thank you.'

She got up and walked to the other end of the classroom. The younger kids used it as a performing space every day, but this group hardly ever left their chairs: adolescence had made their bones and muscles ache (what my mother used to call 'growing pains'), and they were happiest sitting down. But she walked to the back window and stood looking out over the yard. She'd have been happier out there, I guessed, but she'd have to go up a floor and then down the steel steps outside. There was no access from the basement, except through an alarmed fire door.

'What just happened?' Jono muttered to Mel.

'I don't know,' she said, eyes wide, shoulders high. The picture of innocence.

Whenever I went into the staffroom, I was reassured by tales from the other teachers and therapists on the Unit that they too saw spontaneous combustions and meltdowns virtually every day. Arguments, fights and tears were part of the currency of Rankeillor. It happened more often with the newest arrivals, who were still bruised from their old schools and were more likely to lash out at each other and the staff. But every class at Rankeillor had the potential to explode with no warning whatsoever. And the anger or hurt or frustration which spurted from a child was contagious: there were whole days sometimes on the Unit when no-one ever settled because one kid had had a tantrum and then it spread round the building. The walls and floors were thick, yet still the students often seemed to sense when things were awry.

Policemen and doctors will tell you they know when it's a full moon, because the A&E units fill up more quickly than on other nights of the month. Sometimes I would think the same was true at Rankeillor: there was a trigger of some kind – invisible to adults but perfectly tangible to the kids – which would make them all go nuts for a day or two each month; or week, if we were really unlucky. You looked for patterns, but you could never find one. Perhaps there were just too many contributing factors – the lessons, the weather, their families, stuff going on outside of school. I never came close to predicting the days when it would all cave in around me. Usually they kicked off when one kid insulted another. But that day, when Carly burst into tears, was the only time I ever saw it happen because of a play.

Mel shrugged. I decided to try and keep them focussed on their work, but we avoided further discussion of the ending, in the hope that we wouldn't upset Carly further. So I asked them about host–guest relationships in the ancient Greek world, and how things differed now, assuming that no-one could take offence at something so dry. When the bell rang, I walked over to Carly to ask if she was OK.

'Yes, thanks,' she said. 'Except my make-up looks revolting now. Do you mind if I stay here and fix it? I won't be long.'

'No, of course not. I'm sorry we made you feel bad, Carly.'

'I know,' she said, through a tight smile. 'Don't worry about it.'

I left her to repair her face in private. Mel was hovering on the stairs, waiting for her.

'Go back in, if you want, Mel. I'm sure Carly won't mind.'

'Are you alright?' she asked, looking me square in the mouth, as she always did when she was concentrating on what you said to her.

'Of course. Yes. Why wouldn't I be?' I gave her a smile to match Carly's. And because of the way the lesson ended, it was the next day before I noticed that something had gone missing from the classroom.

DD,

Fuck, what a day. I swear to God, if I'd known how today was going to pan out, I would have just pretended to be ill this morning and stayed at home. Seriously. It was our last day on Alcestis, and I honestly thought it was going to be fun. We all had stuff to say about it, and then everything went wrong.

Firstly, Ricky hadn't read it. Alex never tells him off for not doing homework, but you can see that she's disappointed when he's done fuck all. I can see, anyway, even if no-one else can. It's only about twenty pages, for Christ's sake, why can't he just read it? I know he's a slow reader and all that, but even so. So, firstly, Alex is upset about that.

And then Jono of all people, like a fucking hero, steps up. He's read it and he understands it and he's thought about it and all that, and Alex looks really chuffed. It's such a relief to see her again, instead of zombie-Alex. And I'm joining in and it's all going really well and we're having one of these lessons that Annika meant when she asked if we could learn proper stuff this term.

We're asking questions and Alex is coming back to life and it's all really fucking good. And then suddenly Carly wigs out. Literally the last person you'd expect to go off on one. She hadn't said a word to me about not liking the play before today. Just nothing. And then she feels the need to tell the world, especially Alex. She gets caught up in this problem she has about us discussing whether it's definitely better to be alive instead of dead, or whether it might not be. We're all talking about it, really talking about something and working out what we think. And out of nowhere Carly goes nuts and bursts into tears. Anyone would think she's the one with the dead brother.

Except she isn't. She's an only child, she's got two parents, she's got two grannies and two grandpas. She's never seen anyone she cares about die. She's only ever seen a couple of people get hurt, even, and one of those was me and I'm fine now, so that can't be it. But she's not putting it on. So she yells at Alex and you can see, anyone could see, that Alex is horrified. Carly seems to have forgotten completely that it was her who wanted to do this play rather than another one, and now she's gone ballistic because she doesn't like it.

I think the truth is that she'd rather we weren't doing these plays at all. She thinks it was all Annika's idea, and we're just reading them because it's what Annika wants. She thinks it's depressing that we're talking about dying and proper stuff.

Anyway, Alex kept the lesson going, and we all just sat there talking really quietly until the bell went, while Carly sulked in the corner. It was ridiculous, really. Then she waited behind when the others left, so I went back to try and find out what her problem is. And she's still crying about how we're all just being so miserable and horrible and she hates it and I of all people must know why, even though I have no fucking idea what she's on about.

To be honest, I wished I'd gone after Alex instead, to check she was OK – she looked really strung out when the lesson was over – since Carly was just crying snot all over my jumper. And I love her and everything but that doesn't make it any less annoying or gross. And she's trying to tell me what the problem is, but she keeps gulping so I can't make out what she's saying at all, so I'm patting her hair and saying 'Shush, Lee,' because she likes being called that. Her dad calls her 'Car' and it drives her mad. Two syllables isn't much, is it? But sometimes it's still one too many. And all the while I'm shushing her, I'm thinking that I should be with Alex, because she doesn't have anyone.

And just for a moment – but now I can't get it out of my head because it was such a strong feeling – I hate Carly. I think she's stupid and selfish and a whining cry-baby and I want to stop patting her head and smack it instead. Just for a moment, like I said. Then I remembered that she's my best friend and I can't get cross with her for getting worked up over nothing, because it's not like I don't ever do that. I mean, everyone does sometimes. Not just Carly.

So I decide to stop being mad at her and I take her outside and walk up to Clerk Street and buy her a Starbucks and she sits there drinking hot chocolate through a moustache of whipped cream and her eyes are all red and puffy and I remember I don't hate her at all. I feel bad. But not sorry.

6

I know the exact date when that happened, the day Carly got so upset about *Alcestis*. I don't know many dates from that year, because I didn't really keep a diary. My friends wouldn't believe this was possible, because I was the one who wrote everything down and kept lists. Luke always had so many work commitments that came in at the last minute, but my diary was always fixed weeks or months ahead. Previews, press nights, auditions, meetings with writers, producers and venues.

Putting on a play, even a tiny one with a cast of three in a studio theatre, takes a lot of paperwork. And I never wanted to be late or double-booked, because most of the people who work in theatre are impossibly thin-skinned. You can insult someone to the core just by forgetting that they only drink soya milk. Luke would point out that anyone who drinks soya milk is asking to be insulted, but that isn't something I could ever say, as I tried to claw my way into the theatre world.

You can want to direct plays without loving every aspect of the industry, I would reply.

You mean theatre folk? An old actor I had directed in a production of *The Three Sisters* once described himself to Luke as 'theatre folk'. Luke, to his credit, merely nodded, then retained it as shorthand for everything he hated about my job.

But these people had an incredible capacity for perceiving slights. How can they be so sensitive and simultaneously so tactless, I would rage at Luke, when one actor had made another one cry by giving her a line-reading or raising an eyebrow at her unusual bag.

So I kept a detailed diary, for years, and never missed an appointment. Then when Luke died, I didn't need it any more. I didn't have to remember when he had stuff on at work. I didn't need to make sure I wasn't double-booked on nights out we'd arranged with our friends. And I didn't need it for work. I quit the play I was directing, because there was no point continuing with it. The only person I wanted to see it was dead.

My mother said that I was being irrational and melodramatic. She didn't use those words, obviously. She's much too kind to say something so blunt to someone grieving. She said things like, are you sure work wouldn't help take your mind off things, and is it possible Luke would have wanted you to carry on with the part of your life that you've worked so hard for, and that makes you so happy? But I was sure. I believed, even if it sounded silly, that theatre needed to come from the heart. It isn't just an intellectual exercise, it's an emotional one. And how do you put your emotions into anything when the only thing that's keeping you upright is boxing them away and refusing to look?

I couldn't carry on with directing Ibsen, just like I couldn't talk about what had happened to Luke, or eat anything he liked to eat, or hear any music he liked, or walk past his belongings on my way to the kitchen, or open the wardrobe and smell the echo of him on his clothes. I just couldn't.

I also couldn't pay rent with no job, and that's where Robert's plan came in. By agreeing to it, I put myself in a position where I didn't have to do any of the things I found impossible, other than get from the beginning of each day to the end. And in Edinburgh every week was the same. I ran the same sessions with the same kids in the same room at the same times each week. I worked the same days every week. I didn't make plans with anyone, because I never knew if I'd feel up to leaving the flat or not, and I assumed I wouldn't, because I often didn't. I didn't know anyone in Edinburgh anyway, except the staff and the kids.

Sometimes Robert would swoop in and ask me round for dinner, or to see something at the Festival Theatre or the Traverse, and usually I would say yes. He would always ask on the day, never before, so I didn't have time to think of an excuse. He would just produce tickets to a concert from his desk drawer, and brandish them at me until I admitted I was free that evening. Courtesy prevented me from failing to show up, so I just went along with it. I loved that about Robert – he never once asked if I wanted to go out, or if I was spending too much time on my own (brooding, as my mother would call it). He just declared we were going out that night and made it easier to agree than to argue.

But I know that the day Carly got upset was a Wednesday, the 16th of March. And I know that because when I got back to the flat there was a letter from London waiting for me. Almost no-one had my address in Edinburgh, so it could only have come from one of a few people. My mother and Luke's parents knew where I was. Luke's mum used to send me cards every couple of weeks, giving me their news, telling me how Luke's sister Tara was getting on at university, and so on. I replied to about every third letter, even though I never seemed to have anything to say. I used to walk down Jeffrey Street till it became Market Street, and choose postcards for her from one of the art gallery shops: elegant scenes of the city itself, reproductions of paintings, or sometimes a photograph of a piece of unnerving sculpture – a giant Christ-figure on a cross, made entirely from coat-hangers – when I ran out of the more staid options.

I tried to explain that things were going OK, that I was having quite a good time at Rankeillor, that I thought I was making a difference to some of the kids, and so on. As much as you can in a few lines anyway. I used to hate writing her surname, seeing Luke's name squatting there. I would walk up the road to post it as soon as it was written, just to get it out of the flat.

But this letter wasn't from Luke's mum, and it wasn't from mine. It was a white business envelope, with a window that revealed my typed address. I opened it without much thought: could it be a bill? I was paying inclusive rent, so I had no idea when the electricity and gas bills would come through. Besides, they wouldn't be in my name. I unfolded the pages, feeling a sharp burn in the index finger of my right hand as the paper edge sliced it open. I squeezed it between my other fingers to stem the blood, and began to read the typed letter that was wrapped round a sheaf of forms.

It was from the police liaison officer, Sergeant Summers, you can call me Ann. We'd met last year. Dear Alex, it began, I'm sorry to have to tell you.

What could she possibly be sorry about? The police had done a good job in Luke's case. They'd arrested his killer within a week of the murder, a man named Dominic Kovar. He had faced previous criminal charges in Germany, where he'd lived for four years before he moved to London. The police had arrested him, and questioned him, and charged him, and he had been remanded in custody ever since. They had done everything right. Even the tabloids, even the internet vigilantes, hadn't criticised the police for the way they handled this case.

The question people asked, when he was arrested, wasn't about the police, it was about him. Journalists, I mean. How do you feel now Luke's killer is behind bars, Alex? It was perverse: it's not like they could print the question, let alone the answer, when he hadn't yet been convicted. And anyway, how do you answer it? Dominic Kovar's impact on my life was so immense that I felt about him the way people must feel who lose everything to tornadoes or earthquakes. You see them crying, dead-eyed, on the news, standing among the ruins of what used to be their homes, trying to explain to a reporter that this pile of rubble was once a bedroom, a kitchen, a child's room. To everyone on the outside, it just looks like a crazy person weeping on broken concrete. You can't hate the weather.

I read her letter three times before I understood it. She wrote in police-ese, tortuous, full of regret but neatly avoiding blame. Not that I would have blamed Ann. She had tried to warn me, in her own way. She had made gentle generalisations about times when the police brought a suspect to the courts, only to see the Crown Prosecution Service undermine all their good work.

I had nodded and made sympathetic noises, stupidly thinking that she was telling me to get it off her chest. It never occurred to me that she was telling me for my benefit, to prepare me for what might happen. I read it through again. Dominic Kovar is pleading guilty to manslaughter. The CPS have accepted the plea and agreed not to prosecute for murder. He will probably serve less than five years.

It's only a guess, she says, several times. But the sentence is unlikely to be more than eight years. The court will take into consideration the fact that he has saved them time and money by pleading guilty. An expensive trial has been avoided, and that is likely to be viewed positively. He will serve half of that time, and he has already been in jail for five months. So he could be out in a couple of years, and I should prepare myself for that.

Prepare myself. The one thing I have not been able to do in this whole demolition of everything I wanted in my life is be prepared for it. I have tissues and a pen and spare change for the bus and a notebook and lip balm and gloves in my bag all the time: I am a naturally prepared person. But how do you prepare for this? How does anyone? I wanted to write back and ask her, but I knew she wouldn't be able to answer. Why would she know, any better than I do?

ACT THREE

1

So you were angry? Charles Brayford asks. This is our second meeting. As he speaks, he glances at his watch. It isn't even discreetly expensive: it has a huge face set into a metal strap so thick that if he ever decides to swing a punch, he could shatter someone's jawbone with a single blow.

Was I angry? When I received a letter telling me my fiancé's murderer would spend almost no time in jail for killing him? Take a guess.

The words have slammed out of my mouth before my lawyer can intervene. Yes, my lawyer. I took Adam's advice after our last meeting, and called Luke's old firm. His former boss couldn't come today, too busy demolishing some hapless prosecutor in court. In his stead, he has sent Luke's direct superior, Lisa Meyer. I haven't met Lisa before, because she took up her position at Hollis, Butterworth just before Luke died. They must have worked together for six weeks at most. Was she at his funeral? I don't remember. I also don't know what he thought of her, except that she didn't suffer fools. He liked that about her, since he wasn't a patient man himself. When Brian Hollis told me he was sending someone else to meet me, I wasn't too surprised, given how late the notice was. But I was disappointed. I'd hoped it would be him, someone I knew.

And then Lisa Meyer walked into the lobby downstairs, and I

realised she could probably crush Charles Brayford under the heel of one of her knee boots. Lisa Meyer is American. She's very small, five feet tall at most. She is wearing a dark grey Vivienne Westwood suit and the soles of her boots are red and unmarked. They are either brand new or she has only ever worn them indoors, and perhaps once on the short stretch of pavement between her taxi and her office. The other possibility I'm considering is that the ground is afraid of her too. The first thing she says to me is, Alex, I'm Lisa. They will fuck with you at their peril.

When I blurt out my answer to Charles Brayford, her face betrays no irritation. She leans over slightly, so our shoulders are touching, and puts her hand on my arm. She has a wedding ring, I notice, but no other jewellery. Her skin is cool and dry.

Alex, she says, softly but loud enough for all four of us to hear. You don't need to reply to these kinds of questions. They are designed to antagonise and upset you. Why would you give anyone the satisfaction of achieving that goal?

Charles Brayford flushes with annoyance. Adam, who is sitting next to him, says nothing, but his eyes betray him. He agrees with her.

Mr Brayford, says Lisa Meyer, turning her basilisk gaze upon him. You seem to be forgetting that my client has experienced the loss of a loved one in brutal circumstances. She is neither on trial here, nor will she be on trial during your client's hearing. She is, let me remind you, here out of courtesy to you and affection for your client. You will, I am sure, wish to repay that courtesy with some of your own. If not, my client's free time is not limitless, and she will have to put it to a more constructive use.

Charles Brayford loosens his tie slightly. If I were wearing a tie, I would be doing the same thing.

Let's reconvene in two weeks, Lisa Meyer continues. When I have had more time to familiarise myself with the details of your client's case. Your assistant can call me, Mr Brayford, to arrange the most convenient location.

No-one is in any doubt that the most convenient location will be Lisa Meyer's office.

Adam begins to get up, but as she passes him, she adds, We'll see ourselves out, leaving him half-sitting, half-standing, looking foolish. As I hurry after her, wondering how someone so small can cover the ground so fast, Adam nods at me, and smiles.

The day after I got that letter, I walked up to Rankeillor as usual. I wasn't sure how I would cope with the kids today. Not just with the older group, but with any of them. I had spent the night reading and re-reading it, and crying. I was taut with fatigue, but I was too angry, still, to feel tired. I suppose I'd thought that at the point when its entire text was committed to my memory, it might lose some of its power. But not so far.

A few weeks after Luke died, my mother had asked me why, since I was so angry, I didn't shout and scream. The honest answer is that it wouldn't have helped. I'd spent years working with actors who externalised every emotion into noise and gestures, and it didn't help them. They were just as neurotic, just as strung out as ever. Why don't you smash a few plates? she'd asked. Because then I'd be exactly as upset as I was before, and I would also have broken plates, I told her. How would that be better?

I'd texted Robert to ask if he minded if I came in late. I didn't have any classes first thing on a Thursday. I usually had one class of what Robert called 'littlies' at eleven o'clock, but they were on a day-trip that day. So I arrived at about eleven fifteen, I suppose. As I opened the huge front door of the Unit, its black paint coated with a thin patina of dirt from the recent rain, I sensed that the atmosphere was different. There was a fizzing sound from the kids, like you get from opening a shaken-up can of lemonade. A can of juice, as they call it here.

Something had happened. I headed up to the staffroom to get the gossip, but it was empty, which was strange. Brown-ringed mugs were clustered on the table, in defiance of the sign over the sink telling users to wash up anything they used because the cleaners weren't paid to do our chores for us. I walked back down the stairs, past Robert's office. I thought about going in, but I could hear he was on the phone, and from his weary, exasperated tone, the call was not one he was enjoying. I crept past, and went down to the basement.

When the children came in, twenty minutes later, Robert was with them. To be precise, he was with Ricky. Robert looked exhausted. His usually pristine hair was ruffled, his shirt was creased and his tie was askew. The bags under his eyes looked puffy, and I found myself wondering if my eyes were also swollen. I'd stopped looking in mirrors since Luke died. It made me blanch to see my eyes look so haunted, and hollow, like that Munch painting. I hadn't had my hair cut in months, because the prospect of looking at my own reflection for an hour was so unappealing.

Anyway, I couldn't face talking to a stranger, which would inevitably happen if I went to the hairdresser's. And I couldn't deal with perky, can-I-help-you shop assistants. I couldn't deal with sullen, why-should-I-help-you-I-didn't-ask-to-be-born ones either. Generally, I had stopped talking during any kind of transaction. I used self-service tills because I'd lost the ability to make small-talk, and so I avoided every situation where that might come up. It's surprising how quickly you start to look like what my mother might describe as 'a state' if you want to avoid speaking to people.

Recently, though, vanity was beginning to reassert itself. I would feel bad that I couldn't remember when I'd last brushed my hair. Or I would catch a glimpse of myself reflected in a window and see that my jumper was bagging round my elbows and hips, because I'd stretched it out of shape. I'd started to perform high street hit-and-runs: I'd walk over to Princes Street, or the St James Centre and find something to wear that I didn't have to think about at all.

I bought carbon copies of clothes I already wore: grey cardigans, inky-blue jeans, vests that came in twin-packs – black and white, turquoise and navy, pink and maroon – that I would layer, to fight off the Rankeillor basement gloom. No wonder Victorian widows used to wear black crepe, I thought. It performed a valuable twin function of declaring to the world that you were prone to sudden bouts of weeping, and it meant you didn't have to think at all about what you were going to wear for months. It was a better system than wearing black for a funeral and then trying to work out how the hell you should dress afterwards.

I rubbed my eyes, in the hopes that if they were red-rimmed, this would now look like the cause.

'Hello, Alex,' Robert said, tiredly.

'Is everything alright?'

'Everything is spectacular.' He sighed, glaring at Ricky. Ricky shrugged and walked over to his chair. 'Richard needs to be accompanied to and from all his classes today, Alex. Perhaps you might take him up to life skills on the second floor after his lesson with you is finished?'

'Of course I will.' I wanted to ask what was going on, but he couldn't tell me while the other kids were there.

'If you and Richard bump into Donald Brooks on your travels,' he added, 'you might encourage Ricky to turn the other cheek. Or go the other way. Or anything that means I don't have to call the police, or social services, or the children's courts, or anyone's parents. Again. If that's alright with everyone?' His eyebrows had rocketed up to their maximum height.

'OK,' I said.

'And Alex? Come for dinner tonight, please. Jeff has bought enough food for an army, and since the soldiers are out of town at the moment, you'll have to do.'

'OK,' I repeated. It was always best to agree with Robert when he was stressed, or when food was involved.

He nodded, gave Ricky the baleful eye, and left, shutting the door with slightly more vigour than it really needed.

'Robert is obsessed with soldiers. He's so totally a bender,' Jono announced to the room.

'That's a pretty charmless thing to call someone who cares about you as much as Robert does,' I snapped at him.

'Sorry,' he said, looking startled.

I looked over at Ricky, who was examining his grimy fingernails with considerable care.

'Should I even ask what happened this time?' I was trying to sound stern, or at least world-weary, but it was hard to maintain when Ricky was such a model of dejection. He was so skinny, and like most redheads, his skin was translucently pale. When he was angry or upset, he sometimes blushed a clashing crimson, but more often, like today, he just seemed to grow paler still. Bluish-purple veins mapped his temples. His oversized clothes only made him look smaller and more pitiful. I found myself again trying to picture him in combat gear, but the image wouldn't form. Shouldn't you have to be a minimum height and weight to be a soldier? Shouldn't your veins be hidden from view?

Ricky looked up from his hands, and shrugged. He wouldn't meet my eyes, but glared at the floor somewhere in front of my feet. 'I didn't do anything,' he began.

Mel gave a loud sigh, and crossed her arms. 'That's bollocks, Ricky. We all saw you fighting.'

'Snitch,' muttered Jono.

'How exactly is it snitching when Alex is the only person who missed it?' Carly asked, as Mel shot a furious look at him.

'Sorry, isn't it Alex she's currently snitching to?' he asked, mouth curling in contempt.

Annika tutted. 'Yes, because otherwise it'll be a good forty minutes before she finds out from one of the teachers or any of us, and that will make…' She paused for exaggerated thinking time, and struck a furrowed brow. 'Oh yes, that's right. No difference at all.'

'So, a fight? Again?' I asked Ricky. 'With Donnie Brooks?'

'Aye,' he said, quietly.

'Did he start it?'

At this, he finally looked at me. He was chewing on his lower lip. If a casting agent had asked him for a reluctant teenager, Ricky would have aced it. 'Naw, miss. I started it. Well, he started it. But I threw the first punch.'

'And the last one,' said Jono, approvingly. He reached over and bounced his fist gently off Ricky's arm.

'The last one wasn't a punch,' said Carly.

Ricky shrugged and nodded. 'It was more of a stamp,' he said. His accent sounded broader today, and I wondered if it always shifted when he was upset.

'You stamped on Donnie Brooks? On an important part of him?' I tried to keep the alarm out of my voice. I didn't want to add to the cacophony of tellings-off he must have already received.

'Not really. Just his leg. I was aiming for his head, but he moved too fast.'

'He's like a whippet,' said Jono. 'Donnie, I mean. He's small, but he's wily.'

'Well, that's probably something we should be grateful for, if it means Ricky didn't stamp on his head.'

'If you'd met Donnie, you wouldn't say that,' Jono said. Ricky nodded.

'Can we agree to differ on this point?' I asked them. 'I would very much prefer it if you didn't stamp on any body part of any student. Or any person, in an ideal world. Partly because I don't want anyone to get hurt, and partly because I don't want you – either of you – to be in trouble.'

Ricky shrugged. 'Fair enough.'

'So how did he start it?' I asked.

'Donnie's brother stabbed Ricky's brother in the lung,' Jono replied, in a more matter-of-fact tone than most people would have chosen.

'Oh my God,' said Carly. 'Is he OK?'

'He's in the hospital wing,' said Ricky.

'Donnie's brother stabbed your brother? But isn't your brother in prison?' Mel hardly ever asked people to repeat information. It was a point of pride for her: she didn't want anyone to think she hadn't heard properly. But Ricky's feud with Donnie required detailed attention. 'How did it happen? Was he visiting someone?'

'Naw,' Ricky sighed. 'He got remanded there over the weekend. Kicked some tourist in on the Mile at the weekend. Right outside the polis station, too. Donnie's brother is practically retarded.'

'So he got put in the same jail as your brother? I'm sorry, Ricky – I don't know his name. And please don't say "retarded", even if it's tempting.'

'Malcolm, miss. Yes. And then he stabbed him yesterday. Mal's lung collapsed. He said it was actually pretty bad.'

'I imagine it was. I think a collapsed lung is generally regarded as pretty bad, for what it's worth.'

How the hell had Ricky's grandparents not spoken to him about this? I tried to remember Robert's dictum that there is no point blaming the parents, because you can rarely change them. But I struggled to quell my irritation that if they ever paid any attention to their grandson at all, he wouldn't turn up at the Unit without enough clothes to keep him warm, and he wouldn't be prey to other kids and their stupid, heartless bullying.

Ricky looked grateful. 'That's what I thought, miss. But then Donnie…' He trailed off.

'Donnie cornered Ricky in the yard at break,' said Jono, jerking his head towards the window at the back of the room. 'And said Mal was a fucking poof, or he wouldn't have had to go to hospital for one lung.'

'And so you hit him?' I asked Ricky.

'Yes, miss.'

'And now you have to be escorted round the Unit for the rest of the day?'

'Till the polis get here. Yes, miss.'

'The police are coming? Really? Over a playground fight?' I felt like a petulant motorist caught speeding who demands to know why the arresting officer doesn't have anything better to do. Were there so few real crimes taking place in Edinburgh that they had time to get involved in a squabble between two minuscule boys who were already in a unit for children with behavioural problems? Wasn't that enough?

'Donnie called his mam,' Jono said, shortly. 'Like the greeting little cunt he is.'

Now Robert's phone call made sense. Rankeillor had its fair share of scraps and fights, but they rarely involved the police. Generally, the kids saw it as weakness to involve any authority figure in their lives at all. And given how much time most of them had already spent talking to policemen, social workers and enraged teachers, that was hardly surprising. I couldn't condone Ricky's attack on Donnie Brooks. But it did sound as though he'd been ambushed this time.

'Can anyone make an educated guess on how long we'll have before the police turn up?' I asked them.

'They won't be here for a couple of hours,' said Jono. The others all nodded. 'Donnie's not even in hospital, really,' he added. 'It's only Outpatients. That's a lot gayer than a collapsed lung.' Ricky nodded. 'He'll be back by lunchtime, I bet.'

'Well, then I think we should use today to talk about the violence we do to others to avenge our family members, shouldn't we? In honour of the fact that Ricky is about to be questioned by the police for avenging his brother?'

'Alright,' Ricky said. 'I mean, if you want, miss.'

'You don't seem very cross, Alex,' said Mel.

'Cross with Ricky?'

'Cross with any of us. Like Robert is, I mean,' she said, hurriedly, as Jono turned to glare at her again.

'I'm not cross. Why should I be?'

'Because we keep fucking up?' Ricky said. 'Well, I do.'

'I don't think you keep fucking up. Yes, today you fucked up. I think you probably know that beating up another student isn't the best way of being a good brother. And I don't want any of you to get into fights. No-one does. But I'm not going to shout at you or tell you that you should know better, because how would it help? I wish you'd chosen to react differently, but I'm sure you do too.'

Jono opened his mouth to disagree, then shut it again.

'Good choice,' I said to him. He nodded. 'Let's get back to work. Aren't you cold, Ricky? Where's your hoody?'

'I dunno,' he said, looking around him, and under his chair, as though it might be hiding.

'It's gone,' he said. 'They must have taken it back.'

I was just about to ask him who would have taken it back, when I remembered I'd told him it had been left here by someone a few weeks ago. Except, of course, it hadn't been. Someone had stolen it.

2

DD,

I can't go to London tomorrow. Robert busted me for skipping Fridays. Well, he didn't really bust me. He was nice about it and everything. He gave a little speech about how important it is that I show up at Rankeillor every day and make the most of my potential. I'm not even sure if I have potential, but Robert thinks we all do. He loves talking about potential. Sometimes he says it so many times that it starts sounding like gibberish. You stop hearing everything else around it.

My dad used to have a cartoon on his fridge door, which his then-girlfriend gave him. It said, 'What we say to dogs' at the top, and there was a panel with someone saying, 'Come on, Ginger. It's time for you to have some food and then we'll go for a walk. You'd like that, wouldn't you, Ginger?' And underneath there was a second panel, which said, 'What dogs hear', and it was the same speech bubble, but inside it just said, 'Blah blah, Ginger, blah blah blah blah, Ginger.' I don't know why he thought it was funny. He hadn't even noticed that it was clearly meant as a dig at me: I can't hear, the dog can't hear. That was the girlfriend I mentioned before, from last year. She was a complete cunt.

Even so, that's exactly what it's like when Robert gets into his *speech-giving mode. Blah blah potential, blah blah blah, potential blah.*

So I can't really skip out tomorrow, or Robert will think I don't care what he says. And I do. So I'm going to compromise, like our life skills teacher says we should. She might be right about this, even if she is annoying. I'm going to do some research on Alex instead. Whatever I find out, I'll report back here.

God, I hope it's not raining tomorrow. I definitely can't get through a whole Friday there without a cigarette. Well, maybe I could. I'm not addicted or anything. I just like smoking. My dad smokes, actually. He says it isn't an addiction, it's punctuation. That's quite funny, for him.

That evening, I set out early for Robert's. I'd remembered the girls' advice and stopped off to get my hair cut on the way. The hairdresser had gone for fifties chic: a prom dress, purple-framed glasses and an up-do with a perfectly curled fringe. She asked me what I wanted mine to look like, laughing as she pulled a comb through the knots. We settled on 'better', and I left her to it. She cut my fringe back in and bobbed the rest, leaving inches of straggly brown clumps on the floor. She ran straighteners through it, so it looked swishy and neat. As she flipped up a mirror to show the back of my head, I couldn't help smiling. It was, I agreed, much better now. Come back another time for the colour, she said, helpfully. I nodded, and almost meant it. Perhaps I would.

Robert lived out past Rankeillor, past the Commonwealth Pool. By the time I'd walked there, it was almost half past seven. I loved Robert's house. Everyone else I'd ever known in Edinburgh lived in a flat. They had huge ceilings and windows, but they were contained in one floor of a townhouse. But Robert and Jeff had a whole building of their own. The front door was massive, painted bright yellow with a black door-knocker right in the centre. The grey stone bricks had none of the dreariness of other buildings: they were just the supporting act for the mighty door.

As I knocked, I felt suddenly embarrassed. What if it was a terrible haircut? Robert opened the heavy door with a loud grunting sound and stood silhouetted in front of the bright yellow hall, its wooden floors protected from encroaching egg-yolk by elegant white skirting boards.

'Alex, look at you!' he shouted, so loudly that a woman walking past on the pavement jumped. 'You look gorgeous. Did you get that done just now?' He took my coat and scarf, and brushed tiny hairs off my shoulders. 'Of course you did. I'm honoured.'

'It was overdue.'

'Oh, it was, it really was. Jeff, come and look at Alex.'

Jeff sprang out into the hall, followed by the smell of onions, tomatoes and cumin. His cropped grey hair matched his eyes, and he was completely calm. No-one came for dinner with Jeff and found a frazzled host. He always cooked like he was being filmed for a TV series. He owned a restaurant on the other side of town, though he'd hired another chef several years ago to take over the brutal day-to-day cooking. All Jeff's skills were now used to orchestrate dinner parties of incredible complexity for Robert and their friends. Jeff was the only person I knew who would serve a ten-course tasting menu in his own home.

He also had the most intemperate attitude to kitchen gadgets, and you brought him one, or mentioned them with anything other than withering scorn at your peril. Jeff would produce molecular food the day all the other food ran out. The best thing to take him, I had learned, was cheese or other treats from Valvona and Crolla, the fancy deli over in the New Town. So I handed him the box of Scottish cheeses that I'd bought at their shop on Multrees Walk earlier. It contained two I'd never heard of, which was usually a good sign when buying for Jeff.

'You look lovely, Alex. Really well,' he said, glancing at my hair before peering at the cheese. 'And these look marvellous. Thank you so much.'

'He does like your hair, Alex,' Robert said, rolling his eyes. 'He just prefers cheese.'

'It's fine,' I said. And it was.

The kitchen was immense, more a performance space than a room for cooking. Robert headed towards their huge bench dining table, which was lined with imperial purple chairs. The work surfaces were packed yet pristine, just like you hope they would be in a restaurant. Jeff never spilled anything, or left bits on chopping boards that fell off and littered the floor. His kitchen looked better when he'd finished cooking than mine did when it had just been cleaned. There were piles of prepared vegetables, shiny steel pots and pans, all waiting to become the focus of Jeff's attention. Bowls of salted almonds, chilli-stuffed olives and tiny hard-boiled quails' eggs were already on the table, alongside a wooden board of flatbreads that I knew Jeff must have baked that afternoon. It boded well for leftovers.

Jeff handed me a glass of white wine, without asking. He always chose the wine you would drink, because he believed that most people, left to their own devices, decide on a wine because they like the name, or the picture or the writing on the bottle. It used to drive him mad when his restaurant customers picked the wrong wine to go with their food, so he never put anyone else in a position where they might irritate him. I'd brought a Sauvignon Blanc, which the deli guy reckoned would work best with the cheeses, but that had disappeared into his gargantuan fridge, to be paired with something more appropriate another time.

'It's a white Rioja,' Jeff said, as he watched me taste it.

'Lovely,' I said, truthfully. I never ate or drank anything as good as whatever Jeff gave me.

'It's the only thing I'm serving with tapas at the moment,' he added.

'That seems reasonable.' I turned to Robert, 'Did you get through the day in one piece?'

He sighed, and over by the cooker Jeff shook his head slowly, as if the end of the world was nigh and everyone kept failing to heed his warnings.

'He could have done without it, Alex,' he muttered, though his mutterings, like Robert's sighs, were designed to be heard by the back row.

'He's not wrong,' Robert said, reaching over for a quail's egg, from which he picked off tiny speckled triangles of shell before dipping it in black pepper. 'Those boys will be the death of me, Alex. They really will. Donnie Brooks isn't such a bad child, really. And Ricky is sweet, when you can get his attention. But put them in the same building and chaos ensues. And it's not even interesting chaos. It's so bloody...' He exhaled. 'Predictable.' Having coated the egg with a new pepper shell, he put it in his mouth.

'Where did things get to this afternoon?'

He swallowed. 'Ricky has a date in youth court. We'll almost certainly lose him. I don't see how he can avoid a young offenders' institution this time.'

I felt a dull thud of sorrow hit me in the stomach. 'Oh no. Really? That doesn't seem fair,' I said. How would he manage in such a hostile environment? And surely the path to a soldier's life had just got one step closer. But perhaps he had been right all along, and the army was the best place for him. It was better than an institution.

'Things never are fair, for boys like him. We don't always win these battles, Alex. But don't be downcast.' Robert suddenly changed gear. 'You're doing a great job with them all, you really are. Even Jono seems to be flourishing in your classes, a sentence I confidently expected never to issue. And as for Mel, you've transformed her.'

'You think so?'

'I really do. She was such a mess when she arrived at the Unit. A total disaster. Destructive, and, worse, self-destructive. But under your tutelage, she's turning into a very thoughtful girl. I always knew she had it in her, but I didn't expect to see her develop so quickly. I'm delighted, honestly I am.'

'She was a nice kid from the get-go. Well, nearly from the get-go. She's always been the most engaged.'

'But that's your doing. You know, last year,' he lowered his voice and looked from side to side. He wouldn't tone down a performance just because there were only two people in the audience, 'last year, we thought we might lose her altogether.'

'From Rankeillor?'

'From everywhere. She made an attempt on her own life, you see. Slit her wrists. Well, just one wrist, but that's hardly preferable.' The secrets of his filing cabinets were spilling out with wine.

I put down my glass before I dropped it. Then I picked it back up, and took a large gulp. 'I didn't know.'

'Of course you didn't. Why should you? It was a classic cry for help. Her mother had a new partner Mel didn't get on with, her father was more absent than usual with a woman who upset her, and then she and Carly had a row about something. It was Carly who found her, in the girls' toilets. She called an ambulance even before she'd found a member of staff. She's not the sharpest knife in the drawer – forgive the choice of metaphor – but she doesn't panic when it's a crisis,' he mused.

'Mel tried to kill herself at Rankeillor? Are you serious?'

'Yes. And if Carly hadn't been so quick off the mark, she might have managed it.'

'I had no idea, Robert. She seems so…' I couldn't find the word. Functional? Normal? Happy?

He topped up my wine. 'Yes, she does. I agree. She never talks about what happened, either. She obviously decided to try and put it behind her. Though she certainly hasn't always been so controlled.'

'No wonder Carly got so upset when we did *Alcestis*,' I said.

'A young woman sacrifices herself because she thinks her loved ones will be better off without her? Yes, I can see how that might have reminded her too closely of Mel,' he said.

'But Mel was fine talking about it. And Jono. But he must have known that she…'

'Yes, he would have known, I'm sure. But this is what you're supposed to be doing, Alex. Helping them to find ways of talking about terrible emotions and difficulties, without focussing on their own lives all the time. You're doing exactly what I was hoping you would. That's why they respond to you. Mel had a clean slate with you. You came in without knowing her history, and you treated her like any other young person. As a consequence, she's behaving like one.' He broke off as Jeff began piling tiny dishes of sausages and potatoes and beans on the table.

'Tapas,' he said, superfluously. 'I never thought it would take off in Edinburgh, but there you go.'

'Wow.' Thanks didn't quite cover it, with Jeff. You needed to include admiration. We talked about nothing but the food as we ate: it was the least it deserved. After a while, I asked about the restaurant, which was still thriving over in the New Town. 'How many nights a week do you go in now?'

'Never,' Jeff said. 'I do Monday mornings, to discuss the weekend just gone, and Wednesday mornings to discuss the one ahead. But they could manage fine without me. If I went away for a couple of months, the restaurant would be just splendid.'

'Are you thinking of going away for a couple of months?' I caught Jeff and Robert eyeballing each other, and realised that something else was going on. I looked down at my plate, and Robert changed the subject.

'There's a new production of *King Lear* at the Festival Theatre next month, Alex – would you come?' He was speaking too loudly. I tried to bring him down a level.

'Of course. I'd love to. I'll stop off and get tickets on my way in to work tomorrow if you like.'

'Well, that would be ideal,' Jeff said, clearing plates away from the table and shooing away my offers of help. 'You two go together, and then I won't have to.'

'I can get three tickets,' I protested.

'But I can't sit through another crazed king wandering about on a blasted heath, Alex. Not even if I get a tub of ice-cream at half-time.'

'Fair enough. I'll book for two.'

Robert excused himself and walked out of the kitchen.

'Don't mind him,' Jeff sighed. 'He knows I hate Shakespeare. It's lucky he'd finished doing it by the time I met him or we'd never have got together, honestly. How many puns can a man sit through for love? Not many, in my view.'

He came back for the serving dishes and stacked them up his arm, like a waiter, or a juggler. He took them to the kitchen and left them piled on top of the dishwasher. Then he sat back down with me.

'Ach, I'm sorry he's in a mood now. It's because I mentioned us going away, and he doesn't want to talk about it.' He put air commas round the last six words.

'Why not?'

'Because I want to retire, Alex. With Robert. I mean, I want both of us to retire. I want to travel a bit, before these Scottish winters mean my old bones won't allow it.'

'You're not even sixty.'

'I'm not even fifty-eight, thank you, young lady. But, honestly, why not? We've both worked hard for a long old time now. And the business runs itself, really. Kenny is completely on top of it. He has been for years.'

'But Robert doesn't want to leave Rankeillor.'

'He just won't see it. Rankeillor would be fine without him too. He's not indispensable. Well, he is, but only to me.'

'I don't know. He's the soul of the Unit. I know that sounds melodramatic.'

'It certainly sounds like bad sci-fi,' he said.

'But I mean it. The Unit might not exist if Robert wasn't there. He keeps it all going through force of will.'

'I know, Alex. I really do. But using that willpower is eating him alive. Dealing with the children and the parents and the social workers and the police and the counsellors and the youth courts and all of it. It's just too much for him now. You can see how exhausted he looks. He used to look like that by the final week or two of each term, but now it's before he's even halfway through.'

'I don't think he could bear to see it crumble without him, though.'

'It doesn't have to. He's not the only person who could run it, is he?'

There was a creaking sound above us as Robert came back down the stairs, and Jeff broke off.

I stayed for crema catalana, but the atmosphere remained awkward, so as soon as Jeff suggested coffee I made an excuse about being tired, and left early. The rain had given up for the night, so I walked back instead of waiting for a bus. The Festival Theatre was still open, but the box office was closed. I'd try again in the morning. I was so preoccupied, thinking about Mel and Carly and the possibility of Robert retiring, that I was putting my key into the front door at New Skinner's Close before I realised what Jeff had been suggesting.

They were down to four.

'Where's Ricky?' I asked, though I knew what the answer would be.

No-one had said anything about him leaving when I was up in the staffroom at break. The basic skills teacher had lost her purse, and we had all tried to help her find it, before she'd had to cancel her credit cards when it became clear that it was gone for good. Even on the Unit, Ricky had been forgotten.

'He's not here any more,' said Mel. 'He's been chucked out.'

'He hasn't,' Jono snarled at her. 'He didn't get chucked out, Alex.' He turned back to me.

'No,' Mel sighed. 'He's in a young offenders' institution, so I suppose he's just otherwise engaged, is he?'

'His court date.' I remembered Robert mentioning it the other night.

'It's only for a couple of months,' Jono said. 'He'll come back.' Even he didn't believe it. Ricky's chair was still in the middle of the front row, as though we could summon him back by refusing to admit he was gone.

'I'm so sorry. Have you spoken to him? Is he OK?'

Jono shrugged. 'He texted. Says it's not as bad as last time.'

I nodded, not wanting to give away the fact that I didn't know he'd been in an institution already.

'Well, I think we should probably decide what we're going to read next, shouldn't we? Then when Ricky comes back, we can tell him about it, and he'll catch up easily.'

Though Annika's eyebrows shot up above her glasses and I could see she was considering telling me what a pointless delusion this was, she said nothing.

'Is there a play any of you would particularly like to do next?' Last time, I'd let Carly choose, so it was someone else's turn.

'What's your favourite?' Mel asked. I thought for a moment.

'I like the *Oresteia*,' I told her. 'It's about families – parents and children and how they cope with one another. And it's about revenge and retribution.'

'Is it good?' asked Annika.

'Yes,' I said. 'Take a look.'

I handed out copies. Mel had already turned it over and was scouring the back cover.

Jono began flipping through the pages. 'Do you really want to read this? It's gibberish.'

'The choruses are difficult, that's true. But the story is brilliant. We could just skip over the choruses, since they're the hardest bits, and they don't add much to the play.'

'Good,' said Mel. 'I don't like the chorus.' She went rather pink as she said this.

'Lots of people don't,' I reassured her. 'If you were watching the play instead of reading it, the chorus would sing and dance and that would make it more exciting. But they are a bit much when we're just reading it. So, let's look at the first play of the trilogy – *Agamemnon*. What do you know about him?'

There was another silence.

'He's the king of the Greeks,' said Mel.

Carly began ferreting about in a bilious pink pencil tin she'd pulled out of her bag.

'Good, yes. Anyone else? He won the Trojan War: did you know that?'

'With a horse?' asked Jono.

'That's right. They snuck the warriors into Troy inside a wooden horse. That's how the city falls, in the end.'

Carly had found what she wanted in her case, and was using it to file her nails carefully. Her emery board appeared to have at least six different surfaces. I wondered if nails could ever really achieve so many distinct levels of disrepair. She looked up and saw my face. 'I can concentrate on both, Alex. Honest.'

'Do you know what he does when he's won the war? Jono, you must have fought plenty of wars on your Xbox – what does a general do when he wins the war?'

'Kills everyone,' he said. 'Rapes the women first.' He thought for a moment. 'Or after.'

'Gross,' said Carly, admiring an index finger before she started on her thumb.

'Agreed. It is pretty much what Agamemnon does, though. He picks one woman to be his slave, and takes her home with him. Her name is Cassandra. Does that name mean anything to anyone?' They all looked blank. 'Cassandra rebuffed the attentions of the god Apollo, so he cursed her.'

'She did what to him?'

'Turned him down, Jono. Sorry to disappoint. Apollo cursed her to see the future but never to be believed.'

'How did that work, then?' he asked.

'Well, she could always foretell terrible events, but she could never warn people. Doesn't that sound like a terrible curse?'

'Wait.' Annika was frowning. 'Wouldn't people start to notice that she was right all the time? I mean, if she kept telling someone they were going to get run over, and then they got run over, people would remember that she kept going on about it. Wouldn't they?'

'I'm not sure how it worked, but I suppose people misremembered what she'd said, or forgot it altogether. It's a pretty grisly fate for her, don't you think? She would have known that Troy would fall, she would have known that her family would be killed, she would have known that she herself would become a slave of the man who had destroyed her city and caused the death of her loved ones. And she couldn't tell anyone. Or she could, but they would just think she was mad.'

'That's terrible,' said Carly, pausing her manicure. 'She must have been so lonely.'

'You're right,' I agreed. 'It's hard to imagine something more isolating than being surrounded by people who won't listen to you. And then she's captured by Agamemnon, who takes her back to where he's from. A city called Argos.'

'Like the shop?'

'Exactly like the shop, Jono, but only in its spelling. In all other regards, not like the shop. And waiting for him in Argos is Clytemnestra, his wife.'

'She's going to be pissed about him bringing Cassandra home with him,' he said. 'If my dad fucked off for… How long did you say the Trojan War took?'

'Ten years.' Mel answered before I could.

'If my dad fucked off for ten years and then came home with another woman, my mum would go spare,' he said.

'Would you blame her?' I asked him.

He grinned. 'Nope.'

'Well, Clytemnestra feels much the same. And she already hates him – long before he gets home with his girlfriend in tow – because before he left, he killed her daughter Iphigenia.'

'Do you make these names up?' he asked.

'Agamemnon and Clytemnestra had two daughters, Iphigenia and Electra, and one son, Orestes. But Agamemnon offended the gods, and he had to appease them before he could sail to Troy. So he agreed to sacrifice Iphigenia to the goddess Artemis.'

'And then he did it? Honestly?' Mel looked appalled. 'His own daughter?'

'I'm afraid he did. He felt like he didn't have a choice. He slit her throat.'

'Oh my God,' said Carly. She always put her hand on her heart when she was shocked. It was a curious, old-fashioned gesture. I wondered if she'd picked it up from her mother.

'That's parents for you.' Annika shrugged. 'They're selfish.'

'Is that what you feel?' I asked her. As the words left my mouth, I wished I'd said 'think' instead. I didn't want her to start yelling about how boring she found everyone's feelings. To my surprise, she answered the question.

'Of course it is. My parents have dragged me from one country to another, and from one city to another, without thinking about it from my perspective at all. Not once. They didn't think about the friends I was leaving behind in Stockholm, they didn't ask themselves if it was disruptive to my education to change languages midway through, and they didn't ask me – ever – what I wanted. What word would you use to describe that kind of behaviour, Alex? Other than selfish?' She had picked up her pencil as she was speaking, and was tapping it against her notebook.

I saw the trap too late. Answer her truthfully and she could go home and tell her mother that I'd said she was a selfish bitch. Placate her and she would almost certainly erupt in fury. The other three sat in silence, waiting to see how I would get out of it. And for the first time, I found that I really wanted to win one of these battles with

Annika. Not because I didn't want to lose face, again, but because I wanted her to get something out of my lessons. Just once.

'I suppose your father might feel that he needs to go where the work is,' I suggested. 'And that's something they could have tried to discuss with you. I'm sure they must know that they've disrupted your schooling, so I suppose what I'm hoping is that they did that because they felt they didn't have much of a choice, rather than because they didn't care about you, which I'm sure they do.'

'My mother does,' she said. 'I have no idea if my father cares about anyone at all except himself.'

'But your father must care about both of you, mustn't he?' I asked her. 'Or he could have just left you in Stockholm and moved to Scotland on his own. Agamemnon kills one daughter then leaves the other behind with her baby brother. They don't see him for ten whole years – that's a lifetime for a child. Would you really have preferred to know your father didn't want to be with you at all?'

'I don't know,' she said. 'Maybe.' She looked up at me as she thought about it, then gave a brisk shake of her head. I felt an unexpected rush of pride. This was the first time she'd spoken to me about anything she cared about without shouting or being sarcastic. It was the longest conversation we'd ever shared.

'Agamemnon sounds like a massive prick,' said Jono.

All three girls smiled.

'No wonder Clytemnestra hates him,' said Mel.

'Hate is the very word. She's spent the whole ten years that he's been away plotting her revenge. Firstly, she starts having an affair with a man Agamemnon hates. Then when Agamemnon finally returns from Troy – with Cassandra, remember – she pretends that she is delighted to see him home at last.'

'So she lies to him?' Jono asked.

'She gives it everything. She says that he must come inside

for a bath, and she welcomes Cassandra to the house as well.'

'But Cassandra must be able to tell that she's lying?' Mel said. 'If she can predict the future?'

'She can, of course. You'll see when you read it: Cassandra is completely fixated on the idea that she's about to be murdered by Clytemnestra, this terrifying woman pretending to be the perfect hostess. Cassandra is predicting her own death, in bloody detail, and no-one is paying her the slightest bit of attention. She's trying to tell everyone that she's walking into a slaughterhouse, and she might as well be mute.'

'That's so horrible,' said Carly, and she shrugged her shoulders in a tiny shudder.

'Yes, it is. But Agamemnon doesn't pick up on any of it, obviously. He's so pompous and stupid that he buys into the idea that his wife would have got over her dead daughter, and would be over the moon to see him home with a pretty young girl. She really sucks up to him.'

'Steady,' said Jono.

I raised my eyebrows, and caught sight of the clock on the back wall. They seemed to be enjoying discussing this play, maybe we could go one step further.

'OK, well we still have some time before the end of the lesson. Why don't we start reading it together now? Jono, you'd better be Agamemnon, since you're the only man left. Who wants to be Clytemnestra?'

I was thinking about the wrong character, of course. As always, I was looking the wrong way.

DD,

   No-one would believe what I've found out. No-one. And I can't tell anyone, because Carly's being weird. She's been funny ever since that session on Alcestis when she went mental. Now when I try to talk to her about Alex and Fridays and stuff, she doesn't want to know. She says she's 'lost interest' in it.

And she's being really quiet in lessons. I wondered if she was upset about Ricky going. But it's not like they were close or anything. She hardly spoke to him outside of Alex's room. When I went to the toilet yesterday, I came back into the classroom and Carly was talking to Jono. When she saw me, she shut up like a fucking clam. And Jono went bright red. He did that thing where his body crunches together, like he's trying to take up less space. Fat chance.

But they weren't talking about me. You can tell from someone's body language if you've caught them talking about you, or if they're talking about something else that they just don't want you to hear. I can, anyway. People turn away from you when they're talking about you. But when they just don't want you to know what they're saying, they can't help looking at you, to check you're out of earshot. So they must have been talking about Ricky, because what else would they have been talking about? I'll work it out. I just haven't yet.

But that isn't the interesting thing. The interesting thing is about Alex. I thought I'd try and track her down online. I should have thought of doing this before. Well, I did, sort of, when she first turned up at Rankeillor. I looked her up on Facebook and stuff and she isn't there. But this time I tried searching for her properly, although it took a while because lots of people have the same name as her. I found reviews of a few plays she'd directed. The word that people most usually used about Alex was 'promising'. 'Promising young director', 'promising new talent'. She's like us and all our potential that Robert goes on about.

But once I'd gone past the reviews, I found a news story with her name in it. In the Richmond & Twickenham Times. Richmond is in the south-west of London, and Twickenham is next door. The

River Thames runs through them, and Twickenham is famous for rugby. That's what I found out about those places. And Richmond is where Alex and Luke used to live.

They ran a story about him dying, in the paper. He wasn't hit by a car, like I guessed. He was stabbed by a man named Dominic Kovar. This Dominic and his girlfriend Katarina were having a fight in the street, on a small road just behind Richmond train station, it said. And Luke was on his way home. On his way home to Alex. Then he saw a man, a big man arguing with a woman. They were both shouting, apparently: there was a witness who could see them from the window of her bedroom. She saw the whole thing happen. She saw a man she described as 'big, shaven-headed, thuggish-looking' pull back his fist, as though he was going to hit Katarina in the face.

That must be what Luke thought too, because he ran across the road, according to the witnesses, and put himself between the two of them. He probably saved Katarina's life, because a punch could kill you, if you fall and hit your head. But a few seconds later, Dominic Kovar stabbed him twice with a short-bladed knife. The police said Luke was stabbed once in the right lung, and once in the heart. But maybe he wouldn't have stabbed Katarina. Maybe that was just something he did to Luke. So maybe Luke didn't save her life, maybe he just lost his.

The paper said that a passer-by had taken Luke's phone from his coat pocket and rung Alex, but that Luke died before the ambulance even got there. I know the person was trying to help, but I can't stop imagining how she must have felt. She would have seen his name come up, and thought he was ringing to talk to her, but then it was a stranger ringing to say he was dead. That must have been the worst part, mustn't it? Finding out like that. I think it could be the saddest thing that's ever happened to anyone.

4

Lisa Meyer is sitting opposite me in an angular chair. It's slightly lower than her desk chair, but it is the same grey, aerated fabric. It looks brand new. But so does everything in Lisa's office.

It's good to see you again, Alex, she says, and she smiles quickly, precisely. It's from courtesy, not affection.

You too, I reply. I don't know what else to say. She gives me a second tiny smile.

I've done further research, Alex, and I'm afraid my suspicions about Charles Brayford were quite correct. He has taken this case on to try and push himself ahead at his firm. It's a perfect fit: he's extremely ambitious, and this is a notorious case.

As she says this, she brushes an almost invisible thread from her pencil skirt, as though the very idea of such vulgar ambition appals her. I find myself thinking that Lisa Meyer is a consummate performer. Not for the stage, because she's far too contained. But on the big screen she would be perfect. She always plays to her audience, and I realise I can't begin to imagine what she would look like if she were alone. Would she switch from razor-tailoring to slouchy lounge-wear? Would she wear those perfect licks of blue-black eye-liner to go and buy a newspaper? I can't imagine her in any context other than work, because she is playing her lawyer role with such conviction.

Looking round her office gives me no clues about her. No photographs on her wall, no personal things on her desk. She could have walked in off the street for the first time today, if she didn't look so completely in control of the space. Her assistant comes in with two glasses of water, and he bobs as he puts them down on the table in front of us. I am under no illusions that this is for my benefit. He is either in love with Lisa Meyer, or afraid of her. Probably both.

Thank you, she says, without looking at him. This means he can blush unseen, which must be a relief.

I'm ninety-five per cent certain, she continues, that Brayford has decided to get his client off by blaming her actions on you.

I don't really understand what she's saying. On me? I repeat.

Exactly, she says. I think that he is going to go before a judge and explain that you took advantage of his client, that you twisted her affection for you into a destructive rage, that you knowingly led her to London and encouraged her obsession with you and Luke.

Her words are melting before they hit my ears, like tiny flakes of snow. I don't... I can't finish the sentence. Now my words are melting too.

Take a sip of water, Alex, and breathe, she says. I'm sorry this is so upsetting for you. I knew it would be, but there's no other way to prepare you for what's going to happen. We need to be ready to face his arguments; we can't be in denial.

Lisa Meyer is the first person I have ever met who uses audible semicolons.

His job, she says, her eyes on my water glass, which is shaking slightly in my hand, is to get his client off. That means reasonable doubt. A good way to establish that in the mind of a judge is to cast the blame onto someone else. He has a few options: her mother, her father, her schoolfriends. But obviously, you are by far the best target.

He can construct a narrative around you and his client which will sound plausible, even if it isn't true.

I take another sip of water.

Do you understand what I'm telling you, she asks. He is going to try to throw you against the wall to get her off these charges. I'm not going to let him succeed, obviously.

I nod. The very idea that Lisa Meyer would let someone succeed at her expense is demented.

But you need to be aware of what's going to happen, she says. Her voice softens. I don't want it to come as a shock to you.

I nod again. I think it might be too late for that, I say.

She does the smile again. I really am sorry, Alex. If I can keep you out of the courtroom, I will. But it might not work. She picks up the pencil again. We need to decide on a strategy, she says. I need to discredit his argument, and for that, I need you to tell me more about her. She was clearly unstable when you met her. She latched onto you in an inappropriate way, and she concealed that from you successfully. And that is all going to work in your favour.

Wait.

She stops talking and raises the eyebrow again. Her pencil is held perfectly vertical over her paper.

I don't understand. He blames me, and so to get me off the hook, we blame her?

Lisa Meyer gives me an unreadable look. This is the moment that cinema-goers would talk about in reverential tones once the film was over.

That's right, Alex. It's the only way, I'm afraid.

We can't do that, I say.

Lisa purses her lips, but her glossy mouth is so neatly renewed by the action that it looks more like grooming than irritation.

We don't have very many options, she replies.

We can't, though. She's just a child. And none of this was her fault.

Alex, I'm going to suggest that you take some time to think about what's at stake, she says. I understand that you're very fond of her, and that your concern for her is both real and considerable. But I want you to think about what you have to lose.

I have nothing to lose. The words are out of my mouth so fast that I feel my hands move, to try and catch them and stuff them back.

Lisa looks at me sadly. That simply isn't true, Alex. I understand you lost someone you loved. But you must understand: there is always more to lose. It would be better if you took my word for it than decided to test the theory. I realise that it will take a little time for you to come to terms with what is happening. Come back next week, and we'll talk again.

I won't change my mind, I tell her.

She gives a miniature, bonsai shrug.

You will, she says.

Carly had been doing some serious practice: her eyes were lined in bright turquoise, with darker blue lids fanning out above.

'Your eyes are amazing today,' I told her, and she blushed pink, through her sparkly peach blusher.

'Thank you, Alex.'

'Did you all manage to read *Agamemnon*?'

'Yes,' they chorused. Mel didn't notice the look that flashed between Carly and Jono. It was so quick that I barely saw it myself: a crackle of something secret, that no-one was invited to share. Almost instantly, the moment dissolved, and they were facing me, ready to work. I wondered if I'd really seen it. Carly and Jono? So the make-up wasn't practice after all.

'OK, I thought we'd talk about Clytemnestra today. She kills Agamemnon, while he's in the bath. And she kills Cassandra too.

She's drenched in blood by the end of this play, isn't she? Just like Oedipus at the end of his play. Except he's covered in his own blood and she's wearing the blood of her enemies. Are there any other differences between them?

'She's happy,' said Mel.

'Exactly. Oedipus punishes himself for his terrible crimes. At the end of his play, he's wretched. But Clytemnestra really revels in what she's done. She isn't sorry at all.'

'Why should she be?' yawned Annika, stretching her long arms over her head. She looked tired today: tiny grey shadows marked the skin beneath her eyes. I wondered what had been keeping her up late. I hoped she'd been out misbehaving, but it was more likely she'd been arguing with one or both of her parents again. 'I mean, he started it.'

'You are such a psycho,' said Jono, shaking his head. 'You don't really think killing someone because they killed someone else is fair enough. Do you?'

'God, I'm tired,' she said, as if he hadn't spoken.

'But what should she have done then?' Mel kicked the back of Jono's chair to get his attention. 'To get revenge for Agamemnon killing their daughter? Iphigenia, I mean?'

'I don't know. I just think you can't go round killing everyone you don't like,' he said.

'But Annika's right.' No-one looked more surprised by this statement than Annika. As far as I'd ever been able to judge, the two girls tolerated each other, at best. Perhaps Mel and Carly were growing apart, and she was beginning to realise she could do with another friend. 'He did start it.' Mel held firm. 'He killed their daughter, and she hadn't done anything. She thought she was getting married and then he just killed her. He's a horrible person. Why should he be allowed to stay being the king when he'd done that?'

Jono shrugged and turned to face me. 'Didn't they have other kids?' he asked.

'Yes. They have Electra and Orestes. We'll find out more about them in the next play.'

'Well, that's the problem then, isn't it?' He turned back to Mel, triumphant. 'She kills him to avenge her one daughter, but now her other kids don't have a dad.'

Mel looked at him. 'Well, that's a good thing, then,' she said. 'It means they might live to be grown-ups.'

He rolled his eyes and looked away. Carly was completely quiet. Then the bell rang, and Jono sprang from his chair. 'See you tomorrow,' he muttered as he raced past.

Carly turned to Mel as they gathered their books, but her eyes had followed him to the door.

Mel stopped for a moment to ask me about the next play in the trilogy, and by the time she and Carly had gone, I was late for a staff-meeting upstairs. I went to grab my bag, and it wasn't there. I usually hooked it over the back of my chair, but now it was missing. I looked under the desk and in the drawers. Stupid: why would I have put it in a desk drawer? It took me several moments to accept that it had been stolen by one of the fourth-years.

DD,

Ricky leaving has made our sessions with Alex go weird. I didn't really see what he brought to the classes, to be honest. He didn't understand a word we've been reading. He joined in a bit when we talked about it, but he was mostly drawing his endless fucking pictures. But without him, the group feels strange. Uneven, like we're walking with grit in our shoes.

There's me and Jono who like talking about stuff, except that he doesn't always get it. There's Annika, who gets it but doesn't like talking about it much. And then there's Carly, who likes talking, but doesn't like the plays. I'm not sure how much she really understands them, if that doesn't sound too bitchy. And Jono and Ricky were always kind of a double act, and now Jono hasn't got anyone to hang around with, he's like a spare part. Something's going on with him and Carly but she won't tell me what it is. They must have argued about something.

I still can't work out why Alex goes to London. I can't work out why she doesn't go to see her mum. Or why she doesn't go to the place she and Luke lived. At least that would make sense. But whatever the reason, it's a thing she has to do, I get that much. She has to go to London and do the same thing every time, walk through the park to that café, The Regent's Café. I had to look at the map of the park online to find out its name: it seems stupid to be writing about it and not know what it's called. Then she has to wait there for an hour, and then come back to Edinburgh.

I still have no idea who she's waiting for. And why do they never show up? Is it her mum who doesn't come? Maybe they fell out with each other. I know one thing for sure: Carly was way off when she said it might be a new man. If it was, Alex wouldn't keep going when he doesn't turn up. She'd have some dignity, right? Besides, she still loves Luke. She wouldn't want to meet someone else.

But then maybe she doesn't go to meet someone at all. Maybe it's a memorial thing, like my mum visits the tree she had planted in the Botanics on Jamie's birthday. She goes every year at Christmas. She doesn't think he is the tree, or anything mad. She says she just likes somewhere to go and think about him which isn't a graveyard. She says she likes to think of his life, not his death. That makes sense, right? So is that what Alex is doing? Is that why she goes to the park instead of to their old house? Maybe they met in the park? Or maybe he used to take her there? That makes him sound really fucking boring. I hope that's not it.

But I think it's somewhere that was important to them, and she goes there to think about him so that she can come back and be with us and not miss him so much. That must be it, mustn't it?

5

I couldn't ignore this theft. I couldn't get back into my flat, for a start: my keys were in the bag, and the bag was gone. I walked up to Robert's office, and asked Cynthia if he had a few minutes. She waved me through, as always. She placed little value on Robert's sporadic pleas not to be interrupted. She'd probably noticed that he worked best with a deadline, and the easiest way to create one of those was to allow the rest of us to keep disturbing him.

'I'm sorry to bother you,' I began.

'How can I help?' he said, gesturing at the kettle. I nodded, and he walked over and switched it on. He picked up a jar of instant coffee in one hand and a box of tea bags in the other and waved both at me. I pointed to the left. 'Coffee it is,' he said. The kettle growled at him.

'Have you noticed anything going missing?' I asked him.

'More than usual?'

'Yes. I think so. Alison's purse was stolen the other day. She had us all looking for it in the staffroom. Did she mention it?'

'She did say something,' he agreed. The sound of water boiling was growing increasingly loud. 'But she couldn't remember where she'd last had it, so in the end we decided to report it as lost rather than stolen.' Steam was flowing from the kettle, and though it hadn't yet switched itself off, he pulled it from its base and poured. He had no patience for objects which didn't fulfil their function quickly enough.

'There have been a few other things,' I said. 'A hooded top of Ricky's went missing a couple of weeks ago. And now, today, my bag's been taken.'

'Oh no, really? I'm sorry.' He handed me a cup of muddy coffee. 'Definitely stolen?'

'It was on the back of my chair at the start of my last lesson with the fourth-years, and it's gone now. I wouldn't say it if I wasn't sure – you know that – but one of them must have taken it.'

'Right.' He reached for a pen and a pad of paper. Robert must be the only teacher left in Edinburgh whose desk still sported a huge blotter, as though he might set to work with a quill at any moment. 'What does it look like?'

'It's a small purple messenger bag,' I told him. He looked confused. 'You wear it across the body.' I mimed the strap with my hands.

He started to scribble. 'And what was inside?'

'The usual things. Pens, tissues, a notebook, my house-keys.'

'Not your wallet?'

'No.' I tapped my hip pocket. 'I keep it here.'

Robert's face filled with relief. 'So there's nothing irreplaceable there, then. I have a spare set of keys for your flat in my kitchen drawer, unless Jeff's tidied them away. If you give me ten minutes, I'll drive you home and pick them up for you. The bag itself wasn't valuable, was it?'

'No, it's just a canvas bag. It cost about twenty pounds. There was nothing important…'

Robert looked up as I trailed off. 'What have you remembered?'

'Nothing.' I could feel the heat suffusing my face. 'Honestly, it's nothing.'

'Alex, I would rather play poker against you than against an eight-year-old child. What else was in there?'

'It's nothing. I'm sorry.' I could feel the tears coming. 'It's so stupid. My key ring. I'd just forgotten.'

Robert looked briefly baffled, then realisation dawned. He leapt up, shut the door to the outside office, came back and propped himself on the front of his desk. He shoved a box of tissues towards me, and I took a handful.

'Luke gave you your key ring,' he said.

I nodded. 'I'd forgotten I had it. I left everything that was his behind. Everything. I don't wear the necklaces he bought me, I don't have the books he gave me, I don't listen to the music he downloaded for me, I don't watch the films he showed me. I left all of it behind, so that this couldn't happen. So there wasn't anything left to lose. And I forgot one thing and it just was a stupid little leather dog. Do you remember seeing it?'

He nodded the lie. Why would he remember seeing a key ring?

'Oh God, I'm so sorry,' I said. I never cried elegantly. My face was red, my nose was streaming, my eyes were puffing up. I couldn't stop.

Robert handed me another wodge of tissues and I blew my nose. He leaned over and put his hand on my shoulder.

'It's alright, Alex. The only person who could possibly think this is an inappropriate reaction is you.'

'I just want him back,' I wept. 'It's the only thing I want, it's the only thing I'm ever going to want. And I can't have it. He's never coming back, and even though I've run as far as I can from all the people and places and things that remind me of him, it doesn't help. Because I've brought him with me, and every time I think there's nothing more I can lose, I lose one more thing. It's like some kind of horrible test.' I couldn't speak any more. I gulped for air.

Robert squeezed my shoulder. 'I know,' he said. 'I'm so sorry. I'll try and get it back, honestly. I'll interrogate every one of the little sods until they crack.'

'I threw away my phone, did you know that?' He shook his head. 'I couldn't stand having it with his number on it. I couldn't bear knowing he'd never call me again. The last time anyone called me from his number, it was the man who'd called the ambulance. I've never told you that, have I? He called me when he realised they wouldn't be able to save him, not even if they got there straight away. He hoped I was close by, that I'd be able to run round there to be with Luke in those last few moments. And I was nowhere fucking near. I was on the other side of London, in fucking Highbury, rehearsing some piss-poor play that never needed to be put on. It cost me my last chance to see him alive. My last chance.'

I was shrieking now, my voice cracking in the space between shouting and crying.

Robert winced.

'Do you understand now why I won't ever go back to that world? It betrayed me. I gave it everything I had, and when it really mattered, it fucked me over. I could have been rehearsing in fucking Richmond. They have rehearsal space at the Orange Tree. I must have been there a thousand times. But not when it mattered. When it mattered, some fucking histrionic actor couldn't cope with using the Tube, so we all had to trek up to bloody Islington, and look where that got me. Luke used to tell me I spent my whole life bending over backwards to please these impossible people, and you know what?'

Robert shook his head.

'It doesn't matter that I spent my whole life doing it. What matters is that I spent his whole life doing it. I would take it all back, Robert. Every moment I spent trying to be a fucking director, trying to make people happy, trying to be good at something. If I could go back in time, I wouldn't do any of it. I'd just stand next to Luke every fucking second and when anything bad looked like it might happen to him, I'd get in the fucking way and I would keep him safe. And when people asked me what I did for a living, I'd say I loved him. That's what I wanted to do. I thought it was the background, and it was everything. Everything.'

I had no words left. Robert left me to cry for a while. He texted Jeff, who brought the spare keys up to Rankeillor. They walked me home together.

DD,

It's the holidays now. I've never not wanted a term to end before. But this time, I'm fucked off. No Alex for six weeks. Six weeks. Anything could happen in that time. I hate that. I asked her what she was doing over the summer, and she's staying here, in Edinburgh. Maybe Robert will take care of her? She says she's looking forward to the Fringe. Jono told her she can't be a real Edinburgher if she's looking forward to that bunch of self-indulgent southern pricks coming up here in their white-face make-up and wandering about the streets like nutters. She said she knew he was right. And she promised not to go and see a show where anyone had a painted white face. She says she's going to see the National Theatre of Scotland at the Traverse, so doesn't that count for something? He said maybe. I said yes.

She asked what we were doing – Carly's going to Loch Lomond to stay with her grandparents for a bit, and to Spain. I'm stuck here with my mum. But I didn't say that, because I didn't want to sound like a loser, and my mum said we might go away somewhere if she can get time off. Who spends the whole summer at home? I'm probably going to go down to see my dad at some point. He's still deciding what we'll do.

We told Alex we'd miss her over the summer. She seemed happy. She said we'll all be back here in August, and the holidays *will disappear before we know it. I wish that was true, but I know they will drag on forever, like a nightmare. I asked her what I could read over the summer, and she said – honestly – I think you could read anything you put your mind to, Mel. I love that about her. Then she said that next year is our final year at Rankeillor, so we'll need to be preparing for what we decide to do after we leave. I felt cold in my stomach when she said it. I don't want it to be my final year. I don't want to leave.*

It was June. My second term at Rankeillor had sped past. It felt like a few weeks since I started at the Unit, but I'd been there for six months. Time was sliding away from me. I supposed this was the correction, when it had become so heavy and viscous after Luke died. I'd felt leaden every day for months, infected by time, as though it were the flu. But now I could get to the end of the week and every hour didn't feel like it would drag me into the ground.

Outside my windows on New Skinner's Close there were sheets drying all across the courtyard. And they were drying from sunlight, rather than wind-chill alone. I woke up one Saturday and decided to climb Arthur's Seat, just because staying indoors on a day Edinburgh wasn't under full cloud-cover seemed crazy.

I showered and changed into new jeans, a vest and a thin cotton cardigan. I put my key on a leather thong round my neck, and then I double-checked the local weather forecast, to make sure I wouldn't suddenly get caught in a deluge on the way up. But this was Edinburgh, so I tied a thin jacket round my waist, just in case. As I came down the spiral staircase outside the flat, I stopped at the mailboxes. Just one letter, postmarked London, stamped by the Metropolitan Police. I knew what it was, of course. I had been dreading this letter for weeks. I stood still for a moment, trying to decide whether to open it or leave it behind. Then I stuffed it into my back pocket, and carried on.

I walked down the Cowgate and onto Holyrood Road. I went past the *Scotsman* office on my right, and the little BBC building on my left. I kept going until I ran out of road, and then I turned right and began to climb the stony path which would take me all the way from Holyrood to the very top of Arthur's Seat, curving round the green crags as I looped higher and higher. The ground was dry beneath my trainers, not at all slippery. I paused for a moment to rest, and to look down at how far I'd climbed. The Scottish Parliament looked incredibly ugly from above, blocky and mis-shapen. The people who complained still about its incredible cost would be even crosser if they ever clambered up here and took a bird's eye view of the place.

The crags were still quiet at this time of the morning. Even the gulls couldn't be bothered to fly up to the desolate peaks when there were far richer pickings in town. A few keen ramblers passed me on their way back down, greeting me with the cheery, bearded hellos of regular walkers. I nodded and smiled and kept climbing. I was breathing hard by this point, but I didn't want to stop. I needed to get to the very top and look down at the University, where I'd spent so much time so happy. I also wanted to look for Rankeillor, and see if I could pick it out from up here. And then I wanted to sit down on a convenient rock and cry for a few minutes.

It grew cooler as I climbed higher, but I didn't mind: walking was keeping me warm. I had half a memory of reading how Kierkegaard had said that he knew of no thought so burdensome that you couldn't walk away from it. Shows what he knew: the letter seemed to be burning my flesh through my jeans. But then, I thought, perhaps Kierkegaard had assumed you would have the sense not to bring your burdens with you.

Finally at the top of the Seat, I found a flat bit of stone to sit on. I pulled out the envelope and looked at the neat, typed address on the front. I tried to make out the date on the pinky-red postmark. I turned it over, and wondered if the nausea would stop if I just manned up and opened it. I tore along the back and pulled out the letter.

Two pages. It was a long, sorrowful explanation of sentencing procedures, and the impact that a guilty plea usually had on a maximum sentence. It was couched in the blame-free language of the police: we regret if any, CPS guidelines are such that.

The words slid away from my eyes. Remembering my secondary school drama teacher, who would begin no lesson or project without a communal breathe, such was her belief in its meditative power, I took four deep breaths. Unclenching my teeth felt like pulling magnets apart.

I read the letter again. Eighteen months. Dominic Kovar would be out in eighteen months. Luke's whole solid, sinewy, thoughtful, beautiful, grey-eyed life was worth that. Not even a month for each of Luke's years lived. My future, our lives together, everything was reduced to a number. And the number was tiny.

The second page was worse. The sentence was laid out in pre-emptive, don't-shoot-the-messenger detail. Katarina had made a very convincing character witness, it explained. She had impressed the court with her regret over their fight, with her sympathy for Luke's family, with her need for Dominic's income, with her love for him, with her forgiveness for his behaviour. If she had been standing in front of me right then, I realised, I would have pummelled her face into the ground. I would have held her by her ugly, greasy, too-high ponytail and I would have smashed her onto the rocks beneath my feet over and over again. I took another deep breath. Luke's parents had also spoken to the court, the letter went on. They had made an eloquent plea for their son's killer to be given a longer sentence than the minimum. But, perhaps because of a lack of further support, the court had regretfully ignored their request.

I had to read the last sentence three times before I realised what it was insinuating. Dominic had got off lightly because I hadn't attended the trial, because I had run away. My grieving fiancée status might have swung the balance in Luke's favour. One young woman to stave off the pleas of another young woman. Don't come crying to us, they might as well have put. It wasn't the police's fault that Dominic would be a free man in a few months. It was mine.

I didn't want to have these pages in my hands any more. I didn't want them. I began to scrabble at the grass next to me, scratching underneath it to try and loosen a clod. My nails grew black as I dug, but the ground was more solid than I had guessed. I took the key from around my neck and used it to gouge out more of the earth. When I'd loosened the edges enough, I pulled up a lump of grass and soil the size of my fist. I folded the letter into four, buried it in the ground, and replaced the grass on top of it. I pushed the damaged patch back down as hard as I could, and piled the extra soil around the sides, then ground it down with my shoe. Let the worms have it.

DD,

That café that Alex goes to has a website. I should have thought of checking before, because I looked it up, and there it was. Terrible design — clunky, ugly font in browns and greens. They should ask for their money back. It has this Testimonials page where really fucking boring people have said their lemon drizzle cake was exquisite. Anyone who describes a cake as exquisite should be barred from eating it. And then they have a Contact Us button, so you can mail them, I suppose, to complain about the cake if you didn't like it. And a Location button.

And then they have a page marked About Us, and you click on it, and it's got this cheesy letter from the manager explaining that he hopes you have a wonderful time when you visit and how he's looking forward to welcoming you back there soon. They've done a fake signature at the bottom, next to a picture of him with his dark, curly hair, and his tight white t-shirt. I bet that's not even the guy. I bet it's a model they used instead. Because this guy hasn't eaten any cakes for fucking ever, that's for certain.

And then, under his picture are pictures of the rest of the team. The team, for fuck's sake. In a little café. There's only five of them, three women, two men. They all have foreign names: Irina, Dmitri, Alaric, Katarina and Noor.

It only took me a few minutes to find a picture of Katarina, the woman that Luke died trying to protect. They're the same person. Of course they are. It was right in front of me, once I knew what I was looking for. Finally I know why she goes to London.

Alex isn't waiting for someone to come and meet her at all. The person she wants to see is already there.

ACT FOUR

1

Lisa Meyer has a huge bouquet of orchids in the corner of her office.

Come in, Alex, she says, waving me towards the low chairs by the fireplace. She has a fire burning there, to fight off the cold February day.

Pretty flowers, I say to her. She looks momentarily blank, then follows my gaze.

Yes, she says. But I have to keep them at a distance, or they make me sneeze.

Finding out that Lisa Meyer is allergic to pollen is a bit like discovering that it's microbes which take down the Tripods in *The War of the Worlds*.

Have you thought about our conversation last week, Alex? she asks, as she brings a dark, charcoal-grey file over to the table with her. Luke's files were always a shade between pastel and grime – dirty beige, dull pink, yellowed blue. Lisa clearly gets hers from a different stock room. She pings the black elastic bands from its corners, and opens it on her lap.

Yes. I nod. I've thought about it a lot. But I don't know what to do with the thoughts.

Let's start with maintaining your reputation, Lisa Meyer says, arching her one mobile eyebrow. And see if we can't achieve a bit more than that. I've been trying to find out who is paying for her lawyer, she adds, flicking through a few pages from the file. It's taking longer than I thought.

Wouldn't it be legal aid? I ask her. She's just a child, after all. Some-one has to defend her.

Lisa Meyer blinks twice, rapidly. It seems to be her equivalent of a loud sigh.

It can't be legal aid, Alex. Brayford didn't take on this case for that kind of money. Not even for the prestige he imagined he would gain. Someone is paying him, and they must have deep pockets. It is most likely to be her parents, one way or another, but until we do some more digging, I won't know for sure.

I didn't realise it would be so complicated, I say, feeling stupid. I suppose I thought because her guilt isn't in question… I trail off, not knowing how to finish a sentence I wish I hadn't begun.

Things are rarely simple, she replies. We are trying to get a positive outcome in this case, Alex. So I'm leaving nothing to chance. I'm sure you of all people understand that a person's guilt is decided by a court, and that facts are not the only determinants of that decision.

The phone on her desk buzzes once, and she stares at it. It goes silent.

Besides, she continues, as if the phone hadn't dared to interrupt her, her parents know what their daughter did. They will be feeling guilty for what they will surely perceive – correctly, I imagine – to be their poor parenting skills. They may now be over-compensating. But nothing's certain at the moment.

They probably blame me.

Perhaps they do. That doesn't matter, Alex. It only matters if Charles Brayford tries to blame you, in court. He'll need to implicate someone, if they're going to keep her out of jail. So all that really matters is that we make it impossible for him to blame you. Then he might pick a weaker target.

But what happens if he does? What would happen to that person?

I was wrong about the double-blink being her version of a sigh. She inhales sharply, the negative of a sigh.

Then that person would need to get a lawyer, Alex. Just like you did. You need to remember that none of this is your fault. You experienced an awful, life-changing crime and that made you compelling to a teenage girl with an obsessional streak. And as a direct consequence of that, it has become Charles Brayford's job to go through a list of names until he found someone who wouldn't fight back. That used to be you. But it isn't you any more.

I nod again.

Bad things happen to everyone, Alex. She smiles that small, taut smile. We all choose whether to be defined by them, or whether to be who we are in spite of them.

Victim or survivor, I murmur.

Exactly, she says. That's it precisely. You are the latter, Alex. You just think you're the former.

How do you know?

I've spent some time with you. I knew Luke, a little, so I have some idea of what you lost when he was killed. And I've spoken to Brian Hollis about you. He had enormous respect for Luke, and he has enormous respect for you. He tells me you will be the most successful director of your generation, once I've sorted this mess out. I'm very smart, Alex, and I don't make mistakes. That's why they put my name on the door, she says.

This, I think, is Lisa Meyer's idea of a joke. I like the fact that the most self-deprecating thing she can think of is not very self-deprecating at all.

I'm still not happy with the idea of testifying against her, I say.

Let's come back to that, she says. For now, all I need is for you to tell me everything that happened. Everything you remember about meeting her and your classes and her behaviour towards you and her schoolfriends. All of it. If you're still unhappy when the first court date comes up, we can try to come up with a different strategy. Most judges are going to be sympathetic to someone who has been through what you have been through, Alex. They're not monsters. That holds true in this case, too. No judge approaches the trial of a minor lightly, especially not when it's for such a serious crime. But no-one wants to lock her up and throw away the key. It would be inappropriate.

For Lisa Meyer, being inappropriate might be the greatest sin of all.

OK.

I need you to go through any paperwork you have, Alex. I need you to look at a calendar, or your diary, and try to remember what happened when. I need you to make notes of anything you do remember and any key dates that you can tie it to: a lesson one side or another of a bank holiday, for example?

I'll try. But I stopped keeping a diary before I went to Edinburgh. I didn't think I'd need one.

Of course not, she agrees. But you'll be surprised how much you remember, when you start to write it all down. This might help.

She hands me a print-out of last year's calendar. It has all the regular holidays printed on it. But someone – Lisa Meyer's assistant – has added key events that he hopes will jog my memory. News stories, TV programmes, my mother's birthday, which I can't imagine how they know, but they do.

I did go through my first few meetings with her, for Charles Brayford. So I remember that time very well.

That's a great start, she says. But it isn't enough. I need you to really focus on the summer and the autumn of last year. We're looking for more information, and with a different purpose, so I need you to think in a different way.

The difference between looking in a drawer where you think your keys are, and looking in one where you're certain they can't be? I ask.

Exactly, Alex. She smiles. Is there anything else that might help you to remember details? I think for a moment. The calendar from the Festival Theatre, I say. I used to walk past it every day. The show titles will help.

Her eyes gleam. She goes to the door with her name on it, and speaks briefly to her assistant. By the time I leave, a few minutes later, I have in my bag a print-out of the schedule of every exhibition from the City Art Gallery, the National Galleries of Scotland, the dates of all major cinema releases last year, and a list of every theatre show from the past twelve months at every major Edinburgh venue. Lisa Meyer's assistant is determined to impress her.

The school holidays whipped past, as they had when I was a child. Perhaps it was because I had promised myself, when the police letter arrived, that I would stop going to London each week. I was too angry to go the week after I received it, and too sad and weary in the weeks after that. I kept the promise, too; the last time I'd left Edinburgh was early June. And without Rankeillor Street or the trips south to punctuate my weeks, the days all blurred into sameness.

Edinburgh changes beyond recognition during Festival season in August, when the city's population doubles for a month. Every student theatre group, every stand-up comedian with a microphone and scruffy blond hair gelled into artful disarray, every sketch-comedy troupe with a convoluted punning name that plays on an out-dated film title: they all come to town. The supermarkets are suddenly packed, the streets heave with tourists and the Royal Mile switches from being a passable route through the Old Town to a static home for street theatre, jugglers and mimes.

I had experienced all this from the other side, when I first came to Edinburgh all those years ago, with a school play: a production of Anouilh's *Antigone*. We performed for a week in a church hall over by the Botanics, and I fell in love with the city and its pulsing, thronging theatricality. In my memory, it didn't rain once, though that can't be true. We stood in the streets flyering for our show every day, either in costume or in the bright purple t-shirts printed with our show, our school, our venue and our dates and times. Over and over again, we would try to press our leaflets on Festival-weary Edinburgh residents. 'You're awright, hen,' was the kindest phrase of rejection I'd ever heard, and that remained true even when I'd heard it every two minutes for a week.

By the time I went home that summer, I knew I would be applying to study there. I knew I would never want to be anywhere else as much. It was a magical city to my teenage mind: from the Scott Monument and the Castle to the sound of the cannons and fireworks at the Tattoo every night. I even liked the strange smell of the place. I liked the fact that you could blindfold anyone who'd ever been to Edinburgh, then take them to the city, and they would know instantly where they were, just from the thick, yeasty scent in the air. The locals say it's not as pungent as it was before one or another distillery was closed down, but it still smells strong to me. I'd read every Ian Rankin novel, every Christopher Brookmyre book, just to try and keep part of myself in Edinburgh while the rest of me studied for A-levels in Surrey.

Even in 2011, when I was no longer a student but a proper resident of the city, and therefore morally obliged to hate the Fringe, I didn't. I was glad it was coming, glad that Edinburgh would make its annual transformation from sensible Jekyll into rampaging Hyde. Even though I had spent so much time with Luke in Edinburgh – this is where we met, after all, in a bar which had thankfully changed names and décor at least twice since then – I knew that when it put on its August costume, the city belonged to me alone. Luke never stayed here for the Fringe: his landlady would hire their flat out for three times its usual monthly rent, and he would head south, to do an internship in London, or to catch up with schoolfriends and family.

The invasion was the same this year as every year: students in white-face make-up, discs of pink painted on their cheeks, promising a radical new reading of Racine or Kafka, alongside improvisational comedians handing out blank pieces of paper instead of flyers. The baked potato shop on Cockburn Street sprouted queues backing all the way up to the Mile every lunchtime, and around the corner, the Scotsman Steps had reopened as an artwork: every one was a different colour of Italian marble. It felt decadent to walk on something so expensive. There was one step, eight down from the top, that was identical to Robert's steely grey kitchen worktops – except that the steps smelled faintly of urine, because not everyone appreciates public artworks in the same way, I suppose. But the steps were beautiful even when they were pungent: a kaleidoscope of pinks and greens and oranges that didn't fit their surroundings at all, like a peacock who'd wandered away from his formal garden and into the woods by mistake.

The annual craft fair appeared at St John's church, filled with intricate silver earrings, carved wooden bowls and bright felted birds. As I walked round it one drizzly Saturday morning, I saw a tiny wooden spaniel on one stall, which looked exactly like my mother's dog. It was carved from a dark red wood, its polished grain glistening like Pickle's fur. I bought it for her, and walked down Lothian Road to buy a padded envelope from the card shop. Then I thought of the phone call I'd get when she received it – the pleasure in her voice mingled with the sadness that I hadn't seen her all year – and I decided to wait, and take it down for her birthday next month.

DD,

 This has honestly been the worst fucking summer ever. Worse than even I imagined it would be. Here's what I didn't want to do this summer: sit at home every day on my own, not see any of my friends for weeks on end, not know what's going on with Alex. And how many of those things happened? All of them.

 I know. I have a bus pass, I have legs. I could just have gone out whenever I liked. Except I couldn't, because I spent most of the summer with an ear infection. And given that I can't hear, that is about as unfair as things get.

 God, it hurt. It really, really fucking hurt. I don't know where I caught it: my mum is convinced that it was from swimming at Warrender pool. She gets these ideas stuck in her head sometimes, and you can't reason with her.

 The doctor said it was a virus, anyway, which turned into a bacterial infection. He was going to send me to hospital at one point, but I persuaded him to let me stay at home: my mum promised she'd look after me when she wasn't at work, and our flat is warm and dry, which is all they could really offer me in hospital.

 I had to take antibiotics for weeks, which just make me really sleepy, and I felt like crying from how badly it hurt. I would rather have anything than earache. I'd much rather break an arm or a *leg, because it can't hurt as much. The worst part is, it hurts when you swallow. Every single time. I read my Greek myths book a lot while I was lying on the sofa, hurting. And I worked out that this is my idea of Tartarus: the bit of hell where people are punished with the same thing every day. Tantalus is always hungry, trying to reach his grapes that keep slipping out of sight. Prometheus has his liver pecked out every day by a bird. Sisyphus has to push a rock up a hill and every time he gets to the top, it rolls back down, and he has to start all over again.*

And for me, hell would be a middle-ear infection. Every time I eat, or drink, or swallow, it's like someone slicing a razor through my eardrums. I couldn't keep my aids in for more than a few minutes at a time, because the noise was too much. I watched the TV with subtitles on, but after a while, you think if you're going to do that much reading, you might as well just pick up a book.

I stopped eating and drinking during the day, even though I was supposed to drink lots of water. Easy for the fucking doctor to say: I had to press my fists into my ears every time I swallowed anything, even just saliva, to try and dull the pain in the middle of my head, burning through my ears from the inside. If every time you had to swallow, it felt like someone was pressing a lit cigarette into your ear, you wouldn't drink anything either. I said I felt like crying, but of course I couldn't cry. Crying means swallowing, too.

I couldn't go away with my dad to Greece, which is what he suddenly decided we should do. I couldn't go with my mum to see my grandparents. I couldn't even go to see Carly, because I had to stay indoors in case of a secondary infection. The doctor was really stressed about it. He kept making eye contact with me for too long, and saying that if I wasn't very lucky with the antibiotics, I could sustain further irreparable hearing loss. What I wanted to say, but couldn't because my mum was sitting right there, was that I would have willingly swapped my remaining hearing if it would just make the pain stop. It would have been a fucking bargain.

So, my hearing is worse than it was, but it will improve, he thinks. It might never get back to where it was last term, though. The scarring is pretty heavy at the moment, so it depends how that heals up. It was just about the worst possible combination of things: I was in Edinburgh, about two fucking miles away from Alex, and I have no idea what's happening in her life. I haven't seen her since June. Since June, for God's sake, and now it's August. After everything she's been through, she's probably spent the whole time on her own, which is the last thing she should be doing.

I did try. When I was starting to get better, I walked up to where she lives. It was a warm day, so I thought I'd be OK. She stays somewhere off Blackfriars Street – I know that, because I asked her. She would have given me the address before the holidays, for sure, but Jono made some crack about stalking her, and she went all vague. But I already knew it must be around there, because she comes up either Nicolson Street or St Leonard's to get to Rankeillor, so it must be somewhere between the two, mustn't it? I've watched her coming and going from the Unit, she always goes that way. And she's definitely near Waverley, because she walks that way out of the station when she comes back from London, and heads up Cockburn Street. But I still haven't seen her all summer. I waited around for ages in a café on Blackfriars that one day, but nothing. I wandered round St Mary's Street and near there for a bit. I couldn't see her.

I hardly even heard from Carly either. I couldn't use the phone for weeks, and she prefers talking to typing. Plus, she's always busy these days. She said she was helping her mum at work a lot, and then they were all going away to Spain for two weeks. Her mum loves Spain. She takes evening classes, that's how much she likes it. But even when she was here, she wasn't around. I don't know if she's dropped me, kind of, or if I've dropped her. Does that make sense? I mean, we're still friends and everything, but not in the same way. The old Carly would never have been too busy to come and see me if I was ill. The old me would have called her even if I couldn't hear what she was saying. I don't know what happened exactly. I wonder if she could tell she'd annoyed me that day she wigged out at Alex last term. We still look like friends to anyone else, but it's definitely not the same as it was.

And the Fringe is in town now, so everywhere must be fucking rammed. I thought Carly might want to go and see something, but she didn't seem bothered when I asked. And going on my own would be lame. Besides, the tickets aren't cheap, so you have to pick something that isn't going to be shit. But if we'd gone to see some shows, we might have bumped into Alex, and it would all have been worthwhile.

Term starts again next week, though, which is a massive relief. I never thought I'd say that. But I'm so sick of being stuck with no-one to talk to. I've been so bored, I just want to see everyone again. My mum keeps asking about which college I want to go to next year. I keep telling her I'm thinking about it, which I'm not, but now she's started asking about open days and all that shite. Ordering prospectuses. I have no idea where she gets these ideas, but once she's got them in her mind, you can't shake them.

What she doesn't understand, because she doesn't ask, is that I don't want to be anywhere except at Rankeillor. I don't want to have to go somewhere new, I don't want to meet new people and make new friends, which is what college will be like if you ask my mum. She says it will be a chance for me to make a fresh start. But I don't want a fresh start. I just want this one to be better.

The beginning of term in Edinburgh came early. School holidays in Scotland mystified me: why did they finish so early in the summer, and then drag the kids back to school in the middle of August, when the festivals were all in full swing, and the city was full of stuff for them to do?

'It's because it usually rains less in July,' said Jono, when I asked them on the first day back.

'Did you go to see your shows, Alex?' Carly was sitting very close to Jono. I guessed their summer holidays had largely been spent together.

'I saw a few, yes. There are some very good plays at the Traverse, if you can persuade your parents to let you go.'

'You could take us,' said Mel.

'Please,' said Jono. 'We're a bit past school trips, aren't we?'

'Besides, Alex already saw the shows, didn't she?' Carly was quick to slap her down, I thought.

And Mel agreed, I guessed, as she reddened slightly. She looked tired, I thought. And she'd lost weight over the summer too: she was always slim but now she was gaunt. There were dark creases beneath her eyes that I hadn't seen before.

'We could go and see a play,' I said, trying to cheer her up. 'If the four of you would like to, I mean. There's still two more weeks of the Fringe: I'll look into what we could see when.'

'Thank you, Alex.'

As I looked around the classroom, it wasn't just Mel who'd changed over the summer. Jono seemed to be inches taller: for the first time I thought if I walked past him on the street, I wouldn't have guessed he was still at school. Carly had either dyed her hair or covered it with a jet-black wig. She was wearing a pale-blue vintage dress covered in dove-grey beads. If anyone needed a 1920s flapper-girl, she was ready for their call. Even Annika, eyeing Carly's new look with astonishment, had exchanged her glasses for contact lenses. At least I hoped that was plastic, glinting in her eyes.

When Robert had questioned her about the thefts at the end of the summer term, she hadn't even pretended she wasn't guilty. She'd shrugged her slender shoulders and said that if he would just throw her out, her mother would give in and take her away from Edinburgh for good. She would do anything to make that happen: and he could let her go now, or she would continue doing whatever it took to force his hand. She wouldn't be participating in classes till he gave in and promised to let her leave. He'd explained to her that while he was happy to meet with her mother and discuss her concerns, he wouldn't be blackmailed.

All of the stolen objects – the hoody, the purse, my bag, and whatever else she'd lifted from other staff – had found their way to the first bin she passed on Clerk Street as she went home each day. She didn't want any of the things she took. She just wanted to take them away. Robert asked her to apologise to me, in writing, on the first day of the new term. When I checked my pigeonhole before I went down to teach their first class, I found a torn page on which she had written: 'Dear Alex, Sorry about your bag. I hope you've bought a better one now. Annika'. In reciprocation, I scrunched it up as I walked down the stairs, and when I finally reached the basement, I threw it straight into the bin.

'Did you all have good holidays?' I asked.

'Yeah, I s'pose,' Jono said, yawning as though he was still working his way through jetlag. 'I went away to stay at my grandparents' for a bit, in Inverness. It was OK.'

'And Carly?'

'I went to Spain,' she said, happily, shrugging her shoulders and shaking back her newly black hair so I could admire what I pre-sumed were her holiday earrings, in the shape of tiny martini glasses, bubblegum-pink plastic representing their contents. 'You can see what's left of my tan, can't you?' She had indeed turned a pale gold colour, which was nonetheless peeling.

'Did you burn?' I asked her.

She nodded. 'I always do. A Scottish suntan is bright red, Alex, you must know that.'

'Annika?' I didn't really care what she'd done with her summer, but I didn't want the rest of the class to know that.

'Stockholm,' she said. I saw Mel look across, waiting for her to say more, but one word was all we were getting.

'And what about you?' I asked Mel. She curled her lip into an elegant snarl.

'I stayed here,' she said, flatly. 'It was fine. I wanted to go away, but it didn't work out.'

'I'm sorry. Where would you like to have gone?'

She tilted her head to consider it. It looked like she was trying to get water out of her ears. 'A Greek island, or something.'

'Lesbos?' Jono suggested, his face dangerously straight.

'Fuck you,' she replied. 'Sorry, Alex.'

'Let's try and keep things civil, shall we? I haven't seen you all summer. It'd be a shame if we spent today arguing.' I looked over at Jono. I could already see that a relationship between him and Carly was going to make things more difficult than they had been.

'Sorry,' he muttered.

'That's OK. So, are we going to carry on where we left off?' I asked them. 'We finished *Agamemnon* last term, so shall we move on to *The Choephori*?'

'The what?' asked Jono.

'The second play in the trilogy,' I explained. 'Choephori are libation-bearers.'

'Right,' he said. 'Bearers are people who bear things. So that clears things up perfectly. Or at least, it would, if you mentioned what a libation is?'

'An offering,' Mel said. 'A religious offering.'

'Very good.' I smiled at her. I knew it was wrong to have favourites, but she tried so much harder than the others. It was impossible not to feel grateful for her enthusiasm, especially with Annika glowering two seats away from her. 'You're absolutely right. It's a ritual offering of a drink to the gods.'

She grinned smugly at the others. Perhaps the truce was more of a détente.

'Oh right,' said Jono. 'This doesn't sound like one of your more exciting plays, Alex.'

'Well, it's about what happens after Clytemnestra kills Agamemnon. It gets pretty exciting. The libation-bearers are just the chorus: a bunch of old women who go with Electra to pour a libation on her father's tomb. Remember Electra? We talked about her before: she's the second daughter of Clytemnestra and Agamemnon. Sister to Iphigenia.'

'Iphigenia is the one Agamemnon murdered?' said Carly.

'That's her. Electra is the remaining daughter. She's been living with her mother, Clytemnestra, and her mother's boyfriend, Aegisthus.'

'And those are the ones who killed her dad in the last play?' Jono asked, squinting as though he were trying to identify a distant face. 'Don't roll your eyes, Alex, I've had a busy summer.'

'You've still remembered it perfectly. So Electra hates living with her mum because she misses her dad, and she blames her mother for that. And she goes to lay an offering at her father's tomb. And when Electra gets to the tomb, she finds someone else has already left offerings there. And that person turns out to be her brother Orestes. He's been in exile since Agamemnon's murder. But now he's returned to avenge the death of his father.'

'How's he going to do that?' asked Annika, her interest finally roused by the prospect of revenge against a parent.

'Good question. Orestes has an impossible decision to make, which we know often happens to characters in Greek tragedy, right? He is honour-bound to kill the person who killed his father – an eye for an eye, and all that. But he's also honour-bound not to harm his parents, like any good son. You remember last year, when we did *Oedipus*, how important it is that he's killed his father, even by accident?'

'Yes,' said Mel.

Carly and Jono exchanged another glance. It took me a moment to identify the expression on Carly's face, because I'd never seen contempt there before. I needed to add some more students to this class, and I needed to do it before the first new arrivals blew into the Unit over the next few weeks. Would it be possible to merge this class with the year below, or would Robert's timetable implode under the pressure? I carried on, hoping that if I kept talking, the atmosphere wouldn't deteriorate further.

'Orestes is in a bind. His mother is his father's killer. So what does he do? Does he do his duty to his father's honour, and kill his mother, or does he decide he'd rather be a good son to his mother, and leave her alone? What do you think, Jono?'

'He probably kills her, to be honest with you, Alex. Unless this play is a lot shorter than the others.'

'He decides to kill someone else first.'

'Aegisthus,' said Mel. 'Her boyfriend.'

'Quite right, Mel. You must have been reading ahead over the holidays.' She smiled and nodded. I wanted to reward her, but I kept my eyes on Jono instead.

'So Orestes kills Aegisthus, because he has no qualms about doing that. This man helped to kill his father, after all.'

'And he's doing his mum,' Jono added.

'Well, yes. That adds an extra resonance, for sure. But then Orestes and Electra want to kill Clytemnestra, too, which is more problematic.'

The bell rang, and they picked up their bags with the weariness I'd grown used to over the past two terms. Even when they were bored, they considered the actual process of moving to a different classroom to be an exhaustion too far.

'OK, for next time, you could read the play through for me. Those of you who haven't already done so. And maybe you could each write me a side of A4 about Orestes' decision. What should a character do when faced with two irreconcilable evils?'

'Seriously, Alex? It's the first day back.' Jono believed the very idea of homework to be an infringement of the Geneva Convention.

'You can refer to any video game you like in your essay. Tell me what your character chooses to do when there are only bad options available.'

3

DD,

My gran always says you should be careful what you wish for, which is just about the most depressing sentence anyone's ever said. Shouldn't wishes be one of the things you don't worry about? Wishing isn't like crossing the road, you don't need to look both ways before you do it. But I spent the whole summer wishing I was back at Rankeillor, because not being there was so horrible. And now I'm back, it's horrible there too.

For a start, we had a lecture from Robert on the first morning back, about new students arriving during the term. Only about half of us start the school year at Rankeillor. The rest get sent here once they've fucked up their chances everywhere else, so it'll be a week at least before the first ones arrive, and then they'll drip through all term. He gave us the whole you-were-new-here-once talk, about making new arrivals feel welcome and keeping an eye on them and all that bollocks. I could see Jono calculating how many phones he'd be able to swipe from the newbies when they turn up. He's so predictable.

And Carly is still being weird. She's going out with Jono now, apparently, even though she always said she thought he was an idiot. I don't want to talk about it, though. I mean, who wants to know about kissing Jono?

And then there's Annika. Something's going on with her. She was caught stealing last term, you know. Carly told me. But that doesn't explain why she's barely speaking to any of us. And there's more: I think she must have stolen Alex's bag. I saw that Alex had a new one, and I was going to tell her I liked it, but as soon as she walked in to the classroom, she put it in her desk drawer. She didn't say anything about it. But she looked straight at Annika as she shut the drawer and then she threw something in the bin. Annika didn't notice any of this, because she was playing with her phone. But I saw it.

I waited for everyone to leave the classroom before me, and I swiped the paper out of the bin. It's basically the least sincere apology anyone's ever written. Typical Annika. I'm going to try and think of some way to get back at her.

On top of everything else this past week, my mum has gone absolutely bug-fucking mental. Seriously, there are people in asylums who are less demented than her. She spent the whole summer being all saintly because I was ill, and now the lunacy has arrived, right on cue. And it's all down to my dad, who, it turns out, wanted to take me to Greece so that we could 'have a serious talk'. Only we didn't, because I was ill. So he decided to mail instead, because it's just that bit less trouble than coming to see me to tell me that he's getting married again. To someone I've never met, obviously. Which he's sort of managed to make sound like it's my fault: like if I hadn't been ill, he could have introduced me to Lucy. Lucy is twenty-three. She's seven years older than me. It's beyond gross.

At least I don't have to go to the wedding, because they're getting married at Christmas in Bali. Where the fuck? And since when did my dad turn into the kind of person who does things like this?

So I told my mum, even though I knew what she'd do, which is to make it all about her, when it has nothing to do with her at all. She hardly even talks to him now. She hasn't even seen him for two years, when she drove me down to stay with him when she was on her way to a conference somewhere and I wasn't old enough to get the train yet – in her view, anyway. So, basically, she used to know my dad, but doesn't now. Whereas he's still my dad, so even though I don't see him all that often, he's my dad. So when he decides to just marry someone I've never even met, it's a big deal to me.

But obviously it can't be as big a deal as it is to my mum, who went completely fucking ballistic when I told her. How dare he, he's so selfish, cradle-snatching dickhead, etc. Then she moved on to what does it say about her that she was ever involved with him, how is it possible he didn't even mention this girl to me before, and so on. When she gets to the last bit, she gives me a filthy look, like I knew all along and just kept it from her out of spite. Like I've just made up this email for some mindfuck purpose of my own. And that's when I lose it and tell her to go fuck herself, because really, she fucking can. I've had it up to here. It's like dealing with a child.

It's not like she hasn't been seeing someone herself, either, because she's been seeing that freak from her work for months now. Even though he's a cunt who hates me because he blames me for being ill over the summer and keeping her away from him. Like I caught a major ear infection on purpose. I hate him. But it's fine for her to have a thing with him, it's just not fine for my dad to do the same, right? Talk about being a total hypocrite.

She's so busy making it all about her that she doesn't even think to ask how I feel about my dad getting married – and to someone who's only a bit older than me, which is creepy as fuck. She doesn't even ask. Anything he does has to be about her, because she can't

imagine that he might not think about her from one month to the
next. Why would he? If he gave a shit about her, they wouldn't be
divorced, would they? She is completely fucking pathetic. Actually,
they both are.

About two weeks after term began, once the Festival circus had left town
and taken all the clowns, mimes, actors and jugglers with it, Robert
took me out for dinner. The waiter at Ciao Roma looked pathetically
grateful to see customers, now all the tourists had disappeared. I was
still taking off my jacket when the bread appeared. Robert explained
that we would need a few minutes before we'd be ready to order. But
to keep the bored staff busy, he considered a Chianti, then settled on a
Valpolicella, demanding black olives to accompany it.

'Now, Alex,' he said, after he'd tasted the first sip of the screw-top
wine with an expression that suggested he was considering sending
it back as corked. 'Now, Alex.' The cue was unmistakeable. I leaned in.

'Did you have a good summer?' he asked. 'It was quite a strong
year for the Festival, was it not?'

'It was. Yes. I saw some good plays. Nothing earth-shattering, but
plenty of good stuff.'

'Were any of your acting chums in town?'

I hadn't answered their texts, hadn't gone to their shows. I'd avoided
Bristo Square to avoid bumping into them. I had hidden from my
old life, sticking with shows that had originated in other parts of the
country, scurrying in at the last minute before the lights went down,
and rushing out as soon as the cast had finished bowing. If I ever
wanted to be a theatre critic, I'd polished all the necessary skills.

'Yes, a few,' I said. 'Though we didn't really manage to catch up.'
To my surprise, he didn't start in with a lecture about keeping in
touch with my friends and my former profession. If anything, he
looked relieved.

'Is it possible, Alex, that you are happier here, in Edinburgh, than you would be in London, where all your friends are?'

'It's more than possible. It's true. I left London because I couldn't face being there. But now, I don't want to go back. It's not that I can't face it. I just don't want to. I prefer being here.'

'So you would consider a proposal that involved you staying here?'

'What kind of proposal? Are you about to get down on one knee?'

'Too late. I already have,' he admitted, and smiled.

'You and Jeff are getting married?'

He nodded, suddenly shy.

'Congratulations.' I reached over and squeezed his hand. 'We should have ordered champagne.'

'We still can.' He summoned a waiter and asked for two glasses of Prosecco. 'Near enough,' he said. 'It's not like we'll be doing a whole white-dress thing.'

'When did this happen? I'm so pleased for you both.'

'About a month ago.'

'Why didn't you...' I tailed off. I knew exactly why he hadn't mentioned it. I shook my head, and raised the glass which the waiter had just brought over. 'To you and Jeff.'

'To me and Jeff,' he agreed, and our glasses clinked together.

'Speaking of which, where is Jeff?'

'He's giving us space,' Robert explained. 'So I could talk to you.'

'Oh, OK. Wait. What about?' Jeff surely couldn't think I wouldn't be happy for him.

'My retirement,' he said, frowning.

'Really?'

'He won't stop going on about it.'

'So, you're definitely going to leave?'

'At the end of this academic year. I'll leave next June.'

The room tilted slightly to one side. If Robert left, how could I carry on at Rankeillor? I was more than halfway through a one-year contract now, and his successor would want to bring in new people. Then what would I do? Could I get another job up here? I supposed Robert would write me a reference for something. Perhaps I could get a front-of-house job at the Traverse.

'Alex?' Robert was waiting for me to say something.

I started gabbling. 'That's great. It's what Jeff wants, isn't it? Will you travel?'

'So I'll need to find someone to take over from me at the Unit,' he continued, as if I hadn't spoken. I couldn't blame him.

'OK.' Perhaps he was going to ask me who I'd recommend. But I didn't know anyone who would apply.

'And I was wondering if that person might be you, Alex.'

'Oh.' Had I always been this bad at interpreting subtext? 'But I'm not qualified.'

'Nonetheless, I think you'd be the perfect candidate. And I think the governors might see things the same way. You have experience of working at our unit. You know the staff and the students. And unlike some, you don't hold rancorous grudges against other colleagues.'

'But I have no experience of running anything bigger than a cast of eight.'

'But that's not because you can't, it's because you haven't. You'd be terrific, Alex. You like the kids we have at Rankeillor. And that's the secret truth about education. Academics and think-tanks and God knows who else spend years of time and millions of pounds trying to work out how to keep children in schools, how to improve test scores. And the one thing they never stop to consider is: do the teachers like the kids? Do the kids trust the support staff? Does the head like his colleagues? You can announce as many directives as you wish, but in the end, it all comes down to this. I honestly believe it does. It's as true at Rankeillor as it was at the University. It's all about wanting people to succeed.'

I nodded, sipping the Prosecco, trying not to feel hopeful when there were so many obstacles in the path of Robert's plan. 'But the governors will want someone experienced, surely.'

'They'll want someone who wants the job. Rankeillor is not exactly Fettes, is it? They don't have people hammering at the door to be allowed a chance to work with children who are often difficult and sometimes violent. They'll want someone who knows the work of the Unit already, and they'll want someone younger than I was, when I took over, so they don't have to worry about anyone else retiring. They're not going to want someone in their fifties again, are they?'

'I don't know. They might.'

'Yes, they might. But I'm sure I can prevail upon them to see reason. It's the perfect fit, Alex. I'm sure I can get them to agree. But I won't try if I can't get you to agree first. I don't want you to answer now. I don't even want you to think about it now. I want you to put it from your mind, look at your menu and order your dinner. We'll discuss it again in a week or so, when you've had time to think it over properly. And you can't do that on an empty stomach. So…' He reached over and jiggled the menu I was holding, forcing me to look down at it. Robert never lost anyone's attention for long.

Now I'm writing this down for Lisa Meyer, I realise I don't know when the kids found out I was considering a permanent job at Rankeillor. They knew that their original art therapist, Miss Allen, had gone on maternity leave, and that she had been gone, by now, for almost nine months. I don't know if they knew that her child had been born with a minor heart defect which caused her to reconsider her planned return to work and become a full-time mother.

When I first came to Scotland, at the start of the year, I thought that Rankeillor was a temporary measure. And then when Robert asked me to consider something permanent, I didn't know what to make of it. I was afraid of making a decision. If I took him up on the offer, I could stay in Edinburgh. But I would also be giving up on directing, the only thing I had ever really wanted to do. And I didn't want to become one of those people who haunts amateur dramatic societies, muttering about how I could have gone professional if only my life had taken a different path, in between storming out of rehearsals of *Hedda Gabler* because no-one knows their lines.

Was it possible to make a choice which didn't cut off the other option entirely? Could I stay at Rankeillor in the short-term, and then go back to directing in a couple of years? I thought about it for a day or two before acknowledging that I could not. I couldn't treat these kids as a fill-in, biding my time till what I really wanted came along. Even as I thought this, guilt prickled across my scalp. I had already seen them as exactly that. I had gone into their unit because I needed an escape and even now, nine months later, I was still thinking about what I wanted instead of what the children needed.

So I can tell Lisa Meyer one thing I remember: that night in September was the first time in over a year that I really thought about the future, mine or anyone else's. It was also the first time I thought about the kids and what they might want. Not just Jono and Mel, Annika and Carly, but all the children I taught. It was the first time I really, properly thought about someone who wasn't me, or Luke, since he died.

4

The 14th of October was the first time I'd travelled down to London since before the summer holiday. It was my mother's birthday. I took the same train I used to get to King's Cross, then the Underground to Waterloo, which was so crowded it made me gasp for air, then another train to Walton-on-Thames, to my mother's parish. Luke used to tease her about the number of poor and needy people she could find in Walton-on-Thames, which she cheerily admitted was one of the wealthiest parishes in the country. Being my mother, of course, she saw a bright side to this. Certainly the designer clothes and bags which appeared at her bring-and-buy sales were enough to sustain her soup kitchen, her Sunday school refreshments, and plenty more besides. She maintained that fashionistas would trek down from the capital just to trawl through her stash of high-end frocks, all of which she priced up in the belief that charity began at the church hall, right next to the tombola.

When I arrived at the station, she was waiting for me, dog-collar on, dog-lead in hand. Pickle went crazy: I have never been greeted by anybody with even half the enthusiasm Pickle could generate for the postman, let alone a long-lost friend. I tried to hug my mother before dog saliva made the whole process gummily untenable.

'Here you are, darling,' said my mother. 'At last.'

'Happy birthday,' I said, trying not to stiffen at the implicit criticism. We walked down a leafy side-road and past the church to reach her red-brick house, smaller and squatter than the old vicarage, which had been sold to a banker of vast fortune and indeterminate moral fibre some years before.

Her house smelled exactly the same as it had a year ago. Potpourri, dog hair and flowers battled for supremacy. I dropped my bag at the bottom of the stairs, noticed Pickle eyeing its rope handles, and picked it up again. I put it on a chair instead, and dug out the card and the wooden dog, the latter now wrapped in bright turquoise tissue paper, with a navy raffia bow adding a celebratory touch. I kicked off my boots, which were far too hot now I wasn't in Edinburgh, and padded through to the kitchen.

'Happy birthday,' I said again, giving her the card and the present. I'd forgotten how slowly she opened things, as if there was a prize for coming last. No wonder the dog was so excitable: she must have a seizure every time she watched my mother spend three minutes opening a can of dog food.

'Oh darling, it's lovely,' she said, tearing up a little as she finally burrowed her way through the tissue paper to the small wooden statue. 'Wherever did you find it? It looks just like her.'

'It's from the craft fair they hold in the churchyard at St John's,' I told her. 'Carved by a lady who lives up in the Highlands. She had birds and horses and things, but I thought you'd like the dog.'

'I do, very much,' she said, and gave me a hug.

We spent a while catching up, drinking coffee and eating cake. But there was too much space between us: I tried to explain my Edinburgh life to her, and I knew I was failing. I tried to follow the ins and outs of her assorted parish squabbles, but I couldn't keep up. We weren't just living at different ends of the country, we were living in parallel universes.

'You look tired,' she said, suddenly, and I knew she had noticed I wasn't really listening. 'I thought we'd go out for dinner,' she added. 'There's a new Italian around the corner: I've only been a couple of times, but it's very nice. Breadsticks, you know. Like the old days.'

'OK.'

'Why don't you have a lie-down?' she asked.

I went upstairs, not to sleep but just to rest from the effort of talking. My head was thrumming softly, and I lay down on a bed that wasn't mine. My childhood home was long gone, my flat with Luke must have new tenants, my place in Edinburgh was on loan from a man who was avoiding Scotland as if he were a wanted criminal. But it certainly wasn't mine, and he might come back and reclaim it any time, I supposed. I wondered if I should be worried about this, but all I found was a sense of relief that I didn't have to be anywhere I didn't want to be, at least not for long.

Pickle was never one to miss out on a prone body: it almost always meant she would be petted by someone who couldn't be bothered to get up. She nosed her way round the bedroom door, then hopped up onto the bed. I scritched her between the ears, until she reached that Zen state that only dogs and Buddhists can achieve.

Even Pickle would know where home was, if she raced away from my mother in the park. And if a spaniel could acquire a sense of permanence, it shouldn't be beyond me. I thought again about Robert's offer, before dozing off.

Dinner with my mother started badly and grew worse. Her opening gambit was to ask when I was moving back to 'the real world'. As patiently as I could, I explained that Edinburgh was as real as any-where else. But that wasn't what she wanted to hear. She wanted to know when I would move back to London to reconnect with my old friends, and with Luke's, to go back to working in the theatre, to give up on 'children other people are better qualified to work with anyway'. Obviously, she was right about this, but it didn't make it any less crass to say it.

Then we progressed to the 'time-to-move-on' conversation, which my mother felt compelled to have, now it was over a year since Luke died. Even more so, since she had started seeing someone over the past few months, who I would meet tomorrow, and who she was certain I would really like. Again, I tried to explain that while she was ready to move on from my father's death several years earlier, I was not yet ready to consider doing the same thing myself.

The trouble with grief is that once people have survived it, they can develop a hardness, like rough skin: they made it through, so why can't you? And the only honest answer is that you don't know why, or even if you can't move on. You just know you haven't. The nadir came when she reminded me that what doesn't kill you makes you stronger, and I replied that this was not a very Christian idea. Arthritis won't kill you, it only makes you weaker. What if grief works the same way?

By the time we got home, we were barely speaking, and we both went straight to bed. Even the dog ignored me. I got up on Saturday morning and told her I would be leaving a day early, because I knew that things couldn't improve if I stayed. She started to cry, because I wouldn't meet Andrew, and he was looking forward to meeting me. And I started to cry too, because I knew the visit had been a disaster, and that I wouldn't return any time soon.

We hugged as I left, but with resignation rather than warmth.

DD,

Alex hasn't been going to London this term. She's been at Rankeillor on Fridays, and when I asked her why she came in on Fridays now, she said she has a couple of classes in the morning. Like that was the only reason, the only thing that was different from before. I went to the station and checked to see if she was going on Saturday a couple of times, and then on Sundays. I had to keep telling my mum I was going to the shops, even though she knows I don't have much money. Lucky she's too self-absorbed to think about me for very long. Then I thought I'd check Friday again, the day we broke up for mid-term. Just in case. And there she was, just like before.

So I followed her. Fare-dodging was easy. I recognised the guard at Waverley, and I know how he works: he starts at the back of the train and moves forwards. He likes to treat himself to First Class at the end. And he never starts till after Berwick, because otherwise he has to check everyone again after Newcastle, and he can't be bothered. I just hid in the toilet when he did my carriage, and he never came back through again. Like I said, easy.

But nothing else was easy. It was fucking peculiar. Alex didn't go the way she always goes when she gets off the train. And she had a bag with her, which she doesn't normally have. A bigger one, I mean, a tote. She went to the Underground station. I tried to follow her, but she has one of those blue card things, and I didn't have one, and the queue to buy a ticket was about a thousand people long.

I didn't know what to do. So I decided the best thing would be to walk to the park the way she usually goes, and maybe she'd turn up there in a bit. The Underground must go there, right? So I walked the same old walk past the Harry Potter station and the library and everything, and I wondered if she'd maybe just got tired of going on foot. It isn't a nice walk, it's too noisy. The traffic, I mean. I took my aids out, like I always do when I'm walking down a big road, because otherwise they just rumble and rumble and it makes me feel a bit dizzy after a while, and sick.

So I reached the park, only then I realised that there isn't an Underground station in there. So she'd have to walk through the park the same way as usual, to get to the café. I walked past the zoo again – I saw one porcupine, two goats, a camel and three wallabies, which might be a record. It was really warm in London, much warmer than at home. And the park is pretty in October: the leaves are all bright red and orange, and even if it wasn't warm you'd feel warm. They're plastered all over the ground, like that decoupage thing Carly's mum does. It feels like walking on carpet, they're so thick.

I turned left at the top of the park. They have parrots and stuff in secret cages at the back of the zoo. They must be in quarantine or something. They go crazy watching the other birds flying around free in the park, flapping and squawking like mad. I turned my aids back on, actually, to see if I could hear them. There's one small green one like a broken piano: he belts out the same few notes all the time, starting high, dropping low. Shouty fucker, the other birds must hate him. I could hear him all the way to the café, and even while I stood by a tree on the far side, while I decided what to do. Go in, and risk Alex seeing me? Or stand outside all afternoon?

I pushed the door, and nothing happened. You'd think after all the times I've seen Alex go in, I'd know that the fucking thing pulls open. But there was no sign of her. I was kind of relieved, because I have no idea what I would have said if she'd been there. I could hardly have pretended to be just passing, could I? I would have to have explained, and it might have sounded odd. But she wasn't there, so it was all fine.

I sat at a table and ordered a Coke, which cost three fucking pounds, by the way, which is deranged. Three pounds for a can of juice. I drank it really slowly, partly to get my money's worth, and partly to see if Alex turned up later. Maybe the Underground is slower than walking. After half an hour, I stopped being relieved and I started to get worried. Where could she be? What if she'd got lost? Had she gone back to Richmond, where she used to live, or to see her mum, or something? I don't even know where that would be. You get used to a person doing the same thing all the time, you know. And then they do something weird. I couldn't think what to do except to go back to King's Cross and get the five-thirty train she always gets and hope she's on it.

I was just starting to get ready, and then I saw her. Not Alex, I mean. Katarina. She came out from behind the counter with a pot of tea and two cups and saucers for this old couple who were blethering on to each other about something. I couldn't hear what: they were too low-pitched and indistinct. She wasn't there before, when I ordered my Coke. She must have been on a break, because this was definitely Katarina. She looked really happy, grinning away at the old people like they were her long-lost parents or something. I bet Alex didn't grin like that even when she was happy. She's too vague. But Katarina was really definite, right there in the room with her bleached ends and dark roots and thick eyebrows and pale skin. She's tall, and she wears heels, even though her feet must ache after a day waiting tables. She has watery grey eyes, like dirty pools.

She walked back to the counter, with a sort of strut in her step, like she was really pleased with herself for taking tea to two pensioners so well. And then the other lady at the counter, with a headscarf on – the one called Noor – suddenly grabbed her left hand, and squealed. I thought maybe she'd seen a wasp or a bee or something. But then I saw her face and I realised it was a happy scream, not a frightened one. Katarina started laughing and tilting her hand at a funny angle to catch the light, and I realised what she was so fucking pleased about.

Thank God Alex wasn't there.

5

The four of them had been scratchy all term, getting on each other's nerves. Ricky never did return to the Unit, and despite Robert's predictions, no new top-year kids had arrived yet. It was clear that the group no longer functioned. Annika used to be a lightning rod for any room she was in, the quickest route for tension to escape. But now she was refusing to take part in any discussions or hand in any work, she made the atmosphere increasingly uncomfortable. I tried to win her over – though I didn't especially want to – but she was obdurate. And I had hoped that Jono's relationship with Carly might blunt his sharp tongue, but the reverse was true: he would take any opportunity to reinforce their status as a couple. The newly minted tension it had created between her and Mel didn't help either. Robert was sure there would be new arrivals soon and they couldn't come soon enough. The class needed new blood.

We'd spent a couple more lessons talking and writing about *The Choephori*. Jono had produced a smart, funny flowchart of options available to the members of the House of Atreus, revelling in the impossibility of doing the right thing. I asked him if I could photocopy it and put it on the wall, and he hunched in embarrassment and agreed, if I insisted. I did insist. It was about time I started to make the room my own. I'd been here for almost a year. Carly was still a bit out of her depth, I felt, and her writing showed that. But Mel handed in a beautiful story, from the perspective of Electra. It was, I wrote at the bottom, the most moving thing I'd read in months. She had captured the wretchedness of passivity and the tragedy of action. She could have written it about Hamlet. I asked her to wait behind after the session.

'That's a wonderful piece of work, Mel.'

She frowned as I spoke, her eyes on my mouth. Then she smiled and nodded. 'I spent ages on it,' she said. She seemed to need to concentrate much harder to hear me this term. I wondered if she had spoken to her doctor about it.

'I can tell. It's your best writing, really it is. I think you should submit it to a short-story competition. I'll look into it, if that's OK.'

'Yes, it is. Thank you.' Her smile faded a little too fast.

'Are you sure? You seem uneasy.'

'No, I'd like it. I really would.' The words almost fell on top of each other as she gabbled. Usually, she was such a precise talker, every syllable carefully rendered.

'OK, well, if you're sure,' I said. She nodded again, and almost ran out of the basement.

I'd like to say that I realised then that there was something she was trying to tell me. But I didn't, of course. I thought she was late for something, or desperate for a fag, or wanting to catch up with her friends before they left for lunch without her. I read her essays and watched her talking to her classmates, and I thought I knew how her mind was working. In fact, she was just as opaque to me as Annika was. I had no idea that she'd found out so much about me and Luke and everything that had happened. And I had no idea what she would do with that information.

As she left, I realised I'd come to a decision about Robert's suggestion. I had been with these kids for less than a year, and I was making a positive difference to their lives. They were more articulate and more thoughtful this term. They were more capable of putting their hands up in a room of bright students, knowing they were equal to them. They were better prepared for the future and that was, in part, because of me.

So I was going to apply for the job, and do my best to persuade the governors to have me. I was going to help more children realise their potential, and I wasn't going to think about London and my former life again. My mother would come to terms with it, and if she didn't, she would forgive me, because that was in her job description. I walked up to Robert's office and told him, before I left that afternoon, that I would apply in writing as soon as he announced the job was vacant. He beamed at me. Everything was falling into place.

DD,

Which is better: knowing or not knowing something you don't want to know? It looks simple, right? Not knowing must be better.

But it isn't simple at all. You might not want to know if you were dying, but it would be better to know, wouldn't it? So you could say goodbye to people, and make a will, and finish things off properly. Not knowing would be worse. Definitely.

At least, I think it would. But then, take my mum. She didn't want to know that my dad was getting married. She didn't need to know, and once she found out, she went mad. She's been in a foul mood ever since. She's argued with her boyfriend about a million times, and she's been furious with me about everything.

When she gets like this, I just take my aids out and close my eyes. This is what it must be like to be an astronaut walking on the far side of the moon, or in a submarine at the bottom of the North Sea. Totally dark, totally quiet. My mum hates it when I do this: she says it makes her feel like she's seeing me buried alive. She grabs my arm and shakes it till I open my eyes. And then she apologises and starts crying and says she's sorry and it's not about me. It's not about her, either.

So would it be better if she hadn't found out about my dad? It depends. She would have found out eventually, like Oedipus does. And then, wouldn't it have been terrible to find out that it had happened ages ago, and you were the only one who didn't know? Being the last person to know something is embarrassing. That's what Carly doesn't seem to understand about us: I'm not mad about her and Jono, I'm just upset that she didn't tell me until it had been going on for months. Like I didn't deserve to know. Like we weren't best friends. I mean, really, she can do what she likes with whoever she wants, that's fine. It was just horrible of her not to say anything. Not that she cares. And nor do I, if that's how she wants to be.

But maybe it's just me who'd rather know things. Is it? Is Alex better off not knowing about the engagement? How will she feel when she finds out? Won't it be worse the longer it takes? I thought it didn't matter because it's not like I could tell her. But then I realised I could tell her, and it wouldn't even be that difficult. I just need to make someone else break the news.

The following week was the last time I saw the four of them together at Rankeillor. It must have been October the 26th. It was a Wednesday, a week and a half after the disastrous trip to see my mother. That's not why I remember the date, obviously. I remember it because it was two days before.

I arrived at the Unit and hunted around in my bag for a key. Robert had decided that leaving the place open was no longer a viable option, ever since some twelve-year-olds had found an old man sitting in the ground-floor hallway drinking cider on a rainy day last month. Robert's main concern, he explained in a staffroom stage whisper, was that the man might not be able to fight off Donnie Brooks and his little henchmen a second time. Thank goodness his poor old jakey blood was fortified with the Buckfast, he added. A death on the premises doesn't look good.

As I drew out my key, my phone screen lit up. A text from Robert: 'ALEX, see me URGENT'. Things must be serious if he was employing caps lock. I checked my watch. At eight fifteen the kids weren't even there yet: how could there be trouble already? I walked straight upstairs, and knocked.

'Who is it?' he said, warily.

'It's Alex,' I replied, and turned the stained brass handle. 'Is everything OK?'

'Alex,' he sighed. 'Come and sit down.' He gestured vaguely in the direction of a chair. It was so unusual for him not to have total control over every muscle, right the way to his fingertips, I assumed something terrible must have happened. Had he met with the governing body and been told that they wouldn't accept his resignation? Or that they weren't happy at the prospect of me applying for his job? I didn't want him to feel like he needed to protect me from bad news.

'What is it?'

He looked up and met my eyes. He pushed a piece of paper towards me. It was a print-out of an article which had appeared in the *Daily Mail* the previous day. I hadn't seen it. The headline read: 'Lawyer's Killer Gets Engaged...' and then under it, in a smaller font: '... To The Woman He Was Beating Up When He Killed Our Hero Son'. The words began tangling together. I exhaled, realising I'd been holding my breath, growing dizzy. I tried to scan the prose as though I were about to summarise it for another, busier reader.

The journalist had received an anonymous tip-off about the engagement. He'd called Luke's parents for a quote and hit pay-dirt: they'd given him a full interview demanding that Luke's murderer be deported when he'd served his sentence, and that his fiancée be deported sooner, ideally now. There was a quote from a lawyer explaining why this wouldn't happen. Then a hand-wringing inset editorial about the perils of allowing people from violent, lawless territories to enter Britain without controls. And the final sentence that had punched me in the gut so often a year ago that I stopped reading papers altogether: 'Luke Jameson was survived by his fiancée, Alex Morris.'

'I'm sorry,' Robert said, very quietly. I nodded. I couldn't speak.

'Alex, there's something else.' Wasn't there always?

'This page was placed under my office door yesterday evening. I left early for a governors' meeting. Cynthia would have been here till five or so. But when I came in this morning, this had been slipped under the door. I'll speak to Cynthia when she gets in, and see if she can shed any light.'

I nodded again. It didn't seem remotely important to me where it had come from.

'Alex, I'll leave you alone for ten minutes. I'll unlock the place, and then we'll see if you're up to your timetable today. I'll understand if you need to go home. Equally, if you prefer company, we'll be very happy to have you here.'

I nodded again, and he left.

A few moments later, I heard hushed voices murmuring on the other side of the door. Cynthia had arrived, and Robert was quizzing her on the previous evening. He came back in and shut the door behind him.

'Cynthia was at her desk till five, Alex, but she did go up to the staffroom a couple of times. It must have been delivered then.'

'Yes, I suppose so.'

'But who would—' Seeing my face, he broke off. 'It doesn't matter now, though.'

'I'll go down to the basement.' As I stood up, the blood sank from my head, and I drove my nails into my palms.

'Are you absolutely sure, Alex?'

'Yes. Thank you.'

His arms were spread awkwardly wide, like an action figure missing its prop. But today, as so often, I knew that it would be kindness that floored me. The hugs would have to wait till it hurt. They couldn't help now. I patted his arm gently as I walked past, hoping he understood.

I walked down to the ground floor, then down again to my room. The stairs reeked of cleaning fluid, which meant that someone had either thrown up or bled on them yesterday after I'd left. Possibly both. The bulb had been replaced in the light-fitting at the bottom of the stairs: it must have been from a new supplier. The final flight of stairs was now brighter, but greyer than the rest, as if someone had carved out a window onto a vile winter's day.

I sat completely still at my desk, trying to breathe myself calm. In through the nose, out through the mouth, like all those warm-ups that actors do. I pressed my fingers against my thumbs in order – index, middle, ring, little – and then started again, trying to squeeze everything into the space between them, and then squeeze that into nothingness.

By the time the children arrived, I was calm enough. The rumour was racing around the school that I might be replacing Robert at the end of the school year. The smaller children were full of it, excited by the prospect of manageable change. The older ones didn't mention it at all. Stupidly, I thought they wouldn't be bothered, since they would have left by the time I took over anyway.

By lunchtime, I was beginning to share Robert's curiosity. Who wanted me to know about Dominic and Katarina? Why would any of these kids want to upset me?

I didn't come close to guessing the truth. I've never been stupider than I was that week.

I have never come close.

Lisa Meyer has had her hair cut into a blunt fringe. On another woman it might look coquettish. On Lisa Meyer, it looks as if she moonlights as an assassin.

I like your hair, I tell her, as I sit down in her gunmetal chair.

Thank you, she says, and she swooshes it, so I can see how shiny it is, reflective, almost metallic.

Have you made time to do some of your research? she asks. I like that Lisa Meyer doesn't even consider the notion that time might not do my bidding.

I've made notes on everything I remember. Well, everything that seems relevant.

I hand her a stack of notes, which I have made over the past week, typed because I want them to be as neat as all her other paperwork.

Good, she says. I'll go through it this afternoon and see what strategy we can develop.

I've always despised people who use words like 'strategy', but from Lisa Meyer it makes sense, because she views this, and every case, as though it were a war. She leafs through the pages, and stops on the final one. A small line appears across the bridge of her nose. She flips the page over, to check she hasn't missed anything on the back. The line becomes infinitesimally deeper.

Alex, this account finishes on October 26th. I need the last day, too. I need the 28th.

I know.

I realise it must be a struggle, she says, gazing at me. But it's very important.

I nod. She looks briefly at her watch.

Do you know what might be best, Alex? Why don't you tell me about it now? I'll record it, and Jonah can type it up for you later.

I have never known that this is her assistant's name. I nod again.

Lisa Meyer walks over to her desk. She opens a drawer, and pulls out a small microphone, which she plugs into her phone. She walks back, and unfolds a small plastic stand which she places on the table in front of me. She fits the microphone into the stand and taps the phone screen. It starts recording.

I can see the tiny beads of light register her voice, as she says, Whenever you're ready, Alex. There's water next to you – I look down and see this is true – and I just need you to tell me what happened on the Friday. I need to know what you saw and what you heard. Not what you thought or what you wished. What you witnessed. Do you understand?

Yes, I say. Even though I'm speaking quietly, the lights on the phone flicker up. It can hear me.

I'll be over here, she says, and takes a seat behind me. I hear a faint rustling sound and realise she has picked up a pad and a pen, so she can start making notes. I wonder if she's trying to replicate the role of therapist and client, or if she just knows most people find it easier to talk if they're not trying to read the face of their audience.

I take a sip of water. OK, I say. This is what I remember.

6

What I recall most clearly about that day was a bird. But I guess Lisa Meyer would prefer me to start at the beginning, not the end.

I had spent forty-eight hours, by that Friday morning, corroding with anger. How could Luke have been lost, while the people who took him continued to thrive? I wanted to open a window and scream the questions into the crisp night air. What is the point of punishing someone, of imprisoning them, when it takes away nothing but their liberty, briefly, and even that only in its most limited physical sense? Luke's killer had kept everything important: his happiness, his future, his hopes, his lover. He had retained everything Luke had lost. Everything I had lost. I was inchoate, and he was temporarily inconvenienced.

When I called in sick on the Thursday, Cynthia told me to take the rest of the week off. Robert would take my lessons, she said. Everything was fine. But nothing was fine. Yes, I knew; everyone said it, after all. Grieving was supposed to be hard. But this was way past hard. It was in a new category. I took tiny, faltering steps towards a new life, and every time I covered any distance, I got punched in the gut and fell right back to where I'd started. I didn't believe in God, so how was it possible I was living in purgatory?

I spent Thursday in my flat. I wasn't hungry, I didn't go out. I broke my own rule, googled Dominic Kovar, and read the news stories that had bubbled up during his trial and sentencing, the ones I'd worked hard to avoid. I read about his earlier convictions for assault, possession of a knife, grievous bodily harm. I felt my anger crystallise into a tiny solid shape in the centre of my chest. I hated him, right then, with a purity I have never otherwise felt, untainted by any other emotion, unsoftened by mitigation. I wanted justice: the real kind, not the legal kind. And I wanted it to hurt. I didn't want him to lose what Luke had lost. I wanted him to lose what I had lost. I wanted him to know he would never see the person he loved again, that he wouldn't see her smile, or cry, or laugh, or sneeze, anything. I wanted him to understand that this is what loss means.

I left Edinburgh planning to kill her. I walked up to the North Bridge and then down Cockburn Street. I bought my ticket from a machine: I have no idea if it was a single or return. I sat on the train as I had done so many times before, but it felt very different. All those times I'd travelled down there in the past, I'd felt like I was performing a ritual. I couldn't keep Luke alive by loving him, in spite of the platitudes people liked to offer me. I needed to perform an action, to bear my libations, if you like. But not to his grave, a small sad piece of grass in the grounds of the church he attended as a boy. I didn't know that Luke. His childhood was just photographs to me.

I didn't go to a place that was special to us: how could I? I would have fallen to my knees and pounded my fists against the pavement. So I went somewhere that wasn't ours, but belonged to him. If I couldn't go to him, I could at least keep watch on the woman he'd died for. And so I went, week after week, hoping I'd see something that he might have seen – some spark which would make the loss of him a tiny bit more tolerable. He'd saved her life, hadn't he? Didn't that mean she owed him? Didn't she have an obligation to the man whose life she'd cost?

I never spoke to her, never told her who I was. She wouldn't have recognised me: I looked nothing like the snatched photos the newspapers printed of me. But this time, I wanted it to be different. I gazed at the coastline as it sped past. This time, I would go up to her and scream at her. I would put my hands round her thick neck and squeeze until she clawed at the ground. I would have my revenge.

I believed this for the duration of the train journey. My commitment to hurting her – better, killing her – sustained me as I walked out of King's Cross, up the Euston Road, and turned right into the park. I stalked through the park, my head pounding with every step. It looked beautiful that day: I do remember that. The leaves were every shade of red and orange, dropping to form a slippery carpet underfoot. I walked past dog-walkers and joggers and an old couple nestled on a bench. He was reading to her from a dog-eared book. I turned left, and walked past the zoo. The porcupines were scuttling round their pen and a couple of small, dappled goats trotted between the sheep and chickens in the petting zoo.

I had almost reached the northernmost tip of the park. I paused for a moment, then renewed my steps, still heading towards the café. And then I saw the bird. Or rather, I saw what used to be a bird. It was a pigeon, lying next to the path at the top of the park. It lay face up, its too-small head and scabby little feet completely intact, in a pool of tiny white feathers. As I walked closer, I saw its body had been completely pecked away. Crows and magpies, I guessed, had eaten its heart and lungs and everything else. They had parted its tiny ribcage, splaying it out so it was a shell of what it had been. Its wings and shoulders were still there, like a coat wrapped round the back of an empty chair.

And that's when I realised that I could do nothing to Katarina which could make me feel anything other than hollow, no matter how fucking happy she and Dominic Kovar turned out to be. Let them be delirious. It would be easy while he was in prison and it was all stolen moments in the visitors' room, like some cheap romantic film. Easy. But when he left jail, when they moved back in together and faced the grind of rubbing up against each other's bad habits and annoying traits and noisy eating and never doing the washing up, well, let them have that, I thought. We'll see how happy they are then. The last time they were together, they were arguing so violently in the street that a stranger had thought she was in danger, and had stepped in to try and keep her safe. How long would it be, once the forbidden thrill of being together became quotidian, before they were at each other's throats again? Let them have it all. My mouth tasted vile, as though all the hatred in my head was seeping away down my throat. I felt suddenly ashamed at how ridiculous and melodramatic my behaviour had been.

And so I turned round to go home again, because I had nothing left to do there. Revenge was not – after all – something I needed to enact upon Katarina. It was inherent in their being alive; they would see their love crumble slowly, but it would be just as dead as Luke in the end. I started to walk back the way I'd come. I reached The Broad Walk – the big, tree-lined avenue that runs through the park from north to south – and there she was, as if she'd just been teleported into place: Melody Pearce from my Greek tragedy class, standing right in front of me, four hundred miles away from where she was supposed to be.

'Mel?' I was almost afraid. Was it really her? For a moment, I thought I must have conjured her, imposing her face on another slender blonde girl. But it was her, wearing black leggings and a tiny skirt, a green woolly hat over her head, and a small puffy jacket in that red she liked, doing such a poor job of keeping her warm that she was shaking.

'Alex, where are you going?' Her voice was blurred.

'I'm going to catch the train to Edinburgh. What are you doing here?'

'I was following you.'

'I realise that. Why?'

She shrugged, Rankeillor code for any and every emotion.

'Mel, I asked you a question. Would you answer me, please?'

'I wanted to. I wanted to see what you'd do.'

I had no desire to argue with her. I just wanted to go home. I felt utterly spent, every broken night and furious day catching up with me at once.

'This isn't really OK, you know. You can't just follow people because you feel like it. Are you planning to follow me back home? Or do I need to ring Robert and ask him to call your mother to let her know where you are?'

And she reached over and slapped my face, hard. I was so shocked, it took a moment to match the sound to the pain. I put my hand up to feel her handprint burning on my cheek.

'Where are you going?' she said again.

'I'm going home. And so should you. Why were you following me?'

'Because this is it, Alex. Your climax. I came to see it happen.'

'You came to what?'

'You, and that bitch Katarina.'

Hearing Katarina's name said out loud, and by someone from my new life, was so disorientating I felt clammy.

'How do you know about Katarina?' Now I knew where Robert's newspaper article had come from.

'I know everything, Alex. I've known for ages. And now you have to do something about it.'

'I have to go home.'

'That won't be enough.' Her face was blotchy and red. She wasn't shaking from the cold, but with fury.

'Yes, it will. I'm going back to Edinburgh, I'm staying at Rankeillor and I am living my new life – which I'm sure you know is not the one I chose – the best way I can. And none of that will be improved in the slightest if I go and have a slanging match with the woman whose fiancé killed mine. None of it. You can understand that, surely?'

Her face cracked as I raised my voice, and tears started forming in her lovely blue eyes.

'I don't know why you're crying,' I said. 'You hit me, remember.'

'You can't just leave it like this!' she screamed. A woman walking past with a chubby chocolate Labrador gave us a disapproving stare. 'This isn't how it ends, Alex. It isn't fair.'

I was almost laughing. 'You're telling me it isn't fair? Do you honestly believe I don't know that? None of it has ever been fair. None of it. But all of it happened, and I can't demand a recount and get everyone to start again. You're right. It isn't fair. Things aren't fair, and there's nothing to be done about it. Which is why I'm going home.'

I started to walk past her, and she grabbed my arm.

'You can't,' she said. 'That can't be what happens now. You have to have it out with her. If you aren't going to, I will.' And she dropped my arm, and began walking towards the café.

'Mel, this isn't going to make anything better.' I started to follow her. Even though I thought she was behaving appallingly, I couldn't just abandon her.

'Leaving things unfinished isn't going to make anything better,' she snapped, turning back to face me. 'Running away, not saying what needs saying, that doesn't work. I'm surprised you don't know that. Now, come on.'

And I followed her because I thought I could stop her. I thought I could talk to her, and make her see that her behaviour was not just unpleasant, it was unnecessary, because nothing was left unfinished. So I hurried after her, almost running to catch her up. She had grown:

she'd been my height when I first met her, and now she was striding away from me with ease. I kept talking as we drew nearer the café, and she kept arguing that I didn't understand. Suddenly, she stopped dead.

'There she is,' she said, and I followed her gaze. Katarina was walking away from the café, up towards the road, out of the park. I glanced at my watch and realised that it had gone four o'clock. The sky was darkening. I wondered how the hell she could identify someone she'd never even met from this distance, in this almost non-existent light.

'Just leave her alone,' I said. 'Really, Mel, come on. We're going home.'

She wrenched herself away from my hand, and began walking again towards Katarina's retreating back.

What do I remember? I remember that Katarina – a tall woman to begin with – was wearing shiny black heels, topplingly high, with thick, shelf-like platforms. I remember thinking how quickly she was moving, when I wouldn't have been able to take a step without holding on to a rail. I remember that she crossed the road at the top of the park, and turned left to walk past a running track where two weary joggers were circling, hoods up against the increasingly heavy drizzle. Katarina passed them, and Mel was gaining on her all the time, and if I had to describe how I was feeling at that exact moment, it was embarrassed, because the whole thing was so bloody theatrical.

Then Katarina turned right to walk up to the main road, over Regent's Canal. I found out later from the police that she was heading to a friend's flat, just off Avenue Road, a little way north of the canal bridge. She was going to an engagement party which her friends were throwing, because they knew how lonely she was with Dominic in prison. And as she walked over the bridge, Mel broke away and ran up to her. She pushed her hard, in the small of the back.

The railings are so low there. Peeling old brown things, in a crunchy diamond pattern. They must have been built when people were smaller: they were barely at my waist height, and Katarina was tall even without the crazy shoes. With them, her centre of gravity was thrown forwards and up, and so when someone pushed her from behind, sharply and unexpectedly, she couldn't stop herself from falling. And if she'd landed in the canal, the water would have broken her fall. But she was just past the canal, so when she fell, she fell straight down onto the pock-marked concrete canal path, thirty feet below. It happened so quickly, she didn't even scream. I screamed, but she did not.

Mel turned to look at me, and ran. I don't know which way she went. East, maybe. She must have, I suppose, because she made it back to King's Cross eventually. An old couple on the other side of the bridge, grimacing in the rain, looked over at me to see what the fuss was all about. I screeched at them to call an ambulance, and I scrambled round the railings and down the steep bank between the road and the canal, towards Katarina. Tree branches and roots grabbed at my feet, trying to hold me back.

I heard sirens when I finally got to her, and I knew they weren't the ambulance I'd asked for, knew it was going to take too long, in London, in the rush hour. A halo of dark blood was spilling out from under her head, and another under her ribs, and I reached out to her.

'Don't move her!' the old man shouted from the bridge above me. His voice was shaky, but his tone was certain. 'It's important that you don't move her head.'

So I didn't. I took the hand of the woman I hated, and I held it as she died.

ACT FIVE

1

'And that's the last time you saw her?'

Lisa Meyer gets up from her chair, and walks round to the table in front of me. She picks up her phone, and taps the screen once, to stop the recording. She turns to look at me. 'Melody, I mean?'

'Yes. She ran off from the bridge, and I haven't seen her since.' I can feel the skin around my collarbone blotching.

Lisa Meyer pauses. But I have nothing to add. 'So everything that happened after that is the same as in the police report?' she asks.

I try to remember. 'I guess so. The man – the old man, I mean – rang for an ambulance and the police. His phone was in his wife's handbag, so it took a few moments for them to find it, in the dark and the rain. He wanted to come down to the canal, but his wife wouldn't let him. She was worried he'd fall. When the police arrived, they took the three of us to St John's Wood police station. It's very near there – where it happened.'

As I'm telling her this, I'm thinking of everything that wouldn't be in the report. The old man – his name was Mr Hardy – had given me his coat when I'd climbed back up to the bridge, because my teeth were chattering and I couldn't get them to stop. So the whole time I was making my statement, I was worrying that he wouldn't be able to leave because I was still wearing his coat, and it was raining even harder now: I could hear the drops pummelling the window behind me. I kept telling the officer that I needed to return it, and he kept nodding and smiling at me.

Eventually, the desk sergeant knocked on the interview room door. She smiled her apology, and asked if she could have his coat back. I shrugged it off, and she gave me a red fleece blanket in its stead. Only once I'd handed it over did I realise that the coat had smelled of un-smoked tobacco, of red Marlboros, to be exact, and that the blanket smelled nowhere near as good.

By the time the interview was over, nobody could tell me what had happened to Mel – whether they'd arrested her, or even found her yet – and no-one could decide what should happen to me. They asked me to sign the statement which the constable had written for me. His handwriting was round and irregular, like a child's best effort. I felt my throat close up. No-one with a child's writing should be dealing with a case like this.

They didn't think they'd need me again the next day, so I was free to head back to King's Cross. But I needed a different route: the bridge I'd crossed earlier was now blocked off with police tape. So I walked towards Camden, and cut over the next bridge instead. It had been raining for so long that the bridge – which dipped in the middle – had flooded, and I had to wade through water to get over the canal. It seeped in through the soles of my boots, and I could feel blisters form as my wet skin rubbed against the hardened leather.

As I walked past Euston Station, still ten minutes away from King's Cross, I looked at my watch. The last train to Edinburgh had left hours earlier. A grubby-looking hotel with a blue sign offered a good night's sleep from £49. I checked in. There was no minibar, but there was a small supermarket across the street, which sold spirits. I drank half a bottle of whisky that night, cutting it with tap water in a plastic cup. I drank the other half on the train the next morning. At least this wasn't unusual behaviour on the East Coast line.

By the time I reached Edinburgh, I was the kind of drunk where you believe you've circled right back round to sober again, because you feel so much less drunk than you did two hours ago. I was back in my flat in New Skinner's Close before I realised I had no idea what to do now.

Lisa Meyer has poured two fresh glasses of water, and she is looking at me with her tiny frown. 'You're sure, Alex? You haven't seen or heard from Mel since the day of Katarina's death?'

She has framed her question differently, because she knows I'm not telling her everything. I raise my eyes to meet hers, slowly, like I'm still drunk all these months later.

'I haven't seen her, no. I didn't know where I could find her, you see. I didn't even know where she lived. And I couldn't have found out at a weekend, without breaking into Robert's office in the Unit.'

Lisa Meyer nods briskly, although locked doors and high walls would clearly be no obstruction for her. She sits on the chair opposite me, and flips through her notes till the key page realises it can't hope to hide from her, and gives itself up.

'She was arrested the previous night, anyway,' she says. 'The British Transport Police found her on the train at Newcastle.'

'I didn't know that.'

'They continued to Edinburgh, obviously,' she says, glancing down at her notes. 'So her mother could attend the interview with her.' She looks up at me, eyes gleaming under her swishy fringe. 'So even if you'd known her address, Alex, there wouldn't have been anyone there.'

I nod.

'What I'm telling you,' Lisa Meyer says, her reserves of patience ebbing, 'is that there was nothing you could do by the time you got back to Scotland. There would have been nothing you could have done if you'd got back the night before. Melody Pearce was under arrest before you'd finished giving your statement at St John's Wood police station.' I nod again.

'So perhaps it's time you tell me about the letters,' she says, and picks up her pen.

2

L,

I haven't heard back from you. Did you reply? I don't know how much stuff gets through to me in here. You know where I am, though? I said so, didn't I? St Margaret's, out at Newtongrange. Have you ever been out this far from the centre of Edinburgh? I bet you haven't. Or maybe you once went to the Butterfly Farm, that's near here. You'd like it, honestly. I mean, if you came to visit, you would. Who doesn't like butterflies?

I don't think you'd find it depressing. It's a new building – refurbished last year. The staff like to pretend they had it done up specially for us. The kids who are here now, I mean. But it's just coincidence. The girl who has the room next to mine was in a different centre last year. And she reckons this one is miles better. She said the old one was just full of broken stuff: broken kids surrounded by broken pool tables and broken speakers. This isn't like that apart from the kids.

It's not even that far for my mum to come and visit, and she does, every week. It was weird at first, seeing her here. I expected her to cry. But not continually, from the second I saw her to when she eventually left. You know when someone else cries so much that you think you have to cry too, so it doesn't look weird? It was like that. Just one person crying, it's lopsided.

You could get the bus out here, you know. It goes from round the corner from your flat, by Greggs, on the South Bridge. It wouldn't take long: I asked one of the social workers here and she does that every day. She lives in Leith, so she has to get two buses here.

And I've spoken to Carly, and she's coming to see me soon. This week, Carly said. She's going to bunk off school and come, so her mum doesn't find out. Her mum always hated me. She'd go mental if she knew Carly was coming. Totally mental. Did you know Carly had been transferred from Rankeillor? She's at a normal school now, getting ready for her exams. Her mum pushed for that, obviously: she went to see their MSP and everything. But Carly's still dating Jono, so her plan didn't completely work.

I don't even know if you're still at Rankeillor. Are you? I sort of hope you aren't, because I don't like the thought of you being there without us. And I sort of hope you are, because otherwise I don't know where you are at all. I bet you have left. Poor Robert.

My dad just came the one time. The weekend after I was referred here. He didn't cry at all. He was really stroppy with the staff, though. Loads of raised eyebrows and may-I-asks. Like he was some fucking king, coming to inspect the place. I think he thought it would make him look like a better parent. Like, it can't be my fault she went off the rails, look what a disciplinarian I am. It didn't work. They all just thought he was a fucking idiot.

Louise – who's my counsellor here – she says it's quite a common thing they find. Parents worry they'll be judged by the people who clean up after the mess their kids make. But their job isn't to judge my parents. It isn't to judge me, either. It's just to help. That's a nice thing to say, isn't it? You were like that, too. You didn't let us get away with stuff, but you didn't hate us for trying either. Not even Jono. And not even me. At least, I hope not me.

So, I still don't know about this lawyer guy. There were two of them the first time – an older guy and a younger one. The older one was a bit shiny. Too shiny in this place, no matter how new it is. Do you know what I mean? No-one here wears a suit. And the fabric was wrong – it reflected too much light. You get used to everything being less garish here – it's all dull colours like you used to wear: jeans and tees and hoodies and stuff. I think it's because it's so brightly lit in here – fluorescent lights everywhere and white walls. You have to cancel that out a bit, or your eyes would go funny.

I wouldn't see the lawyers the first time they came. I didn't want to, and Des said I didn't have to. I like Des. He's one of the social workers. But then the younger lawyer came on his own, and with a message saying you'd sent him. So I wrote to you to see if that was true. It didn't sound right. But why else would he say it, right? Louise says it's OK for me to have trust issues (she talks like that), especially with strangers. I don't know why. It's not like I'm here because I got in the car of someone I didn't know, is it?

But I haven't heard back from you yet. So I still don't know if it's true or not. And now I'm wondering if the letter even got to you. I hope this one does. I'll send it care of Robert, because I'm sure he will find you.

D

'The letters?' Lisa Meyer prompts me.

'She's been writing since two weeks after she was arrested. Quite often,' I say. 'But she isn't supposed to contact me, I don't think. Is that true?'

Lisa Meyer does the closest thing to a frown that she can, given that she has decided never to incur a wrinkle. 'I don't see why not. Has her lawyer told her that?'

'I think so. She started writing to me at Rankeillor, and Cynthia used to forward them to me. Since I'm…' I don't need to finish. Lisa Meyer knows that I'm not at Rankeillor any more. That I'm not even in Edinburgh. Robert's retirement plan has suffered a major setback, though he and Jeff have never once mentioned it.

'Do you have them with you?' she asks. I nod, and get them out of my bag, a small bundle of letters to which I have never replied. Lisa Meyer takes them in her perfectly manicured hand. Her nails are a shiny putty colour, like shells. She skim-reads the first three letters.

'She started writing to you using your real names,' she says, flipping back to double-check the first two. Then she changes to D and L – why is that?'

She changed the address, too,' I reply. 'She sends them to Robert at his home address now. I have no idea how she knows where he lives.'

Lisa Meyer says nothing, but simply waits for me to answer the question she originally asked.

'She started writing to me openly, I think, because she wanted to, and it doesn't often occur to her not to do what she wants. Then she became more secretive because she's been told by her lawyers that she can't be in touch with me.'

'They've told her a lot of things,' Lisa Meyer remarks. 'They seem to have told her that you've hired them, for a start.' She looks up. 'Which I'm presuming is untrue.'

I'm blushing, even though I know that I'm not the one who's been lying. 'Yes, of course it is. I don't know who hired them. Her mum, maybe? Her dad? And I have no idea why they told her it was me.'

'Think about it,' Lisa Meyer says. 'Her lawyers were trying to implicate you. For that to work, they needed to know a lot more about you. And for that to happen, they needed to ask Melody about you. But she's devoted to you. So they simply found a way round that.'

'Is that even legal?'

She shrugs. 'It's certainly unethical. Why D and L?'

'Teenagers always abbreviate names, don't they?'

Lisa Meyer, a woman whose own parents probably call her by her full name and job title, looks uncertain.

'Carly and Mel were close, and they had nicknames for each other. They used the last syllable of their names – Lee and Dee – because everyone else used the first syllables – Mel for Melody, and Carly is really Caroline, you see.'

Lisa Meyer is unconvinced.

'They're best friends, and they're teenagers. They have secret nicknames,' I say, hoping she will remember what it's like to be sixteen.

She nods, slowly. 'But L doesn't stand for Lee here,' she says.

'No, it stands for Lex. She's just using the same system on my name as she did on Carly's.'

'No-one else calls you Lex?' Lisa Meyer asks. She looks deeply suspicious, as if I have suddenly revealed an alter ego, mid-costume-change in a phone booth.

'No-one.'

'It's not a very sophisticated code,' Lisa Meyer mutters, skimming back through the letters.

'She just wants to believe that the letters will reach me. And she's disguising her identity and mine because they've persuaded her that she shouldn't be writing to me. But no, she probably won't get a job at MI5.'

'Brayford has taken a big risk. He must have known there was a strong chance she'd check. Have you written back?' she asks.

'No.'

Lisa Meyer tilts her head. She is testing the weight of my answer.

'I think you might have to,' she says. 'I want to know who told Brayford that lying to his client is a reasonable course of action. It can't be her mother, I don't think. More likely to be the father. But if it is him, and he's the one trying to use you to ameliorate his daughter's position, I want to know for sure.'

'Does it really matter?'.

'Information is always better than a lack of information,' she says simply. 'The more we know, the better prepared we will be. You need to write back. Use your real name. Tell her to reply via my office if you don't want to give her your address.'

'No, it's fine. I don't mind if she knows my address.' The unsaid words hang in the air between us. What's she going to do – come here and murder someone in front of me?

'If you're sure,' Lisa Meyer says.

'She's just a child. She made a mistake – a terrible mistake, I know, but it was still a mistake. She's not a homicidal maniac, she's a sixteen-year-old girl.'

Lisa Meyer's face is unreadable.

'OK,' she says. 'Write. Tell her you don't know anything about her lawyers, and you certainly didn't send them. Tell her she should try and find out who did, because they're lying to her and they're lying about you. And if you possibly can, do it before the final post today,' she adds. 'We're on a deadline, Alex. The court date is only a few weeks away, and you need to bear in mind that knowledge is crucial. Not just for you. For Mel.'

Dear Alex,

I got your letter! I wish I could send you mail, but our computer time is all checked and stuff here. No phones or laptops or anything much. I don't mind as much as I thought I would. If you'd asked me if I could go without the internet twenty-three hours a day, I'd have said no way. But it turns out that you just do things differently – now I'm writing letters instead. And it's really exciting when the post comes in the afternoons. Well, it arrives in the mornings, but it has to be checked through before we get it. I don't know why. It's not like you'd be sending me a map of the building and its weak spots, is it?

I didn't know you were living back down south again now. It was nice of Robert to forward my letters. I'm sorry you left Rankeillor. They must really miss you there. I bet they blame me, right? For you leaving? Do you blame me, too? I know that must be why you left. Because you were going to stay, weren't you? You were going to stay on there permanently and now you've had to start a new life all over again. Or have you just gone back to your old life? Do you have another job? Have you seen your mum? Tell me everything. It's boring here, so any news from outside is more exciting to me than it is to you.

I'm not bitching though, honestly. I like it here. Well, maybe not 'like'. But it's OK, is what I mean. I don't prefer it to being at home or anything, but it is kind of easier being here. At first, you think everything's decided for you: you have to be at this place at this time for this thing, which makes me feel a bit itchy. I don't like being told what to do. But actually, the people who work here are really nice. So if you tell them that you don't want to have counselling first thing in the morning, they try and change it so that you get it after lunch. They like us to feel like we have control over our lives. Or as you'd say, agency over our fates. Right?

So, that's weird, about the lawyers. You didn't send them, but they definitely said you had. I told the Centre head here that I wanted to see them again, and she passed the message on, and the young one came back. His name's Adam. You said you'd met him – he's pretty hot, isn't he? I like the way his hair curls into his collar, and his eyes are almost green – did you notice that? Cute, anyway.

Plus he blushes when you ask him why his boss is a fucking liar. He goes all burbly, um, er, well, I can't imagine how, I mean, well, er, yes. I told him point blank that he could either tell me the truth or fuck off out of my life so I could have some peace and quiet to read a fucking book. And then he saw I wasn't kidding, and said it was my dad who was paying him, but that my dad had asked them to keep that hidden from me, 'if at all possible' (he put little air quotes round that like a total numpty), in case it 'antagonised me further'.

How fucking bizarre is that? My dad hasn't even visited me here beyond once, because I wouldn't take his phone calls and I ignored his letters. And I don't miss him, because I hardly ever saw him anyway, because we don't even live in the same city. And then suddenly he's all Jason fucking Bourne subterfuge. That's the right word, isn't it? Subterfuge. I like the sound of it, but actually it looks even better written down. I've looked it up: it comes from Latin. It means to escape secretly. You probably know that already, though, don't you, Alex?

Anyway, my dad is clearly busy with his girl-bride, isn't he? Isn't it weird how the plays we were reading began to happen in real life? My mum hates him enough to be Clytemnestra, easily. So I suppose that makes me Electra, doesn't it? I don't mind that – it's a pretty name.

Actually, I wonder if he is still planning their wedding, or if I've spoiled that for him too. Maybe she's left him, because of his scary awful daughter (that would be me). It would be hilarious if that had happened. Wouldn't it? If he'd gone all mid-life-crisis-cliché and then she'd left him when she found out what kind of father he is. It must look really bad, having a daughter about to stand trial for murder. You couldn't mention that on a first date.

But I'm definitely not going to see him again now I know about this whole lawyer thing. Why would they say you'd sent them? I asked Adam, but he was really vague – just muttered about how they wanted me to feel safe talking to them, and that obviously my mother hadn't sent them so his boss had to think of something else. Really fucking dubious. He said they had a few questions about you, but I told him he'd have to fuck off until I'd spoken to you. He said, and I quote, 'That was the very thing we were hoping to avoid, Miss Pearce.' Like a fucking vicar would talk. When I asked him why he didn't want me talking to you, he just blushed and burbled again.

Write back soon. Tell me how you are. What's it like where you're living? Is Reigate in London? Or nearby? Are you working in London? Tell me everything, but don't spend ages replying, because I'd rather hear from you soon and have you miss things out than wait ages for a letter. Please, I mean.

Love, Mel

PS Adam tried calling me Mel, but I told him we weren't friends, so he could call me Miss Pearce. You'd have been proud of me. I think. I hope.

x

3

I meet Lisa Meyer at Edinburgh Airport. I have flown in from Gatwick, and she's come from City Airport. My plane arrives an hour before hers, so I wait in Arrivals, surrounded by presentation bottles of Glenmorangie and toy bears in tartan capes. I haven't been in this airport for ages – I'd forgotten how small it is. It doesn't seem possible that planes can fly from what appears to be nothing more than a tiny shopping mall, but they do. Lisa Meyer steps into the Arrivals hall with a silver travelling case hovering behind her. I wonder how much she had to pay for one which never snags its wheels on the uneven flooring or tips to one side.

'Alex, you're here,' she says. I'm not sure if she was worrying I wouldn't come because I'd be scared, or because she has deemed me the kind of person who misses flights, caught in a maelstrom of lost passports and misplaced boarding passes.

'Yes,' I say. I have given up trying not to state the obvious when talking to her. I think perhaps very beautiful people have that effect, so that their lives are filled with people describing the weather, or commenting on the furniture. It's possible Lisa Meyer's existence is duller than I have previously considered.

At the exit, there's a man to our left, holding up a piece of A4 paper on which he has written Lisa Meyer's name. Of course she has booked a cab. I can't even see her on a bus in my imagination. The driver takes us across the road outside and into the ground floor of the car park opposite. His taxi is one of those minivans that could hold eight people, easily. He takes Lisa's case, swings it expertly onto the back seat, then stands back so I can untangle my bag and put it on the seat myself. Lisa has already given him the address and he is soon pounding towards the city centre. As we drive down Corstorphine Road, past the zoo, I feel a brief pang. I would like to go and see the pandas, which made the national news when they arrived after I'd left Edinburgh. But there is literally no-one I could go with: even Robert wouldn't want to go to the zoo, unless there was an outdoor production of *A Winter's Tale* by the bear enclosure.

The driver turns down Lothian Road, heading towards Bruntsfield. I can't tell if I'm car-sick or just frightened. But by the time we pull up outside Mel's building, I can feel sweat dotting my forehead. It isn't a warm day. Lisa Meyer takes her case from the car, and tells the driver to wait. He glances up at the parking sign, which demands a residents' permit, but he doesn't say anything. She slams the door, and looks over the roof of the minivan to me.

'Are you alright, Alex?'

I nod.

'Just breathe,' she says, as she walks past me and crosses the pavement. She scrutinises the bells and presses 1F2. A moment later, there's a faint buzzing sound and she pushes the door open. Upstairs, the large red front door of an apartment is being held open by a woman I have never met, who must despise me. She looks very much like her daughter: she's tall and slender, and she dyes her hair the same shade that Mel's is. The colour of set honey. Her eyes are puffy but not red. She has cried for days, but not yet today.

She looks straight past Lisa Meyer to me, and says, 'You must be Alex Morris.' I nod, and she says, 'I'm Eleanor, Melody's mother. I'm so sorry.' And she disintegrates like wet paper.

There's a beat before Lisa Meyer takes charge. She holds the door for me to follow her, and produces a pack of tissues from her handbag that she hands to Eleanor, who claws at it for a moment before realising it's unopened. Finally Eleanor peels away the plastic and wrenches one out. She covers her whole face with it, and stands there for a moment like a vandalised portrait. Then she presses it to her eyes and nose, stands perfectly still for a few seconds, and scoops it away.

'I'm sorry,' she says again. She offers Lisa Meyer the remainder of the tissues, but Lisa waves them away.

'I have a bag full of them,' she says. 'April is the pollen season.'

Eleanor nods, and leads us through to her kitchen. She switches the kettle on, and it boils in a few seconds. She pulls three mugs off a mug tree, and looks hopelessly at a jar of coffee and a box of tea bags.

'Tea all round?' Lisa Meyer says, briskly. 'Let me.'

Eleanor sits at the kitchen table, and I do the same. Lisa doesn't ask if anyone wants sugar or milk. She just makes them black, and puts the milk carton on the table.

'Mrs Pearce,' she says, calmly. Eleanor blinks hard, and only one small runnel falls from each eye.

'Call me Eleanor,' she whispers. 'Please.'

'Eleanor,' says Lisa Meyer. 'Alex isn't going to yell at you, and neither am I.' She looks to me for confirmation, and I nod, vigorously. I have no plans to yell at Eleanor Pearce.

'I just feel so awful,' she says. She's breathing slowly and deeply, trying to control herself. She looks at me. 'You were there, when she…' And she breaks off again.

The tiny line across Lisa Meyer's nose has appeared again, and I suspect she is calculating which flight she will make, given that this afternoon is clearly going to take longer than she'd hoped.

'Yes,' I say. 'I was there.'

'And now I hear from Melody that Martin's lawyers have been

trying to…' She begins to crack and then regains composure. 'He wasn't like that when we were married. He really wasn't. He's changed.'

'People do,' says Lisa Meyer. She's hoping that if she talks in generalisations, it might reduce the potential for weeping.

'I know you're right,' Eleanor says. 'But how dare he?'

I haven't really considered things from this perspective before. And it hasn't occurred to me that Mel's mother would, either. I have been braced for her fury: how dare I have encouraged her daughter to read murderous plays, how dare I have not noticed Mel's growing obsession, how dare I have waltzed into her daughter's life and then danced off again once the damage was done? And instead, Eleanor is all apology, guilt and grief. Just like me.

'We really need to know a bit more about how Melody's getting on,' says Lisa Meyer. 'Her trial date is quite soon now.'

The mention of practicalities is what finally dries Eleanor Pearce's tears.

'Yes,' she says. 'What do you need to know? She's going to plead guilty, of course.'

Lisa Meyer nods, as though this is exactly what she was expecting to hear. It isn't at all what I was expecting to hear.

'Guilty of murder?' I'm appalled.

'Manslaughter,' Eleanor corrects me. 'Well, she says she's going to plead guilty to murder, but her lawyers are hoping the court will only ask for manslaughter. I mean, not hoping, exactly. It depends on… I mean, if she hadn't… But maybe if—'

'But won't she be locked up for years?' As Eleanor is trying to work out what she wants to say, I blurt the words out. Eleanor breaks off, sobbing, and Lisa Meyer gives me a weary look.

'She did kill an innocent woman,' she murmurs.

'Excuse me.' I get up to find the bathroom, which is next to the front door. I pour cold water onto my hands and pat my face and the back of my neck. I sit on the edge of the bath for a moment. There is a small glass bowl with tiny silver discs in it. I can't work out what they are, and I have to reach over and pick one up before I realise they are batteries for a hearing aid. Of course I knew she would go to prison or a secure unit or something. But she could plead guilty to manslaughter. Surely that would be enough? How punished did we need her to be?

I walk back into the kitchen to find Lisa Meyer and Eleanor still discussing the consequences of Mel's guilty plea. In the six months that have passed since Mel was arrested, Eleanor has come to terms with the fact that her daughter will be incarcerated for several years. And nothing ever surprises Lisa Meyer. It's just me who is shocked.

'But she didn't mean to do something terrible,' I say, so loudly that Eleanor jumps. I moderate the volume. 'I know she didn't. Your daughter isn't a bad person.'

Eleanor dips her head, not noticing Lisa's single, tiny head-shake.

'Have you got her diary?' I ask. I am certain that this will reveal her to be the decent girl I think she was, before everything went wrong. Wouldn't that help?

Eleanor frowns. 'No,' she says. She thinks for a moment. 'Mel used to write all the time, last year. She started it after you asked them to, didn't you?'

'I don't think any of them really bothered except her. Maybe Carly kept one for a few weeks. But Mel used to mention that she was writing hers.'

'She must have taken it with her into the secure unit,' Lisa Meyer says.

'Yes, she must,' Eleanor agrees. 'But you can check her room if you want.'

As she leads us along the hall, Lisa Meyer glances discreetly at her watch. She is clearly regretting that she didn't have this conversation on a conference call.

Mel's bedroom is ordinary: two shelves of books, mainly young adult novels; posters of actors and of a band I don't recognise and couldn't name; a desk with a few ring-binders lined up along the wall, their spines neatly labelled with the subjects she studied. There are a few books, an illustrated Greek myths, a book about tragedy, a pile of magazines. Her computer is unplugged, and the desk shows a discoloured patch next to it: the police must have removed it, I realise, and then brought it back and put it in the wrong place. The bin hasn't been emptied since she was arrested, I don't think: there are tissues and a broken ring-binder in it.

Eleanor notices me looking, and puts her hand up to her hair. 'I'm sorry it's a mess,' she says, though it isn't. 'I haven't managed to…'

'It's OK,' I reply.

This doesn't look like the room a murderer lived in. It looks like a room a child lived in.

'Could you ask her, when you next visit?' I ask. 'Ask her where the diary is?'

'Yes, alright.' Eleanor nods, and the floating strands of hair which she had placed behind her ears come free again. 'Unless you wanted to visit her, while you're up here?'

'Alex has to be back in London by tonight,' Lisa Meyer says, quickly. 'Another time, perhaps.'

We're there for another hour, drinking more tea, trying to comfort her. When we leave, Eleanor hugs me, like a daughter. I squeeze back, because I don't know what else to do. The car is waiting right outside, and the driver springs out of his seat to open Lisa Meyer's door for her. He begins the return journey to the airport. Lisa Meyer asks once if I am alright. Then she opens her shiny silver case and removes her laptop, making swift notes as we drive along.

Hi Lex,

That's a pun. Did you get it? An ilex is the Latin word for an oak tree. Are you impressed I know that? You should be. I haven't started gardening, before you think I've lost my mind. God, imagine if that was the therapy here. Fuck, that would be lame. I've started a course in Latin. The Centre head here is really cool. A bit like Robert, actually. Except she's a she. She asked me what I was interested in, since I didn't seem 'engaged in my learning plan'. Yeah, I know. It's like they have a weird condition.

I told her I wasn't engaged in it, because it's basically more fucking collages (Jono would love that). And I prefer learning stuff to being bored. So she's found this online course for me to learn Latin. I don't know if they'll let me learn Greek so I can read your plays properly. That might be good. Or maybe not.

Speaking of Jono, he and Carly came to see me yesterday. That's why I didn't write then. It was weird seeing them after all this time. Really strange. They seem exactly the same, whereas for me, everything's different, isn't it? It was all a bit awkward at first – lots of stilted hellos, and Carly hugged me and Jono didn't know what to do and then he hugged me too, which was unexpected. I think he's got fatter – I could barely reach round him. And then he said, you're not armed, are you, and Carly jabbed him with her elbow, but I thought it was funny so I laughed and then they laughed and it was OK.

I don't want you to think I'm laughing about what happened, though. I do know, Alex, that it isn't funny. Honestly. But sometimes, when I think about that day I don't know how to feel. It's like something I dreamed or watched, something that happened to other people, not to me and you. When I talk to the counsellor about it, she says it's a dissociative state. She says it will take a long time before I can come to terms with what I've done. And she says it's OK that I don't know how to process it at the moment.

Do you think that's true? Because there are moments, tiny flashes, like a migraine, when I feel really, really awful. And then they flash away again, just as fast. And if you asked me what I'm afraid of, and I told you the truth, I would say this: I'm afraid it's those moments that are real and the rest of the time is the lie. And that what she means when she says I'll come to terms with it is that it'll switch round, and I'll live in those bits, the migraine moments, and the good stuff will be what happens in short flashes – with Carly and Jono, or learning Latin, or writing to you. Just tiny bites of happy, and the rest of the time will be bad. Is that what happens when you do something terrible? And if it is, how do you learn to live with it? How do I?

You visited my mum last week, didn't you? She liked you – she said so. She said you might come and see me sometime, but it probably won't be here, will it? I'll be moved after my trial. Or maybe I won't for a bit. No-one knows yet. But you can still come, you know. I'll send you the new address.

My mum said you were upset that I am pleading guilty. I don't want you to be upset, Alex. You of all people know I have to plead guilty, don't you? That's how it works – you do something bad and then you have to pay. Like Orestes and Electra in your plays. We never got that far in class, did we? But I read it anyway. I brought the book with me, and I read the final play of the trilogy in here. The Eumenides, I mean. That's a pretty word, isn't it? They sound nicer than they are. The Kindly Ones – that's what it means, isn't it? Except they aren't kindly at all. They're terrifying vengeful goddesses with black fire all around them. I've been drawing them in art class (I can't get out of all the collage bullshit, you see). I've enclosed a sketch of one here. It's not that good, but I'm getting there.

The trick is to do it in charcoal, you see, and not pencil. That was Carly's suggestion, actually. She was always better at art than me.

Anyway, I want you to understand that I'm not pleading guilty because I want to be punished, I'm pleading guilty because I have to be punished. It's in the play, Alex – if society doesn't punish its criminals, the gods do.

I don't think that black-fire-breathing monsters will come after me, or anything. I'm not crazy. But those flashes, the moments of blackness – those are my Eumenides. And I can't live with them, not if they get any bigger. I'll be better off in prison, honestly. You have to let me do this. I can't really explain it to my mum – she pretends she understands, but I know she just thinks I'm mental. She hasn't read all the plays that we have, Alex, so she doesn't get it. But you have, so you should understand.

My mum says you want to find my diary. You won't find it, you know. Not if you looked for a year. I want it that way – it's private. My mum says you think it will show the jury that I'm just an ordinary girl who got a bit confused, or something. But I don't want it found, I don't want it read, and I don't want it in court. It wouldn't help, anyway. And even if it would, that isn't what I want.

I hope I haven't upset you. I just need to do this properly. I need to do things right, for once. Write soon, though. Tell me you're OK with everything. I'll be worrying about it till I hear from you. My counsellor says that kind of statement is passive-aggressive. Jesus.

Love, Mel

4

Adam is in the coffee shop when I arrive, drinking something frothy and eating what might once have been a muffin. On second glance, I'm not sure if he's eating it, or merely rendering it down to crumbs. He has a messenger bag on the floor between his feet, and his right leg is twitching so fast it makes his whole leg quiver. He's gazing at the muffin remnants.

'Hello.' I stand in front of him, and he starts to his feet.

'Alex,' he says, reaching out a hand covered with crumbs, which he brushes onto the table. We shake hands.

'Do you want anything?' I ask him.

'No, thanks. I mean, let me.'

'It's fine.' I walk over to the counter and order a latte. By the time I return to the table, Adam has jettisoned the plate and swept the crumbs from the table to the floor.

'How are you?' he asks.

'Worried about Mel,' I reply, and he nods vigorously.

'Can I help?'

'I think so. You know she intends to plead guilty?'

He nods again, but smaller.

'I think her diary would prove that she isn't...' I can't find the words.

'Isn't what?'

'Isn't a monster. She kept it for the whole year, almost. She wrote her feelings and worries and everything in there. She wrote stories and things for class.'

His nods have scaled back so much, they are almost invisible to the naked eye.

'I just think if you could find it, if you could show it to the court, then they would realise that she's not a terrible person. They might not lock her up for so long. She doesn't deserve to lose her whole youth, does she? She's just a kid who did something terrible, which isn't the same thing, is it?'

'No, quite,' he says. 'She hasn't mentioned a diary in our,' he pauses, 'admittedly brief meetings.'

'Maybe you shouldn't have lied to her about me?' I suggest.

He tugs at his collar. 'I'm sorry about that. I don't have much say in the choices my boss makes. But I admit that was a terrible idea, and I should have told him so.'

'Charles Brayford made a stupid choice. It means she doesn't trust him, and she only half-trusts you.'

He brightens. 'Do you think she does?'

'She thinks you're cute. So she told me.'

'Well, that's better than before, then,' he says. He pats away the milk from his top lip with a napkin. 'I can ask her for the diary, Alex. I can go to her flat and search the place. But you've tried that, haven't you? So she probably threw it out before she was arrested, don't you think?'

'Probably. But maybe not: a diary is a very personal thing. People who keep them care about them. And she wants to be a writer. I think it would have been agony for her to throw it away. It's at least possible that she kept it.'

'OK,' he says. He reaches into his pocket for a phone, and brings up a yellow screen, thin grey lines running across it. 'What does it look like?' His finger is poised to make notes.

'I don't know. I've never seen it.'

'Ah.' He switches the phone back off, and returns it to his jacket pocket. 'But you're sure it exists?'

'She told me she wrote in it.'

His face is almost completely motionless, only one eyelid flicking betrayal. I remember that he is a man who spends a great deal of his working life with liars.

'Why would she lie about it?'

'To impress her favourite teacher?' He shrugs.

'Her mother says she was always writing in it.'

'Ah, so she knows what it looks like.' He's relieved.

I shake my head. 'She never saw it either. Mel just told her that she was writing a diary.'

'Well, then.' He presses his lips together for a moment, then continues. 'We'll find it. But you have to understand that it might not help her. You do see that?'

'Yes.'

'She wants to plead guilty because she committed an awful crime,' he says, quietly. 'That's her right, Alex. Even if we're doing our best to reduce the time she serves.'

'It was just an impulsive moment,' I reply. 'She was with me, she was angry and upset, and she did something impetuous and stupid and someone died.'

'It wasn't completely impetuous.' He's talking so softly now, that I have to lean in to hear him over the sound of the steamers and milk frothers.

'What do you mean?'

He looks perplexed. 'You must know, Alex. You were there.'

'She just pushed her. If the woman hadn't been wearing those stupid shoes, she'd have probably kept her balance. No-one could have seen that she would fall, not even Mel. And even then, a few seconds earlier and she would have fallen into the canal, and she wouldn't have been hurt at all, probably. A second or two later, and she'd have fallen into some shrubs, and the worst that would have happened is a few scratches.' As I say this, I feel the branches on my wrists and ankles again, poking their way in up my coat-sleeves and between my jeans and my boots. I rub my wrists to ease the phantom itching.

'But that's not all she did,' he says, and looks at me in a manner which would surely be full of meaning if I had any idea what he was talking about.

'I don't understand.'

He takes a deep breath, and exhales. He's gazing at me so hard that I begin to think I have milk or something on my face. I put my hand up to check.

'Has no-one ever told you? The police, when they questioned you, they didn't ask you if you saw the knife?'

My brain tells me my ears must be malfunctioning. 'The knife?'

'I'm so sorry, Alex.' He reaches over and grabs one of my wrists. 'She stabbed Katarina Prochazka in the back as she pushed her. In her left kidney, to be precise. And although that didn't kill her, there's little doubt that the blood loss from that wound contributed to her death from the head injury she received when she hit the towpath. The police never found the knife. Mel said she'd thrown it somewhere. And since she didn't know the route she'd taken back to King's Cross, the police didn't manage to find it. But I suppose they didn't need to, when they had her full confession. Are you alright?'

He starts digging about in the messenger bag for one of those miniature bricks of tissues that Lisa Meyer always has. He opens one out, and hands it to me. I haven't noticed I'm crying till then.

5

Dear Alex,

You don't give up, do you? I said I didn't want the diary found, and I don't. And it won't be. So could you stop hassling my mum, my lawyer, and everyone else I've ever met? This is what the therapist here calls a boundary issue. As in, you're overstepping my boundary.

You're probably thinking that's rich coming from me, right? That's fair enough, I suppose, but you have to let this go. You're not helping — you're making things harder. My mum's upset now, and Adam-the-lawyer has gone all soft-voiced, just-trying-to-help-you-Mel-don't-make-me-the-bad-guy. It's exhausting. My days are long enough in here without everyone adding to it.

So please, let it go.

Adam says I'll see you in court. Are you really coming? Because you know I'm pleading guilty, don't you? It's not like a proper trial at all, really. It's just, well, I don't know what it is, exactly. It's just the thing that happens next.

So maybe I'll see you there.

Love, Mel

PS The fact that I put 'love Mel' doesn't mean I'm not still pissed off with you.

I have many regrets about what happened in the aftermath of Luke's death. One of them has always been about his killer's trial. Should I have gone? Would it have made a difference if the jury had seen me in the gallery? A grieving widow. Except I wasn't a widow. I wasn't Luke's wife, so there is no word to describe what I became – or rather, what Dominic Kovar rendered me.

But as I sit waiting for Mel's sentencing hearing to begin, I am glad that I spared myself the first trial. I arrive at the court with Luke's parents, with whom I was briefly living after I left Edinburgh. They have always been kind to me: from the beginning, when they offered to pay the rent on the Richmond flat after he died. They realised far more quickly than I did that the financial things wouldn't wait till the emotional crisis subsided. It's not like our landlord wasn't sorry about what had happened, but it was a buy-to-let, and the rent we paid covered his mortgage. So he needed me to move out, even if I'd wanted to stay.

And I didn't want to stay, because no-one should have to live on the same street as the faintly discoloured paving stone which marks the place where the person they love bled out. At first, people put flowers there, propped up against the wall, and tied to a lamp-post: limp carnations and dying roses. But the offerings don't stop people stepping there, dropping gum and walking dogs. Treading on his blood. To them it was pavement, to me it was desecrated ground. I would have taken the paving stone if I could. I would have dug it up and marked his grave with it.

When I moved out, I headed to Edinburgh with just what I could carry, and his parents took in my things, mine and Luke's. They boxed up our DVDs and books, our saucepans and plates, marked the boxes 'Fragile'. They moved them into their garage in Reigate, and parked their car on the drive instead. I told them I would never need any of the stuff again, and they didn't argue, or tell me I might change my mind later. They simply nodded, took the boxes away, and didn't mention them again. And when I called them all those months later, from Edinburgh, to tell them what had happened, because I had to tell someone, they invited me to stay.

When I got there, his mother had made up the spare room for me, across the landing from Luke's old bedroom. I peeked round the door that evening, and saw that the room was, as it had been when Luke was alive, a study. People in Reigate have studies. The only sign that it had once been their son's room was a photograph on one bookshelf. He was smiling and ruffling my hair. I was laughing, and trying to move his hand. I went to pick it up, then decided to leave us there, in peace.

It was a day or two later when Luke's mother, Alice, asked if I wanted any of my clothes from the boxes. She said she needed to sort through them, to work out what needed keeping and what she should throw away. So we ploughed through each box, emptying and re-boxing things for the charity shop. We kept one box with a few of Luke's clothes inside, because when we opened it, it smelled so strongly of him, of lemon and basil and cleanness, that I couldn't breathe. He could have been standing behind me. Neither of us could have thrown it away. So we closed it up and put it on a shelf next to the boxes of Christmas decorations.

After a few more days, Luke's father, David, said that the theatre in the nearby town of Redhill was looking for a new artistic director, and that he'd suggested they ask me. He did this in such a matter-of-fact way that I didn't even wonder about the coincidence. It wasn't until some weeks later, when I was helping to stuff programmes into envelopes, that I saw their names on the list of Friends and Angels. I wondered how much he'd donated.

So I went to have a look at the theatre with Alice, with no expectation of being offered the job, and then it was so small and perfect, and they were so keen, that I said yes before I'd even thought through the consequences. As we went to have coffee and a bun to celebrate my new job, Alice gave me a set of keys to what she described as 'the granny flat' at the end of their road, which they had bought long ago for when David's mother became frail and unable to manage on her own. She had never set foot in the place: a flurry of minor strokes killed her in less than a week. They had rented the place out since then, and their most recent tenant had just moved up to London to ditch her commute.

Everything had fallen so neatly into place that I was beginning to wonder if Luke's parents had missed their calling in organised crime.

My own mother offered to come to Mel's sentencing hearing, but I told her not to worry. I would be fine with David and Alice. And when we arrived at the Old Bailey, it seemed strangely familiar: all those news broadcasts I suppose. I'd spoken to Adam twice more between our meeting and today, and he was cautious about the way the case had progressed. Mel had remained determined to plead guilty, but the Crown Prosecution Service had decided to charge her with manslaughter, rather than murder, even though she'd used a knife. Adam saw this as a victory for him and Charles Brayford: murder charges were almost automatic, if a knife had been used. But because the coroner had cited the head injury as the cause of death, the CPS had made a rare exception.

Adam was disappointed that he had come no closer to finding Mel's diary. Asking her for it had simply ensured that she wouldn't speak to either of her lawyers. Adam said she would tell him he was wasting her time, remove her hearing aids, and wait until he left. He offered to find her new counsel, but she ignored that too.

So neither man knew for certain what would happen at the first hearing. She did exactly what she had promised she would do, and entered a guilty plea. It was only then – for the first time in many months – that I was no longer in Charles Brayford's sights. Whatever he had been hoping to throw at me made no difference now. She had been determined to protect me one last time.

She was remanded back to the secure unit in Edinburgh, pending her psychological evaluation. Those evaluations, Adam said, were now submitted to the judge, so her sentence could be decided. I called him the day before and asked him how long she would be imprisoned. He had no idea. I asked him to guess. Too many variables, he said.

And now, David, Alice and I are sitting outside the courtroom, waiting to go in. The courts are bustling with people, all carrying papers and briefcases, wearing suits and striding past with a visible sense of purpose. No wonder Luke felt at home in this world. I don't ask Alice if she's thinking about him. Neither she nor David ever ask the other what they're thinking about. They both know the answer already. It's always him.

I wish Lisa Meyer was here. Once Mel entered her plea, Lisa's job was done, and I haven't seen her since. 'That's a good result,' she said, slicing away from the courts to go back to her office. 'I hope I'll see you another time, Alex, in happier circumstances.' She gave me a nod, because Lisa Meyer prefers not to shake hands, as she never knows where other people's hands have been.

I wanted to give her a hug, but the dark glint in her eye told me this would be a huge mistake. And since she could probably fell me with some lightning move if I even so much as moved towards her in a hug formation, I just said goodbye to her, awkwardly, giving her a small wave, because somehow goodbyes demand that we do something with our hands.

'Will she come past us?' Alice asks, suddenly.

'I don't know,' I tell her. 'They might take her in through a different door. But I don't know.'

We fall back into silence, and after a while a clerk tells us we can go through to the public gallery, so we follow her directions onto the courtroom balcony, which is smaller than I'm expecting, and darker. It's almost empty inside. Mel's mother is already there, downstairs, with a man who has his arm around her shoulders. At the opposite end of the bench seating, two rows behind her, is a dark-haired, middle-aged man who must be Mel's father. He's alone. I hope he doesn't see me. Or at any rate, I hope he doesn't talk to me. I'm not surprised that he blames me for his daughter's predicament: I blame myself. But that doesn't mean we have anything in common.

The judge arrives and takes his seat. He places a pile of papers in front of him. When he directs the clerk to bring Mel into the courtroom, her mother straightens up, shifts out from under her friend's arm, and slides an inch or two away from him.

Mel looks older, after all these months. She's maybe an inch or two taller, and her hair has been cut into short feathery layers. It suits her. She clocks the gallery and gives her mother a small wave. She blanks the boyfriend, and doesn't even look in the direction of her father. I wonder how she knew where he would be sitting, to ignore him so completely. Finally, she looks up to me, David and Alice. Her eyes flick over them, and I know she's trying to work out who they are. She knows they can't be my parents, because she remembers my father is dead. It takes her a second, if that, to catch on. She puts her thumbs together and arches her fingers above them to make a heart shape, which she holds as she looks at her mother again, and then at me. Her mother starts to cry.

The whole thing is over in a matter of moments. I'm an idiot for not realising there would be no courtroom drama scene: she has already been convicted, after all. It's just her sentence that needs to be decided. The prosecution reads out a statement from Katarina's mother and sister, in a monotonous voice. Mel doesn't react as he drones through a paragraph about how their lives will never be the same again, and how she lit up the room just by being in it. I feel guilty for wondering if the clichés were in the original Croatian, or if they appeared in translation. His voice is like a fly stuck between a net curtain and a closed window. There is no statement from Dominic Kovar, the bereaved fiancé. Perhaps we only care when grief is visited on the innocent.

Charles Brayford, dressed in a suit which is too silvery, respectfully reminds the judge of the sheaf of papers they have submitted in advance, from Mel's counsellors, psychologists and psychiatrists at the secure unit. The judge tells the court that he is weighing all these things in his mind as he considers the appropriate sentence, and Mel sits completely still throughout. I wonder if she can have taken her hearing aids out. I can't see her ears through her hair, but her hands are suspiciously clenched, as if she is holding something small. She doesn't seem to hear anything Charles Brayford says. And she doesn't react when the judge starts talking again. He asks her to rise, and she ignores him. He asks again, and the clerk reaches over and touches her forearm. She jumps.

The judge asks, loudly and slowly, if she can hear him, and then looks around helplessly, wishing someone would suggest a solution. Mel is enjoying herself. Wrong-footing them all with her deafness, using it as a mechanism to undermine them.

He asks if anyone might be able to provide a sign-language translation for her. She replaces the aids while he's looking the other way, at the clerk, and says slightly too loudly, which would annoy her if she knew, that she can hear him perfectly well, thank you. The judge looks flustered, and asks if she is sure. She gives him a look of such comprehensive contempt that the judge, who has presided over some of the most challenging murder cases in the past decade, according to Adam, physically blanches. The threats and rage of a hardened criminal are as nothing, it seems, in comparison with the utter scorn of a teenage girl.

He gives her a sentence of eight years. David murmurs in my ear that this means she'll be out on licence in four, less the months she has already been on remand. He's an expert on sentencing now, of course. The judge tells us he has made his decision in the light of excellent reports on Mel's behaviour from the secure unit staff. He is mindful that her disability will make any period of incarceration more difficult for her. He is taking into account the fact that her plea has saved the court and the family of the victim from the expensive and painful process of a trial.

Her face is motionless, so I have to look to Charles Brayford and Adam to see if they're interpreting that as good news. They're both smiling. Charles Brayford raises one hand up to head-height. It is possible that he is considering a high five, I think. As Adam turns away to put papers in his briefcase, Brayford morphs the gesture into tidying an imaginary stray hair. I find myself wondering if Dominic Kovar's lawyers would have done the same thing, celebrated their triumph, last year.

Mel smiles at her mother. She leaves the court without speaking, and she managed to get through the entire hearing without ever looking at either her counsel or her father. By the time we get downstairs, her father has left. Her mother is across the lobby, sitting on a bench, sobbing. I don't want to interrupt, so I leave her to her boyfriend, who is standing awkwardly next to her, holding a small plastic cup of water which I doubt she can even see. He holds it for a little longer, and then he starts sipping it himself.

I duck into the Ladies, to feel cold water on my hot hands. When

I come out, there's a clerk looking for me. Mel would like to speak to me before she leaves, he says. She's waiting behind the courtroom.

I follow him down one corridor, and then another. She's waiting for me, next to a grey-haired man whose creased face suggests that he spends more time laughing than I would ever have guessed from his expression.

'You have two minutes at the very outside. And only because you asked nicely,' he tells her sternly. And then he pats her shoulder. 'I'll be listening,' he says.

She looks at me, and I realise it's the last time I'll ever see her.

'I just wanted to say goodbye,' she says.

I nod. I don't want to cry, because I know she must be sick of everyone crying at her by now.

'Thank you,' I tell her. 'For making things...' Not easier. She certainly hasn't made my life easier. I think for a second, though I know we don't have long. 'Thank you for keeping them from hurting me,' I say.

She gives me that smile that used to raise my hopes in the classroom, the one which shows she knows she understands something better than anyone else in the room, and that I have noticed.

'Bye, Alex,' she says. 'I'll always remember you.'

The guard looks at me, and taps his watch.

I have run out of words. I make my right hand into a ball. I place the underside in front of my heart and make a circular movement. It's the only piece of sign language I know.

'I'm sorry too,' she says.

EPILOGUE

It's three o'clock on a Saturday afternoon, and I am in the theatre café, which is deserted, because there's a children's show going on in the auditorium, and everyone is in there. There's the faint sound of tinny music bleeding out through the double doors. The café looks like a piñata has been smashed overhead: there are bits of brightly coloured sweets and icing and crayon pieces and plastic everywhere. Laura, who has a master's degree in behavioural psychology and is running our café until the job market catches up with her, is surveying the room.

'Is it worth cleaning up now?' she asks. 'Will they all come back here in the interval?'

'They will.'

'Then I'm just going to do the tables,' she decides. 'The floor can wait till all the buggies have gone.'

Adam walks in five minutes later.

'I'm sorry I'm late,' he says, shaking my hand firmly like I might be interviewing him for a job. 'The train was held up at East Croydon.'

'It's fine,' I tell him. 'What can I get you?'

He asks for coffee, and I head over to the counter to make it, but Laura beats me to it. I carry the two cups over to the table that looks least like a crèche.

'Sorry.' I sweep a few stumps of coloured pencil into a plastic container.

'No problem,' he says. 'Children's show?'

'No, it's a touring production of *Coriolanus*.'

He looks briefly alarmed, then smiles. 'You're teasing me.'

'Yes.'

'Because you're wondering when I'm going to stop the small-talk and tell you why I asked you to meet me?'

'Yes.'

Laura comes over with a small plate and two cookies. She puts them down in the most theatrically subtle way possible, a perform-ance that would not have gone unnoticed by the toddlers in the main house. He thanks her, and she goes back to cleaning the tables.

'I have a letter for you,' he says. 'A final duty to discharge for my client.' He reaches into the messenger bag he has parked on a seat.

'Here,' he says, and hands me an envelope on which is written the single letter 'L'.

I reach over and take it, but I misjudge and my fingers touch him instead of the paper. It falls on the table.

'Sorry,' I say, and pick it up quickly. I turn it over, and notice that it's not sealed. The flap has simply been slipped inside the back. I begin to slide my fingers under it.

'Stop,' he says, and I drop it on the table. 'Sorry, I mean, please would you do that later?'

'Why?'

'She asked me to ask you. She asked me to bring the letter in person, and she told me to ask you to wait until I'd gone before you read it.'

'Why didn't she just post it?'

'She's not allowed to write to you any more.' He begins the process of dismantling the cookie into individual crumbs of raisin and oats. I wonder if he ever eats anything which is still solid. 'Well, rather, I should say, she's agreed that it's best if she doesn't contact you any more. The staff at the secure unit believe that she can make real progress there. She's studying. She's doing well.'

'OK.'

'But she said there were a couple of things outstanding, so she wrote this and gave it to me when I saw her last week.'

'Will you see her again?'

'Not for a while, no. The firm will continue to advise her over parole and so on, as and when it comes up. But she may prefer a lawyer who's closer to her geographically.' He looks at the second cookie, which is wearing a fine dusting of the first. 'Did you want that?' he asks. I shake my head. 'It certainly slows things down, having to travel up there from London.'

'Yes, of course. It was kind of you to bring it. I mean, I would have understood if you'd just posted it.'

'Ah. You might have understood, but Miss Pearce is made of less forgiving stuff,' he says.

'You're honest, for a lawyer,' I tell him.

'I'm sure it won't hold me back. Actually, it might. But I hope it doesn't. When does *Coriolanus* finish?' He glances at the clock on the wall above the counter.

'The interval's at four.'

'OK, well, then I might leave you to the melee,' he says.

'Thanks again, for bringing this.' I pick the envelope up again.

'My pleasure,' he says.

'Did you read it?'

'No,' he says. 'She gave it to me like that. I promise.'

'I believe you. Bye, then,' I say. Out of the corner of my eye, I can see Laura gesticulating frantically, but I look away. I put out my hand.

'Bye, Alex.' He takes my hand, but he doesn't shake it. Instead, he leans in and kisses my cheek.

'This is going to sound odd,' he mumbles into my ear. 'But I will kick myself all the way back to Clapham if I don't say it. So I'm just going to do it and hope you don't laugh. I'll be here on the first Saturday of next month, at the same time. If you want to meet me for coffee, I'd like that very much. If you don't, I'll wait for an hour, and then I'll piss off and you can have the place to yourself. If you don't show up, I won't come again. I'll leave you alone, because one thing you don't need is another stalker.'

And he turns around, gives Laura a jaunty wave, and walks out.

Dear Alex,

This is my last letter to you. But I bet Adam's told you that already. I have to do all those therapeutic things they talk about: move on, draw a line in the sand. Is it any wonder I still like your Greek plays when everyone else talks in clichés? See, now it sounds like I'm being a bitch, and I'm not really. They're good to me here. And I want to get better. Scratch that, I want to be better. And for that to happen, I'm going to give some of their clichés a try, just in case they're clichés because they're true.

So here's what's going on in my life. My mum is less upset than I thought she'd be, with how everything worked out. She's realised I won't be gone for as long as I might have been, so she's counting her blessings, she said (you see what I mean, about everyone using them?). I don't see her too often, but she comes every other week or so, and we're getting on way better than we did before.

I haven't spoken to my dad. He rings the secure unit sometimes, but I don't want to talk to him yet. They're great about that kind of thing here. They just tell him I'm taking my time (another one) and all that stuff. Maybe next year, huh?

You really did get obsessed over my diary. OK, I'll put you out of your misery. I never had a proper diary, like Anne Frank or whatever. I mean I didn't use an actual book, because I didn't have one. I just wrote it on sheets of paper from a pad. I kept them in a folder, because I didn't want to lose the pages. But I didn't want my mum or someone else reading it, obviously. So even before that day in London, I'd started taping the pages into the illustrated Greek myths book my mum bought me last year.

When she said you were asking after it, I thought I'd get found out. So I asked her to bring a few things in, including the book. I knew she wouldn't look in it. She hates all that stuff. She thinks it warped my mind. I told her it takes more than a play to warp a mind, but she's adamant. Anyway, she brought it, and she never knew. And as for what happened to it next, me and my room-mate Rhiannon used it for roll-ups. I know, my precious diary, right? Literally gone up in smoke. And not literally like they say on the news. Actually literally. And I don't mind telling you, Alex, those cigarettes were fucking inky. Though that's more likely to be from the illustrations than from the diary, I guess. But don't feel sad, anyway, because I am going to start a new one for my therapy in here. Probably I will, anyway.

I might be given a new identity when I get out. Isn't that odd? I could give up being Mel Pearce and become someone completely new. I've been thinking about that a lot. What would I like to be called? At the moment, I think I'd go with Amber. Do you know what the Greek word is for Amber? It's Electra.

I'm going to ask Adam to bring this to you. He totally likes you. Do you remember what Jono said never happens in your plays, Alex? No-one ever lives happily ever after. But you know what I think? I think we will, you and me. I don't know if you believe it yet. But I bet you I'm right.

Love, D